Under the Influence

CHOSEN PATHS BOOK 2

L.B. SIMMONS

SPENCER
HILL
PRESS

Please visit www.lbsimmons.com

First Edition: May 2015
L.B. Simmons

Under the Influence: a novel / by L.B. Simmons—1st ed.
ISBN: 978-1-63392-098-9
Library of Congress Cataloging-in-Publication Data available upon request

Summary: By the age of thirteen, Dalton Greer had already experienced abuse unfathomable to most. So by the time he was finally rescued from the latest of his long string of foster homes, he was already traveling down a very dangerous path. Indebted to a known drug lord as a means of protection, he chose the life of the streets, thinking that was all his life had to offer . . . until he met *her.*

Five years later, she's the only bright spot in his very bleak existence. There's nothing he won't do to shield her from the evil he's experienced, and he wants nothing more than to protect her from the life he's chosen, as well as from himself.

The day Spencer Locke found Dalton sitting on her porch, she felt his pain and understood his rage. They were bonded by both, though he would never understand why. He had been lost while she was found, and in that moment, she vowed to help him find his way too.

As the years pass by, that initial bond becomes something deeper. Spencer loves Dalton regardless of his past, in spite of his choices.

One night is all they have before fate makes its own decision. Dalton is forced to choose the path he will travel, and Spencer is left not knowing why.

This is a journey toward the discovery of true friendship as it blossoms into first love, the experience of crucial sacrifice and ultimate betrayal, and the endurance of agonizing heartbreak on the way to finding lasting redemption. And when all secrets are unleashed, two fractured souls find solace . . .

Under the Influence of love.

Published in the United States by Spencer Hill Press.
This is a Spencer Hill Press Contemporary Romance.
Spencer Hill Contemporary is an imprint of Spencer Hill Press.
For more information on our titles, visit www.spencerhillpress.com

Distributed by Midpoint Trade Books
www.midpointtrade.com

Cover design by: Hang Le
Interior layout by: Scribe Inc.

Printed in the United States of America

Chosen Paths Series

Book One: *Into the Light*
Book Two: *Under the Influence*
Book Three: *Out of Focus*

Part One

Addiction

Prologue

Dalton

I am not a good person.

And I don't pretend to be.

There may have been hope for me at one point, but now, as I stare back at the hardened face and vacant eyes in front of me, there's no denying the truth. All hope for me was lost years ago, stripped clean from my mind as they broke me. The life I'm indebted to now is one packed with corruption and polluted with lies.

I try to breathe in deeply as I rinse the freshly spilled blood from my hands, but I begin to feel the bitter pang of disappointment in my chest. It seeps along the previously etched grooves that line it, burning the hollow channels created with each punch to my stomach and blow to my ribs.

I rarely have these moments of weakness, when I wish I hadn't allowed myself to be drawn into the darkened path that is this life. But right now, I wish I had been strong enough to brave my childhood on my own. That I had been able to fend off the monsters that lurked in dark rooms and reeked of alcohol, able to protect myself from the multitude of broken bones and black eyes inflicted by the hands of those who were supposed to fucking *protect me*.

But I wasn't. And now I'm stuck, hopelessly adhered to a life in which I have chosen to forgo conscience for security.

Little did I know that the day I met Silas Kincaid, I'd be making a deal with the devil. That I would be forever bound to a life from which there is no escape.

Although I started out as his lackey, I grew quickly—both physically and within the hierarchy of his organization—to become his weapon. Not only his muscle, but a tool that has many uses. His most-prized possession.

And now here I am at eighteen years of age, long since graduated from errand boy. I watch the familiar streaks of someone else's blood swirling around yet another porcelain sink. Someone who also made a deal with the devil but didn't deliver on his end.

I always deliver.

After drying my hands, I curl my fingers over the lip of the sink and place my palms flat on the cool surface, silently watching the reflection in the mirror. Cold, dead eyes stare back at me. Not a spark of life left in them.

Not anymore.

In fact, Spencer Locke is the only bit of humanity I permit myself to indulge in. She's the one thing, the one person whose mere presence provides some sense of relief from the constant sense of asphyxiation I feel.

She is my reprieve.

My air.

Spencer Locke is the *one* slice of happy I have in this shit pie I call life. Silas Kincaid is a ruthless motherfucker.

The two will never cross paths.

I would, with absolutely no hesitation, lay down my life to make sure that never happens. Spencer's safety has been and will always be my concern—no, my priority. And in order to ensure that safety remains, she must never know the real me. The cold, calculated, hardened criminal that I am. She will only know the Dalton Greer I permit her to know.

Just like everyone else I come into contact with.

To Rat, I'm the entertaining best pal. To Spencer, I'm the over-protective friend. And to Silas, I'm the lethal weapon.

None of them truly know *me*.

Because the truth is, there's nothing more frightening in my world than those who know you—who *really* know you. The ones who know your deepest, darkest secrets. The ones who know what you're going to do before you do it. The ones who know not only what buttons to push when they seek your attention but also the ones that can be used to completely incapacitate you.

They can be your strength.

But they can also be your weakness.

And just as a chameleon changes color to blend for protection, I've learned to evolve into the person I need to be in order to survive the situation at hand, all while keeping people at arm's length. Yet sometimes I can't help wondering what my *true* colors would have been had I not been subjected to this life. I question what it would be like to just let someone in, to tell them my unforgivable truths and discover they still love me in return. *Something so unattainable.*

I find myself utterly fascinated, awestruck even, that there are people actually capable of truly loving someone without wondering when and how they'll be betrayed. However, the knowledge of their existence also saddens me because the cold reality is, I will never know that type of love. I will never know the freedom to just *be* with someone—without pretense or fabrication, without the endless lies and untruths.

Maybe that's why I keep holding onto Spencer when I know I shouldn't. When all my instincts scream for me to let her go, to cut those ties and just let her be.

I can't.

I'm too selfish.

Therefore, I will plaster on my overprotective big-brother face so I can see her again, just to get my fix of relief she provides. And in turn, I will continue the lies.

I will continue telling myself the *only* reason I insist on my frequent visits is because I want to see to her protection.

I will continue convincing myself the things I say to her are merely *pretenses* that accompany my facade.

But in this rare moment, I will also concede that like a moth to a flame, I'm *drawn* to her.

To her innocence.

To her kindness.

To her ability to love.

To all the things I wish I was capable of but have sacrificed in order to survive.

Because just seeing her willingly share those traits with me and with others, the knowledge that the ability to do so actually exists in a world outside of mine, somehow frees me—no matter how temporarily—from the chains that bind me here in this suffocating place.

Yes, Spencer Locke is indeed my air.

I desperately hope the immorality I've chosen to bury deep within my soul doesn't one day pollute her very essence.

Chapter 1 ✴

Spencer

"Soooo . . ." Cassie says as we make the trek from track practice to Londonderry Street.

I glance to the right and warily eye my friend. Her long brown hair is pulled tight in a low ponytail that whips in the wind as we walk, and her face is flushed from our recent five-mile run. And, of course, in typical Cassie style, her track shorts are about three inches too short and barely cover the cheeks of her ass. She grins slyly as she swings her gaze to meet mine.

The skin on my shoulder objects to my heavy backpack, so I sling it over the other one before the nylon strap saws off my arm.

"Soooo?" I can only imagine what is going to come out of her mouth next.

"So," she begins subtly, then screams, "Jonathon Hawkins asked me to prom!" Her pitch increases as she begins to rattle off the details and my face falls with lack of interest before totally tuning her out.

I tend to zone out a lot when it comes to Cassie. It's not that I'm uninterested or don't want to hear what she has to say, but there are so many needless details she insists on including. She's one of those people who begins a story only to become sidetracked by another one, then another, and before long there are so many subplots going on I have no idea what she's talking about.

It's easier to listen for key words when she speaks and then piece them together on my own. That way she thinks I'm listening and I avoid losing my ever-loving mind. Plus, I tend to have a lot of inner monologue going on, so there's not a lot of extra room to store her stories in their entirety.

For example, with this conversation, it would go something like this:

Locker. (Meaning it happened at school)

Roses. (Pretty standard)

Serenade. (Nice touch)

Sex. (Time to pay attention)

Gah. She gets me every time with that one.

"Wait, hold on. Back up." I cease walking and turn to face her, dumbfounded. "You had sex with him? Outside the school? Before homeroom?"

She giggles and eagerly nods. I just shake my head back and forth to clear it because her recent revelation is just so ass-backward. "Aren't you supposed to wait until *after* prom to have sex with your date?"

Cassie shrugs her shoulders. "I guess, but what would be the fun in that?"

"Cass—"

"I mean, prom is like *two* months away. There's no way I'm going two months without sex. Absolutely not happening."

My eyebrows rise in question. "Okaaaay, so are you and Jonathon exclusive then? Like, sexually exclusive?"

She scoffs and looks at me like I've sprouted another head. "Um, I'm not sure what *he's* doing, but I plan on living it up for the remainder of this year. And that means *muy* drunken sexual encounters in my near future."

She places her hand on my shoulder and squeezes. I'm dumbstruck. "We should work on getting you laid too. Being a virgin in college would be *no bueno*, my friend. Trust me on this."

I close my jaw and, in hopes of a much-needed topic change, I say, "Excellent use of the Spanish language there, Cass. Your Spanish teacher was a fool for failing you."

She grins. "Right?" She looks toward the sky and exhales loudly. "Coach is an asshole. He was just pissed I wouldn't sleep with him. My Spanish is just fine."

Instead of sheer horror, I'm strangely relieved by this statement.

She takes another deep breath, then looks back at me. "Ready?"

I nod and shift the backpack yet again as we begin walking. Soon after, we turn onto Londonderry and make our way toward my house. A very familiar 1969 Camaro Z28 is parked in my driveway and the driver sitting on my porch, patiently awaiting my arrival.

I lift my hand to shield my eyes from the sun. Taking in his appearance, I'm whisked away from the present and deposited in my past. Five years ago to be exact.

"Hi."

My voice is small and unsure as I attempt to speak to the boy sitting alone on my front porch. The crackle of the gravel under my feet, however, is the only answer I receive. As I hesitantly approach, I mentally peg him as being only a year, maybe two, older than me.

The tips of his sandy-blond hair gleam brightly as the setting sun strikes, highlighting both the top of his head and the strands that peek at me from behind his ears.

Receiving no response to my presence, I watch silently as dust takes flight when he drags his foot through the dirt. My eyes fall to the tops of his shoes, the shredded holes displaying his gray socks underneath. Slowly I notice the frayed patches of his faded blue jeans, the brown stains on his white tank top, and finally the yellowing bruises lining the right side of his jaw.

Internally I cringe, but my voice remains steady as I offer gently, "My name's Spencer. What's yours?"

His body stiffens before he lifts his piercing blue eyes to meet mine. My breath stills at the sight of them. They're the most fascinating color I've ever seen.

So light blue they're almost gray.

So clear that I immediately recognize the pain he's trying to mask.

He watches me cautiously for a moment, taking in my appearance before his face pinches into a scowl. "Spencer? That's a boy's name."

I nod. "Yeah, not the first time I've heard that one."

His expression tightens before he finally breaks eye contact to focus on the much more interesting soil below him.

This isn't the first time we've had a foster kid show up at our house. I might be twelve years old, but I know a lot about this kind of stuff. I know his life has been difficult. His annoyed and hardened response isn't something I haven't dealt with before. Therefore, instead of being insulted like most girls my age, I simply take a deep breath and sit next to him, saying nothing else while we watch the sun set in front of us. Both in complete silence.

Once it has disappeared below the horizon, the boy blows out a long, deep puff of air, as though accepting his current situation, then drags his fingers through his messy hair before turning to face me. The side of his mouth barely curves upward into a subtle, yet playful, version of a grin.

"So . . . Spencer, was it?"

I finger the strands of long, blonde hair that have blown across my face and pull them away while offering him a tiny nod. He gives me a slight nod back and then jerks his chin in my direction before he speaks.

"Well, Spencer. Wanna get high?"

And that's the day I met Dalton Greer.

A wide, goofy grin crosses my face at the memory.

Right after he asked his question, I punched him in the arm. *Who in their right mind would offer weed to a twelve-year-old girl they just met?* Then I proceeded to take him up on his offer, catching him completely off guard. He busted out laughing, I took the first puff of many, and we've been friends ever since.

My heart springs to life as he rises, donning his typical playful smile and his ever-present Yankees cap, pulled low to hide his eyes. Although he still strongly resembles the kid I met that day, he's about a foot taller and definitely more man than boy now. Once standing, Dalton stretches broadly and the white V-neck T-shirt clinging to his chest lifts a couple of inches, exposing a small sliver of his muscled stomach. His frayed jeans hang low on his waist, so I also catch a glimpse of the glorious *V* marking his hips as he passes his hands through his longish, shaggy blond hair.

I sigh out loud.

I know we'll never be more than friends, but my heart is relentless. And a traitor. It abandoned me that day on the porch, leaving me to suffer in silence with my unrequited crush.

"Girl, you are in so much trouble with that one," Cassie mutters under her breath as we pass my mailbox.

I shoot her a sideways glare. "Shh . . ."

As usual, my attempt to shush her delivers the exact opposite effect.

"Dalton is so gorgeous, Spence. You know, you should totally cash in your V-card with him. I'm willing to bet he would take very, *very* good care of you." She sighs. "I hate that he graduated last year. I used to watch him walk down the halls. That ass in those jeans . . ." She actually moans after the last word and I elbow her in the ribs.

Clearly insulted, she stops and gasps. "Ouch, bitch!"

"Shut. Up. You know it's not like that with us," I snap. My tone is harsh, but when I catch a glimpse of her wide-eyed expression, I struggle to hide my amusement.

Narrowing her gaze, she leans into me and whispers, "You and I"—she gestures between us—"are going to figure this out. I'm going to go home and come up with a plan, like now. And then I'm going to come back over tonight and we are setting this brilliant plan I haven't even thought of into motion." She giggles and wraps her arms around my neck, pulling me into a tight embrace.

I hug her back, laughing in her ear. "You know, you make absolutely no sense, but I love you anyway."

A giggle sounds before she responds, "Love *you*, times two."

Releasing me, she turns to cross the street to her house, evidently to concoct the plan of the century. I smile as I watch her cross safely, then turn toward Dalton, who is making his approach. He grins crookedly at me and reaches to take my backpack. I hand it over willingly.

"Thanks," I state, rubbing my shoulder. Dalton switches the backpack to the other hand, then curls his fingers over my shoulder and begins to knead my aching muscles.

"Anytime," he answers, still smiling. With his hand still massaging, he urges me forward.

I glance up at him and squint. "Why do you always wear your hats so low?" I reach up and tug the bill of his cap. "It hides your eyes."

He frowns. "That's exactly why I wear them that way. If you can't see my eyes, you can't see me watching. And I watch everyone. All the time."

I snicker. "Okay, because *that's* not creepy."

He shrugs as we continue to walk. "What's Daisy Mae up to these days?"

I laugh. "You know that's not her name. And you know she hates it when you call her that."

The previous tension in his face fades as he grins and angles his head. The cap on his head fulfills its purpose and shields his bright-blue eyes. "I also know you hate it when I call you *Pencil*, but that doesn't stop me either."

"It's only cute when it comes out of the mouth of a five-year-old little girl who can't pronounce Spencer," I remark, straight-faced, as memories of little Anna Grace from the shelter fill my mind. She wasn't there long, but during the short time, she lovingly gave me the nickname *Pencil*. Although Dalton is the only one who uses it, so I guess she gave it to *him*.

His laughter echoes around me as we make our way to my porch. "Stop lying to yourself, Pencil. You think it's cute when I say it too."

I do, but that shall remain unsaid.

"Plus, if Cassie doesn't want to be called Daisy Mae, she needs to wear longer shorts."

I nod in agreement. "To answer your question, she's up to no good," I answer truthfully.

His features draw taut and he turns to look at me with his face now hardened. Protective. "You know she's not a good influence."

I bark out a laugh and shake my head at his blatant audacity. "That's rich coming from you."

Dalton narrows his eyes. "What's that supposed to mean?"

"You, my friend, have introduced me to pretty much everything my mom has warned me to stay away from. You're not the best influence yourself."

Finally at my porch, Dalton shakes my backpack off his shoulder and onto the front step as we take our usual seats. His on the left and mine on the right.

I inhale deeply and turn to face him, and as I do, I watch his expression morph from that of protection to one of internal argument. I can see it so clearly in his blue-gray eyes when he's warring within himself. I've seen this struggle frequently over the past five years, and I've yet to figure out a way to help him through it.

My eyebrows draw together, and without hesitation, I lift my hand and tug on the bill of his cap. "Hey, what's going on with you?" I ask softly.

My hand falls to his shoulder while he continues to stare off into the distance. I remain silent, allowing him the time he needs. We've danced this dance many times before.

The day he showed up on our porch, something happened while we watched that first sunset together. I don't know how or why or if I can even put it into words, but we became forever connected. My hidden pain cried out for his, and his fiery rage searched for mine. It was as though the most deprived parts within each of us sensed the other's, then reached out and grabbed hold, essentially melding us together and making us whole.

I know it because I felt it.

I felt *him*.

And soon after, the number of sunsets watched became too many to count, the amount of easy laughter shared immeasurable, and the quantity of weed and alcohol consumed between the two of us . . . *copious*.

Yet with all this time between us, amid the sunsets and laughter, not once did we dare discuss our pasts.

As far as Dalton knows, I'm the only daughter of Deborah Locke, and my father is deceased. I'm a habitual visitor of domestic violence centers, alcohol/drug rehab clinics, and homeless shelters because my mother volunteers nonstop. With no one else around, since I was a little girl, I've had to traipse wherever she went and sometimes still do. I have seen horrors that no one should ever have to witness during these visits, which obviously had the intended effect because I'm actually very thankful for my life. Thankful for the chance I've been given, and thankful I have a loving mother.

While Dalton is aware of all of this, there's also a lot he doesn't know. But he has his skeletons too.

Dalton is very secretive about his former life—or *lives*. I know nothing more than I did the day he showed up on our porch. My mom, however, was provided in-depth knowledge of the various reasons he was removed, because as his emergency foster parent, she *needed* to be privy to the information upon his arrival. She has never shared that information with me out of respect for him, and I would never ask her to do so, for the same reason.

Every single child that lands themselves in our spare bedroom is given that same respect. But I know enough to understand that if they have found their way to our house in need of emergency foster care, the situation is never a good one, as it's typically needed for the child's protection.

We only housed Dalton for a matter of weeks before he was placed with the Housemans. My mother worked closely with Dalton's social worker to have him placed within their care. Through the relationship built while volunteering at the local abuse shelter, she knew from experience that they were very kind people with vast experience when it came to fostering abused children.

The bond Dalton and I formed that very first sunset strengthened over his four-week stay into our friendship today. Even after he left for the Houseman's home, he was still near enough to stop by whenever he wanted. His visits never ceased, and even though he "aged out" of foster care last year, they still continue.

In the time we've spent together, I've vowed to try to help him. To teach him the lessons I've learned. To find a way for him to let go of the past that so clearly haunts him, which means I must have patience during times like this.

And I will wait as long as he needs.

The corner of my mouth lifts into an encouraging smile. Breaking his eye contact from the ground to meet my patient gaze, he hesitantly reaches up and removes my hand from his shoulder to encase it in his own.

"I just worry about you, Spence." He shakes his head in frustration. "I mean, you said it yourself, I'm not the best influence. I've never pretended to be. But what you need to understand is people like me, like Cassie, we find ourselves unintentionally drawn to you because deep down, we want *you* to influence *us*. Not the other way around."

Familiar storms brew in his eyes. "You're such a *good* person, Spence. I just worry that one day, being surrounded by people like us, well . . . I worry that what makes us who we are will eventually destroy the person you are meant to become."

I hold his gaze, assessing him, then smile. "Dalton, I'm not a freaking piece of china. I'm not some delicate, fragile *child*." I laugh boldly at his assumption. "*You* are not going to destroy me. *Cassie* is not going to destroy me. *No one* is going to destroy me."

I shake my head. "We're all just *people*, Dalton. People make mistakes. Some more than others, but every person deserves to be judged on how they learn and adjust from mistakes made. Not defined by tragedy or happenstance. I know who you are *now*, Dalton, and that is a good person who just happened to make some crappy decisions along the way. That's all. Same with Cassie."

He remains expressionless, but when his jaw clenches, I sense his objection. Shrugging my shoulders nonchalantly, I add, "You know, I'm always here if you want to talk about *before*. You never do, but I just wanted to let you know while we're having the 'no discriminatory judgment' conversation."

I watch as his eyes soften and the storms within them calm, before Dalton, in typical Dalton style, completely disregards my offer by deflecting. "I also worry about you alone in that goddamn high school. St. Louis Parochial High School is full of nothing other than rich, pansy-ass douchebags whose brains are capable of processing exactly two things: spending their daddy's money and satisfying their dicks. I'm one hundred percent sure Cassie's no help in the latter department, either."

Laughter bursts from my chest. "Um, I go to that school, so that blows both your theories, since I'm clearly lacking in those areas. I'm only able to attend that school because Mom works there and well"—I look at my lap and shrug—"I'm clearly lacking."

He fights a smile. "*You* aren't like anyone else in that school."

"Cassie isn't either, and neither were you."

"I don't even want to know what Cassie had to do to get in that school. And I only got in because your mom pulled strings to get me some obligatory we-care-about-poor-people-too scholarship."

"That's not true and you know it, Dalton." And it's not. He had to be tested before he was accepted, and his scores put him right at the top 10 percent of his class. Mom did relay that information to me.

Dalton returns his gaze to the ground in front of us and mumbles, "Yeah, well, I hate that I'm not there anymore to watch over you."

I grin. "You are aware that it's March, right? I've already made it through the majority of the year unscathed. I think I'll be okay for two more months."

He nods stiffly as I continue, still smiling, because I kind of find this whole thing adorable. "Is that why you come by? To make sure I'm surviving without your *protection*?"

His face becomes solemn as he releases my hand, relaxing back onto his elbows and stretching out his long legs. Facing forward, he stares at the horizon.

"Not the only reason," he answers softly. "I miss our sunsets."

Without a word, I lean back and mirror his position, stretching my legs to match his. We watch together in shared silence.

Just as the sun begins to set, I whisper, "Yeah. I miss you too, Dalton."

He continues to look forward, face blank, no words spoken. They never are. But I know he heard me when he finally releases a long, contented sigh, because my own heart warms in response.

I know because of the bond we share . . . That's what it feels like when Dalton's heart smiles.

Chapter 2 ✳

Dalton

An involuntary breath passes through my lips. As much as I want to hide it, to act as though her presence has no effect on me whatsoever, I can't deny my body's response. Familiar warmth coats my chest and soothes the constant burn, temporarily salving the open blisters it often leaves behind. I know the pain will be back. It always comes back. But instead of focusing on the inevitable, I take a brief moment to relish in the serenity that floods me. The peace that only she can provide.

I maintain my forward stare for fear she will see my weakness—my overwhelming *need* for this feeling. The pure ecstasy it brings is better than any drug I've ever done.

I crave it.

I crave *her*.

After a while, she releases a sigh, and without thinking, I glance to the side. The breeze kicks up and the sweet, citrus scent of Spencer fills my lungs. Our gazes lock, her blue eyes meeting mine, and I'm mesmerized by the innocence staring back at me.

The tranquility of the moment is soon broken, because just as quickly as my relief was found, her purity strikes a match that sets my chest aflame. Guilt reemerges, a fiery blaze of sins and transgressions committed. All oxygen vanishes and I can no longer breathe.

I need to go.

I shouldn't be here.

Rising off my elbows, I scoot into a seated position. Just as I open my mouth to tell her I'm leaving, her freckled nose crinkles in a very familiar way. In a way that tells me she's about to ask me to do something I won't want to do.

Spencer sits up and smiles, her blue eyes lit with anticipation. "Come to the shelter with me," she proposes. "Mom is there and she'll want to see you. Plus, the kids love it when you come." She laughs, then knocks my shoulder with hers. "Even though you pretend you don't like them, I know you secretly do."

"I can't," I answer quickly. "I need to get back."

She narrows her eyes and pinches her mouth, disappointed by my response. But then, her expression turns thoughtful and I watch as her lips move to the side.

"Hmm . . ." she hums, tapping her finger on her chin. "I think you should come to the shelter with me," she repeats.

I fight the urge to smile. "I have to go, Spence."

"No." She shakes her head, unrelenting. "I think you *need* to come to the shelter with me."

I know exactly what she's doing, and damn if it's not working. Laughter climbs its way up my throat.

"I. Have. To. Go," I respond, enunciating each word. I even add the motions of sign language, since she's clearly not hearing me.

The lyrical sound of Spencer's giggle douses the fire in my chest. She twists her body to face me. "You"—she points at me, then scissors her index and middle fingers in a walking motion—"come with me."

My jaw tightens as I swallow my laughter because she really, *really* sucks at sign language. She grins widely in response. She knows she's about to get what she wants. I'm helpless to do *anything* but give it to her.

The sight in front of me—Spencer's smile and wide eyes filled to the brim with excitement—breaks my composure. My shoulders bob as my laughter breaks free, a response only she and Rat are successful in eliciting.

I shake my head, grinning as I concede. "Fine."

"Yay!" she screams, then jumps up, snagging her backpack. "I'm gonna put this up, then we can go."

As soon as the screen door shuts, my head falls into my hands. I cannot believe I let her talk me into this. Every time we visit the abuse center, I'm forced to relive my past. The one I've been trying to forget since the day I was born. The helplessness in the eyes of the mothers and their children—their fear, their uncertainty, their desolation, their scars (inside and out)—it's all so fucking familiar. It makes me sick to my stomach.

Spencer thinks my being there will help me come to terms with my past, to find some measure of healing by helping others, but it doesn't. All it does is piss me right the fuck off.

But I endure it because making her smile is just another facet of my addiction. When it's me who brings that smile to her face, so full of undeniable joy, it's easy to pretend *my* reality doesn't exist. That instead, I'm the person she believes me to be—believes I *can* be—rather than the monster I've become.

What I wouldn't give to live in that world.

"Okay! I'm ready," Spencer shouts.

Reluctantly, I stand. After plastering a fucking fake smile on my face, I gesture to my car in the driveway. Spencer takes my calloused hand into hers and I revel in the skin-to-skin contact as we walk, releasing her only to open the door.

When she's tucked safely inside, I close the door, cursing to myself until sliding in next to her. I stick the keys in the ignition and fire up the engine. My Camaro growls to life, the roar reverberating all around us. The side of my mouth kicks up and I glance over at Spencer, her face beaming with mutual appreciation.

"I love this car, Dalton. I can't believe you restored it so quickly." She smiles and runs her delicate hand along the dash. "It looks like your time at the garage is paying off. I'm so proud of you."

Ah, yes.

The *garage*.

My job as a lowly mechanic, the same as Rat. I eye the pride in her expression, and the truth squeezes my chest like a vise. I don't have the heart to tell her this car was actually taken as payment in full from one of Silas's customers.

Over 200K owed, we took whatever cash he had available and the Camaro for our time. I broke my hand during the acquisition and Silas gave me the car as a reward. I happily accepted it because (1) you don't argue with Silas Kincaid and (2) it *is* a fucking pretty sweet ride.

As far as Spencer knows, my broken hand was the result of a jack slipping from underneath one of the cars at the garage. Being a mechanic seems to be the main source of my *accidents*. In fact, to her, I must seem like the most accident-prone mechanic ever.

After putting the Camaro in gear, we make the fifteen-minute drive to the center with minimal conversation. I park the car and leave it idling, focusing on a woman as she enters through the front door. It's not until a warm finger curls around the bottom of my chin that I look away.

Spencer redirects my attention and my stare falls directly to her mouth. It's so unbelievably wrong, but it's the only thing my eyes seem to want to see. She swallows deeply, nervously raking her teeth along her bottom lip, and I force my gaze to meet her eyes.

She smiles shyly, clearing her throat. "You're not going to back out on me, are you?"

A grin tugs at my lips, persistence one of her most endearing qualities. "No."

Her mouth broadens into a relieved smile. "Good. Now come on, Mr. Grumpy McGrumperton, let's get in there and change some lives."

Through a breath of laughter, the words fly out of my mouth before I can think better of it. "Your incessant positivity is wearing. Don't you ever get tired?"

Her mouth falls, drawing her lips tight. "Actually, Dalton, what exhausts me is constantly hauling you out of the cesspool of negativity in which you insist upon drowning. It's an endless, tiring job." She sighs. "But I continue to do it because I believe in you *that* much. And if it means I have to drag your ass to see a bunch of kids—who happen to adore you, by the way—in order to get you out of one of your many funks, then that's what I will do."

My head jerks in surprise and my brows rise as I stifle my laughter. I forgot how hilarious it is when she's pissed. My little yapping Chihuahua.

"Don't laugh at me," she warns. "It's not funny."

"It's kind of funny, Spence."

She just stares, face blank.

I roll my eyes. "Fine," I groan. "Let's go."

Once again, her eyes fill with delight and she beams at me. "Okay," she shrieks, then throws open the door.

I snort, actually *snort*, with laughter before my own feet hit the ground.

As we approach the center, I note how extremely unassuming this building is. But as Spencer enters the code for our entrance, I'm reminded of why. Its anonymity is necessary for the safety of those stashed inside.

Upon entry, Mrs. Locke greets us as she passes by the front desk. With her glasses askew and her long light-brown hair piled in a messy heap, she focuses her caramel-colored stare directly on me. A smile breaks across her face, and she wraps her arms around me, enveloping me in one of her bear hugs. I stand awkwardly while Spencer giggles.

Once released, Mrs. Locke steps back and addresses me. "Dalton, it's so good to see you. It's been a while. How have you been?" She watches me closely, her sharp eyes missing nothing.

"I'm good, Mrs. Locke. Keeping busy at the garage," I lie, pushing whatever starved remnants of conscience I have left out of my mind.

She tightens her gaze. "Hmm, I see." After a few seconds, she voids her face of suspicion and adds, "You can call me Deborah. You know that."

I smile and nod. She grins back, then turns to Spencer, brows raised. "Homework done?"

A light blush creeps across Spencer's cheeks. "Almost?"

"I've got one more hour here and then we can head home." Mrs. Locke turns to me. "Thank you for giving her a ride, Dalton. You're free to go if you like."

Tempting, but after the lengthy lecture I just received, I think it's safest to make an appearance. "No, it's fine," I answer. "I'm going to visit with the kids for a while."

Ms. Locke's smile widens. "Excellent. They're in the game room. Have at it." After another quick embrace, she hastily disappears into the kitchen.

Spencer knocks me with her shoulder, indicating the direction of said game room, and once inside, I take in the familiar sight of coloring book pages, painted palms resembling animals on construction paper, and various drawings and sketches covering the walls. Though the hand-painted clay pots lining the windowsills are a new addition. In front of me, three kids are engrossed in a mean game of Super Smash Bros. I recognize two of them.

"Dalton! Come join the game. You can be Princess Peach," one yells, bursting with boisterous laughter.

"Hey, *I'm* Princess Peach!" Spencer shouts, then darts in front of the TV to snatch the last controller. She sticks her tongue out at me before refocusing on the game.

I grin as I watch her play. Just as she shouts "BOOM!" while taking out some repressed anger on poor Donkey Kong, my gaze wanders the room. I spot a little girl sitting by herself at a table tucked into a distant corner. Light-blonde hair conceals her face as she scribbles furiously on the paper below her. Completely enthralled by her presence, I walk to where she's seated. She continues coloring, and although my instinct is to stay away, to leave for her benefit, my feet remain rooted to the ground.

She pauses in her efforts, shyly glancing up at me before returning her attention to the table. She grabs another crayon and continues coloring. With her eyes just as bright and blue, I find myself staring at the exact image of what I believe Spencer would have looked like at six years old.

Surprising the shit out of myself, I ask, "Do you mind if I color with you?"

Without looking at me, she carefully flips the pages in the coloring book until she finds what she's looking for. Then she tears out the page, sliding it in front of the seat next to me before searching her box of crayons. Once satisfied, she pulls out a select few and places them on top of the torn paper.

All without saying a word.

Taking my seat, I remain silent as I pick up the blue crayon and begin to color the bodysuit of the one and only Superman. Several minutes pass, and just as I switch to red for the cape, she finally speaks. "You're a good colorer."

I grin and tear my eyes away from the almighty Kal-El to look at her. And that's when I see it. The faded bruise high on her cheek and the red welts lining it. A slap mark.

I force a deep breath through my nose and crack my neck, my natural response when stricken with memories from my past. The rage I feed upon, the anger that fuels me to perform on a regular basis, skims dangerously close to the surface. Instinctively, my fingers tighten around the crayon in my hand.

Her innocent eyes remain locked with mine. She watches me closely for a moment, studying me intently, then rises and leans her tiny body across the table to place her palm on my cheek. Normally I would strongly object to anyone I don't know putting his or her hands on me, but I remain frozen. The warmth of her fingers seeps into my skin as tears of understanding rise in her eyes.

"You're one of us. I can tell."

She flattens her palm against my chest, the burn beneath my ribcage strangely anesthetized by the contact. "I know." She nods, focusing on her touch. "It hurts here. Where they break your heart."

I'm barely able to nod and my throat clogs with emotion I haven't felt in years. I swallow it deeply, watching her gaze lift to mine before she speaks. "Yeah, I feel it too."

She offers me a small, shy smile, then grips the paper she gave me minutes ago, flashing it in front of my eyes. Superman stares back at me as she states, "You're good like him. A hero. You just don't know it yet."

It takes every ounce of willpower not to bark my denial, but I force myself to remain silent. She places my Superman on the table, then reaches for her own page, pulling it in front of us before climbing into my lap.

As the little girl silently resumes her coloring, I see Spencer watching out of the corner of my eye. I, however, keep my attention focused solely on what's happening at this very table. I don't dare to interrupt this moment. Something inherent within me recognizes that this gesture, this demonstration of trust, is just as important for her as it is for me. So instead of looking away, I simply reach around the tiny body in my lap and pick up right where I left off.

Just as she finishes her picture, which is a very green version of Wonder Woman, she twists her neck to look at me, seeking approval.

"Is that the Green Giant?" I ask, offering her a teasing smile.

Her eyes brighten as she giggles. "No, dummy. It's Wonder Woman!"

I narrow my gaze, pretending to evaluate her work. "Is she sick? She's looking a bit green."

She bursts into laughter. I don't even bother trying to fight my grin as it breaks across my face. "You're funny . . ." She pauses. "What's your name?"

"Dalton. And you are?"

"I'm Penelope. Penelope Owen, but you can call me Penny 'cause you're my friend."

I dip my head in thanks, then grab the black crayon from the table. "Well, Penny. I colored this Superman just for you." Before giving her my artwork, I jot a couple of things down on the paper.

"This"—I point—"is my name. And this"—I gesture just below it—"is my phone number."

I fold the paper and hand it to Penny. "I want you to put this in your pocket, or your backpack, or wherever you will always have it. And if you need anything, you just open this and dial my number. Okay?"

A mischievous grin crosses her face before she rises to her feet, glancing around for any onlookers while shoving the picture in her front pocket. Once done, she wraps her arms around my shoulders, squeezes my neck, then completely annihilates my world as she whispers . . .

"See, I told you. You're a hero. You chased the pain away."

Chapter 3 ✳

Spencer

"It was the weirdest thing, Cass. I could see it all over his face. He opened up for like two seconds, then *bam*! He gets a text and completely shuts down."

The memory of him whispering something into Penny's ear right before announcing a very terse good-bye to me skates through my mind. I watch from a seated position on my bed as the chair at my desk spins at neck-breaking speed.

"Stop it, Cassie. You're making me dizzy."

The chair slows, Cassie's eyes trying to focus on mine. "Who do you think the text was from?" she asks.

I shrug. "Who knows? Probably one of those *girls* he dates."

My tone is flippant, but I can't deny the pain clenching my heart. I don't know if I'm merely frustrated with the lack of morals of the girls Dalton goes out with or if I'm simply disappointed that I'm not one of them. There's a lot about my reaction to Dalton's *extracurricular activities* I don't understand these days.

"Dalton doesn't *date*, Spence. You know that." Her dark-brown eyes narrow on me. "You *do* know that, right?"

"Yeah." I sigh. "I mean, I know we're *just* friends. We've been friends for years now. I guess there's just a line that shouldn't be crossed. But to be honest, it hurts that he doesn't look at me *that way*."

I fling myself backward and close my eyes. Covering my head with a pillow, I groan.

Cassie's shameless cackle fills the air. "Spencer, that boy is so into *you* but you have absolutely no idea. It's endearing really." I remove the pillow and open my eyes to find her standing directly above me, knowing smile on her face. "Dense and incredibly naïve, but endearing," she adds thoughtfully.

My face falls slack at her pitiful attempt at encouragement while offering my most clever of responses. "He is *not*."

She giggles again, then hurls herself right next to me. Centering her face above mine, she cocks her brow. "He *is*."

Definitely not one of our sharpest repartees.

Rising, she sweeps her long brown hair over her shoulder, then folds her legs underneath her teeny-tiny pajama shorts. Her intent eyes narrow on mine. "You guys are always touching each other. Haven't you noticed that?"

My lips pucker in thought. "Well, yeah, but we've always done that. That doesn't mean anything. I hug you all the time."

"That's different and you know it," she barks. "You're openly affectionate with exactly *two* people. Him and me. And he touches *no one* besides you. Don't you think that's odd?" I crinkle my nose and she grins as she adds, "That's what I thought."

"Cass—"

"And that's where my plan comes in."

Oh, yeah. The brilliant plan of the century.

She grins wider. "You need to go on a date."

I give her an incredulous laugh and roll my eyes. "You have officially lost your mind."

Cassie maintains her calculating grin. "If you go on a date, I guarantee what you'll find regarding Dalton and his feelings will surprise you."

"Cass. No one wants to go out on a date with me. Trust me."

She shakes her head before bursting into unnecessary, heinous laughter. "You really have no idea, do you?" she asks, wiping her eyes. "Every guy at school has a hard-on for you, you fool. They're just fucking scared to come near you because of Dalton. He let it be known that if they did, he would deal with them."

"Oh my God! You have no idea what you're talking about." I laugh uncontrollably. She really has lost her mind.

Cassie shakes her head. "I'm totally serious, Spence. I swear on my Kindle."

At this, I take in a sharp breath and sober immediately. To Cassie, her Kindle is as sacred as the Bible.

She nods dramatically, allowing me time to grasp the severity of her statement. Right hand raised, she states, "On the overabundance of trashy romance novels within my possession, I solemnly swear that Dalton openly took out a vendetta against any male in our school who should dare approach you."

"He did what?" I screech, catapulting into an upright position. Anger ignites and my face heats wildly as realization dawns.

This whole year—in fact, my whole high school career—no one would even look at me. No one asked me to come to parties, to go on dates, to go to prom. Not that I would, but being asked would be nice, ya know? Okay, I probably would go. I mean, it's a rite of passage, right?

Two black-painted fingernails snap directly in front of my face, jolting me out of my inner thoughts. "Hooker. Pay attention."

I shake my head and refocus. Still seething, I whisper, "This whole time, I've thought it was me. That I wasn't dating material or pretty enough. Four years, Cass. Four years of feeling like I wasn't good enough." My molars grind together. "It all makes sense now."

Cassie waves her hand dismissively. "We're getting off track here. I have found someone who, luckily for you, seems to have recently acquired a death wish."

I stare blankly and she nods her head slowly in emphasis. "Jase Williams."

My eyebrows hit the ceiling while my jaw falls slack. "Jase Williams? As in the quarterback of the varsity football team? The unbelievably hot and completely drool-worthy boy with the killer smile who every single girl in our school would give their left boob to go out with? *That* Jase Williams?"

Cassie's head dips in affirmation. "*That* Jase Williams."

My face scrunches in thought because this I find very interesting. The idea of me actually going on a date, while exciting, is also intriguing. I would be lying if I didn't admit that part of me wonders if Cassie is right. Maybe Dalton's overprotectiveness is simply his way of masking unspoken feelings. Maybe, *just maybe*, Jase Williams will be the catalyst needed to break through Dalton's titanium-encrusted shell and force him to actually feel *something* for *someone*. To feel something for *me*.

But there's another, less dominant part also forced to concede that maybe this is exactly what I need *for me* to finally feel something for someone *other than* Dalton Greer. For me to bury this useless schoolgirl crush and focus on the possibility that there may be someone out there who actually reciprocates my feelings.

Yet even with that acknowledgment, my foolish heart leaps with hope for the former.

My pulse kicks up a notch and my stomach churns with anticipation. "All right," I grant, my mouth curling downward as I nod. "I find myself intrigued with your theory. Therefore, I shall go out with *that* Jase Williams."

Cassie's face breaks into a goofy grin and her eyes light with anticipation. I raise my hand to calm her excitement before adding, "For research purposes only, of course."

Her expression falls into mock seriousness. "Of course," she repeats.

I fight a grin, but eventually smile as Cassie does the same, her brilliantly concocted plan evidently in full effect.

Mom's voice halts our devious activity as she shouts from the hallway. "Cassie. Your mom called, sweetie. Time to head home."

Cassie reaches forward to envelop me in a Cassie-embrace before whispering, "I gave Jase your number already."

She climbs off my bed and heads toward the window, her typical method of both entering and exiting my bedroom. I giggle and shake my head as she unlatches the lock, climbing her way onto my lawn.

"I don't know why you find it impossible to use the door like everyone else in the world."

She stops midstride, straddling the ledge before giving me a toothy smile. "Why would I want to be like everyone else in the world when I can be me?"

"Agreed. Wholeheartedly." I grin. "Be safe crossing the street, crazy ass." She grins back and winks. Just before she lowers the window, I add, "Love you."

Blowing me a kiss, she says, "Love you, times *two*," then shuts the window behind her.

My feet hit the floor and I watch her make her way like a ninja in the night. I'm latching the window when I hear Mom's voice.

"Cassie just leave?"

She's standing in my doorway, worn pink robe wrapped tightly around her body. I glance once more out the window before closing the curtain.

"Yeah."

"Homework done?" she asks, turning down my sheets.

"Of course, Mom." Laughing, I climb into bed, the familiar smell of clean linens surrounding me as I snuggle in. "How dare you question my work ethic?"

She grins and takes a seat beside me. Extending her arm, she tucks a strand of blonde hair behind my ear before leaning and placing a gentle kiss on my forehead. "Just making sure," she states with a wink. Her smile fades before she continues. "I know I've been busy. I hate that I haven't been here as much as I should lately."

I shake my head. "It's okay. I know there are kids out there who need you."

"You need me too, Spencer. I should be here more."

We have this conversation often. Between her day job at my school as the guidance counselor and her volunteer work in the evenings, I don't see as much of her as I would like. But I can't be selfish. There are kids out there who need her more than I do right now.

"Mom, it's fine. I'm fine. School is fine. Stop worrying." I grin reassuringly.

She smiles back, then takes my hand into hers. "I don't know how I got so lucky, but I'm blessed to have you."

She squeezes my fingers gently. After another light kiss to the top of my head, she stands, tucking me in tightly before heading toward the doorway.

Just as she passes my desk, I remind her. "The light, please."

I don't miss the hesitation in her movement. We also have *this* conversation often. Without having to see her face, I already know her expression is etched with concern because at seventeen years of age, I still sleep with a light on and the door wide open. A habit not even my mother has been able to break. Not for eleven years.

She leans, pulling the cord on my lamp, then twists to face me. "Movie night. We need a movie night this weekend."

I smile and nod my agreement. She dips her head, flicking off my overhead light before leaving me alone in my room. Reaching under my pillow, I grab my phone and plug it into the charger before putting in my ear buds and hitting play on my Gabrielle Aplin acoustic album. As "Ghosts" begins to flood my ears, I find myself lost in the excitement of Cassie's theory and the eagerness of Dalton's response. Seeing him with that little girl today gave me hope that there's still a part of him that is alive. A very viable piece that he keeps hidden from the rest of the world. A small section awaiting someone's discovery.

I just really hope that person is me.

After glancing once more at the lamp, I close my eyes. Anticipation mixed with the sounds of Gabrielle's guitar keep the demons of my darkness at bay as I allow sleep to finally take me.

Chapter 4

Dalton

A deep, familiar voice and the sound of a lock being sprung wakes me from the most uncomfortable attempt at sleep, ever.

"Well, you're free to go. *Again*."

I pry open my good eye and shift my neck to peer across the room. I'm met with a disapproving stare—something I've become quite used to with this particular officer of the law.

As I slowly awaken, the pain begins to ebb. *Jesus*. My fucking head is killing me. And my ribs. And my back. In fact, every single part of my body aches and this metal slab I'm lying on is doing absolutely nothing to relieve the discomfort. I take in a deep breath, praying to the gods of pain for mercy before hauling my ass up.

And as I rise, my world falls off its axis.

"Fuuuuuck . . ." is all I can manage as my feet hit the ground.

After a quick pass of my fingers through my matted hair, I respond, "It's about time."

Damn. Even my hair hurts.

"Let's go, Greer. Your other half is waiting for you."

My face is in no shape to smile, so I grin inwardly at the remark. It's no secret that Rat and I frequented the Fuller County Jail often throughout our youth. Although, this is my first time outside the juvenile holding area.

I inhale again in preparation before finally standing. My fingers clench, my body objecting to the movement, and my steps are slow as I walk toward the open door of the cell. Officer Kirk Lawson invades the space, clad in his typical dark pants and polo-shirt combo, his keen brown eyes watching.

"What?" My tone is clipped.

Lawson shakes his head and exhales. "You're in a completely different arena now, kid. A legal adult. You keep doing this shit, you're going to land your ass in prison. In fact"—he pauses to close the door behind me—"with the charges brought against you, that's exactly where you'd be headed had they not been dropped."

His gaze narrows and his face tightens into a stern expression. "Assault with a deadly weapon is no joke. It shouldn't be taken lightly and neither should prison. I've watched you grow up on the streets, in and out of the juvenile detention center, petty crimes here and there. All of which will be sealed in your file because of your age at the time. But this, this is an entirely different game. A game for which there are no winners."

He shakes his head once more in emphasis. "Mark my words, Greer. If you keep playing, you *will* lose."

I stare blankly at him, his words having no effect as they ricochet off my hardened armor. "We done here?"

His features relax, slowly transforming from frustration to concession. "You're tough, Greer. There's no doubt about it, but you're also smart. You could do so much more, *be* so much more, than this life. And as a *man*, that's now your choice to make. You can either hold onto the rage that consumes you, or let it go and break free."

I scoff at his ridiculous delusions. When the hell was I magically whisked away to become part of yet another fucking after-school special? I'm growing increasingly weary of this same PSA and my recurring role in it every time I see Lawson.

My eyes narrow. Although I typically have a certain amount of restraint when it comes to his mind-numbing lectures, tonight it seems too much for me to contain. Fury boils at the surface and the words spew sharply through gritted teeth.

"You don't fucking know me, and you sure as hell don't know my life."

My voice trembles and my fists clench to suppress my anger, but fury finds its exit as it erupts along my skin. "Contrary to what you and your fucking fairy-tale existence have led you to believe, I am *not* given a choice. I'm not awarded that luxury because of what I *had* to do in order to survive. That was the path I was *forced* to take, and on that path I *have no choice* but to remain. Don't come at me like you know me. Know my life. You don't know shit."

Lawson's eyes remain trained on me, not once breaking away during my tirade. He watches me thoughtfully, taking in every word I speak. Once the last word leaves my mouth, he leans into me and quietly offers, "You're right. I don't know your life. But I know mine and because of that, I know you *do*, in fact, have a choice. No one gets to pick their circumstances, Greer. The choice lies in what you do in response to them. It's not *awarded* to you, but it is yours for the taking."

He holds my stare for approximately two-point-five seconds more before finally turning away. No more words are spoken between us as he leads me to release processing.

Once all my personal effects are again within my possession, I exit the jail, Lawson's speech still looming in my mind. The pain begins to numb as I force myself to concentrate on his words. Yeah, it worked for a do-gooder like Lawson, the theory that I can dig my way out of this grave in which I will undoubtedly be buried— probably sooner rather than later. But what he doesn't realize is that there is so much soil on my head, so much blood on my hands, there's no way out for me now. Even fucking Hercules couldn't tunnel his way out of the mess I've made of my life.

The door slams shut behind me, and I'm greeted by the pearly white, shit-eating grin of my partner in crime, Anthony Marchione III, a.k.a. "Rat." "Rat" actually being short for "No-Good Hoodrat," a name given him by many a store clerk back in the day. With deft quickness I'd never before seen, he lifted food from every corner store in the neighborhood. He was pretty much the only reason I ate some days. He's still fast as lightning, and Silas uses that speed to his advantage.

Rat's thumbs are hooked in the belt loops of his frayed jeans as he approaches, the gold chain around his neck glistening along with his trademark Italian horn as both rest against his black thermal T-shirt. With his hazel eyes and olive complexion, the smile on his face lights up like a beacon when I head in his direction.

"Did you tell Lawson I said hi?" he asks, laughing and moving to clap me on the shoulder. I duck out of the way to prevent the contact, then wince, my body screaming from the movement.

Rat's face draws taut and he tightens his gaze. "Let me see your face, brother."

Reaching up, I thread my fingers through my hair and pin the layers against the top of my head, the length no longer able to obstruct the injuries. My right eye is now completely swollen shut, and I taste blood when I run my tongue lightly over the gash in my bottom lip.

"Motherfuckers," Rat breathes. "What happened?"

I shrug, releasing the hold on my hair. "After you went with Jamieson, I don't remember much, man. I just know as soon as you left, I was surrounded by at least ten of his men. The rest of it is a total blur."

This is pretty typical actually. When I'm in *my zone*, I see nothing but the monsters of my past. It's their faces that my fists connect with, their ribs I break, and their wrists I snap, all in the name of retribution. My payback to all those motherfuckers who felt the need to knock around a helpless child. My fucking vengeance as it rains down upon them.

That's what makes me so valuable to Silas. I have no conscience when it comes to what I do. Because deep down, I know the men I beat senseless are nothing more than the same scum I feared growing up. The difference is, now I'm no longer a helpless child. And I make good and goddamn sure they're aware of that fact.

I will concede that Lawson was right about one thing. The rage. It's always there, lying just beneath the surface, waiting for the floodgates to open.

And tonight, those gates flew wide the fuck open. Except, it wasn't about *my* retribution. It was about Penny's. My mind was inundated with visions of her tiny little body being knocked around like a rag doll. Of her sweet, angelic face marred by some monster's hand. By the very men surrounding me.

That's all the fuel I needed.

I siphoned every bit and used it until not one of them was left standing. I don't even remember where the baseball bat came from, but I do know it came in handy.

"Brother."

Rat's deep voice pulls me into the present.

"We need to go. 'Caid wants to see you."

I still don't know how we've managed to get away with calling *the* Silas Kincaid 'Caid over the years.

After a relenting sigh, I reply, "Yeah, I figured."

Together, we turn toward the parking lot. I pull my cell out from my pocket, the cracked screen reminding me it was broken during my *attempted assault*.

My eye rolls, trying to bring the other with it, which results only in a tremendous amount of pain.

Rat throws me a sidelong look. "After we're done, you're gonna need to get some ice on that. And I would lie low if I were you. You don't want your girl poking her nose where it doesn't belong, and she will when it comes to you."

I nod my agreement but say nothing. Rat and Spencer have been friends ever since the day I introduced them when we were kids, and I know he watches out for her almost as much as I do. He's also smart enough to keep our affiliation with Silas a secret and happens to be employed at my fictitious garage.

"What's up with you two, anyway?" Rat asks.

I take a brief second to enjoy the evening air, allowing it to numb my throbbing face before we round the corner of the police station.

"Spencer? Nothin', man." I glance toward Rat and notice his skeptical expression. I dip my head in the direction of his illegally parked Caddy before reaffirming, "Nothing is going on. She's like my little sister."

His head jerks back and both brows disappear behind the jet-black curls that hide his forehead before he barks out a laugh.

"Dude, if I looked at my sister the way you look at Spencer—no, just no." Shaking his head back and forth, he continues. "Let's just forget I said that."

"You're delusional, man. The only way I look at Spencer is *like a little sister*." The last words are enunciated slowly so his highly deluded brain has time to process them.

He snorts. "Right, man. Whatever you say."

We both stop at the side of the car, and he grips the door handle, grandly gesturing for me to enter. I happily take him up on the offer, sliding into the passenger seat. He rounds the front of the car, then opens his own door. Just as he hits the leather, he adds, "She looks at you the same way, brother."

The car takes off and I inhale a long, deep breath of calming air. "Seriously, Rat, what's up with this newfound obsession with my love life? Are you jealous? I mean, I know I just got out of jail, but I'm no one's bitch. Not even yours." My lips twitch as I add, "It's not you, bro; it's me."

We coast to a stop at a red light and he turns to face me, his green-brown eyes full of intensity I've rarely seen. "I'm tired of this game you play, D. I've been your best friend since we were six, and we have been through hell and back, *together*. If I see something good for you—something to give you that piece of happiness, that *home* you crave—I'm going to not only point it out but call you out for being a stupid motherfucker if you can't see it for yourself. And you are, without a doubt, being a stupid motherfucker right now."

I say nothing as he absently swipes the sleeve of his thermal, clearing it free of lint. He sniffs and then adds, "Plus, you're really not my type. You're too fuckin' pretty."

Just as the light turns green, I fight the threatening smile and respond, "Shut the fuck up."

Rat's answer is a satisfied chuckle.

"Speaking of *sisters* . . ." I throw him a deadpan look to properly indicate the segue. "How's Trinity?"

He smiles genuinely, pride replacing the previous intensity. "She's great, man. 'Bout to graduate, actually. She'll be the first in our family to make it through high school."

Just as we pull into the too-familiar warehouse, my mouth curves upward at the corners and I nod in agreement. "That's good, man. Real good."

"Yeah, well, we can't all be geniuses like you, D. Not all of us were able to graduate from the likes of *St. Louis Parochial High School.*"

I involuntarily snicker and my ribs throb in protest. I wrap my arm tightly around them. "Spencer's mom is the only reason I was awarded that scholarship and you know it. I'm not a genius, fuckwad."

"You are too. You read Aeropostale and Pluto."

My shoulders shake with laughter, my mind clearly ignoring the pain in favor of humor. "You mean, Aristotle and Plato?" I clarify as he throws the car into park.

Rat shoots me a peeved glare. "That's what I said."

Grin still intact, I lean forward and jerk the door handle. "Nah. I don't read Aristotle or Plato. Dante maybe, but that's because I find it comforting that someone else's hell was worse than mine."

As soon as I'm standing, Rat's door closes behind him and he makes his way to the front of the car. "But he makes it through, right? I mean, he eventually goes through purgatory and then to heaven."

One look at the surprised-as-shit look on my face and Rat snorts in response. "CliffsNotes, man. I read one paragraph of that old, worn-out book you had on your desk and it was interesting shit, but I didn't want to spend the next twenty years of my life trying to deciber what the dude was talking about."

I press my lips together. "Decipher?"

"Right." His eyes narrow impatiently. "That's what I said."

Rat continues. "I can see why you read it, but I like to think we've already made it through our hell and we're just kind of chillin' in purgatory for now."

Once we reach the door to enter the warehouse, Rat yanks it open. I shove my hands in my pockets, answering as I pass him by, "Yeah. You just keep telling yourself that. Maybe one day you'll even get a pass to heaven."

"You never know, brother. You never know."

The door closes, encasing me in a narrow hallway, confirming that we are indeed *not* in purgatory. Because as we travel its length, slowly entering the ninth circle of my own personal hell, I know it's only a matter of time before I come face to face with Satan himself.

Chapter 5

Dalton

Our boot-covered feet pounding against the cement floors are the only sounds we hear as we make our way to Silas's office. Two left turns and a set of stairs later, we finally reach our destination. Taking our seats in front of his desk, I eye Juan, his number two, as he stands next to our boss like the loyal puppy that he is. With his slicked-back hair and beady black eyes, he glares at me from across the room, looking ever the henchman. His black blazer is stretched to full capacity as he crosses his arms behind his back, his gaze never leaving mine. In fact, it's not until Silas mumbles something inaudible that he disengages, nodding briskly before leaving his post. The door shuts quietly, and we watch the back of the chair we've been staring at slowly turn, finally revealing the man in question.

Silas silently stares for a moment, then rises and rounds the corner of his desk, positioning himself directly in front of us. After rolling the sleeves of his designer dress shirt to his elbows, he leans and crosses his arms over his chest. The predatory look in his eyes tells me we're definitely not here for a friendly chat. The olive-colored skin on his face is drawn taut, his light-green eyes are hard, and the muscles on his forearms are flexed with obvious frustration. His head is cleanly shaven, and the only bit of hair visible is that of the goatee circling his tightly pinched mouth.

"What. The. Fuck. Happened?"

Rat opens his mouth to explain, but Silas silences him with his hand while his eyes remain pinned on me. "I want to hear it from him."

"I was jumped," I state matter-of-factly with a shrug of my shoulders, then recline lazily into my chair.

His eyes tighten. "And how the hell did *you* manage to get jumped by Ed Jamieson?"

I inhale deeply, knowing my answer is not going to be well received. "It wasn't Ed. It was his men, I think. It was a setup. It had to be."

"A setup?" Silas's dark brows rise in question. When I nod back, he calmly states, "A setup. Very interesting." So calm, it's eerie.

He turns his attention to Rat. "And what the fuck were you doing while your friend was getting the shit beat out of him?"

My body jolts upward, almost launching me from the chair. The bitter ache in my ribs is excruciating, but I ignore it. Just as I open my mouth to announce that there was not *one* man left standing when I was through, Silas slides the hand of silence in my direction, effectively cutting off my defense. Just to add a silent exclamation point to my almost-protest, I slam my body back into reclining position, pain be damned.

Rat clears his throat. "I was led to Jamieson's office, where I retrieved payment. I was headin' out the door to get back to the main floor where I'd left D when I heard the cops. So I got the fuck out of there and stashed the cash. By the time I got back, he was already in custody and there was nothing I could do, so I left, grabbed the money from where I stashed it, and threw it in my trunk before calling you."

"And where, may I ask, is *my* money?"

"Like I said, it's in my trunk."

Silas's eyes narrow into slits. "You mean to tell me you have been driving around town with 300K of my money *in your trunk*? Unprotected?"

Rat's lips curl into themselves and I fight the urge to shake my head. Silas, however, does not as his head moves side to side before he glances back at me. He arches one eyebrow and I shrug, silently pleading the fifth. He turns his attention back to Rat, glaring for another uncomfortable moment before finally leaning backward over his desk, extending his arm and pressing a button on his phone.

"Boss?"

Silas finally frees us from his stare. "Juan. Please escort Rat safely to the *trunk* of his car. After retrieving my money, deposit it in the safe where it *should* have been this entire evening instead of taking a fucking joyride on I-10."

The sound of Juan's snicker travels through the speaker. "On it, Boss."

I glance over at an unusually pale Rat before looking back at Silas, who has ended his call and is once again sitting upright, arms crossed. Now one would think, given Rat is obviously skating on extremely thin ice, he would remain silent. But then again, it's Rat. So instead of demonstrating his thanks to Silas for sparing him an epic beatdown from Juan, he decides to poke the grizzly in front of us with a short fucking stick.

"I think we should be allowed to carry, 'Caid. We have no protection except for Dalton's fists and my feet. And although we made it out alive tonight, if this happens again—"

"It *won't* happen again."

Silas's voice is unyielding as he presses himself off the desk, rising to his full six-foot-four height. "Ed Jamieson will be taken care of. Mark my words. What happened tonight was a direct fucking insult to me and my organization. If he is not punished for that very unwise decision, I lose respect. And respect is *everything*." He bends, now eye to eye with Rat, their faces inches apart. "I will not be made to look like a fucking fool. You hear me?"

Rat nods once, clearly nervous. Silas eyes him before finally rising out of his personal space. "And regarding your . . . *request*." He turns to me. "I cannot allow Dalton to carry until he can control his temper. Otherwise, he'll undoubtedly shoot the first motherfucker who crosses him, which will land him in jail. And he can't very well do what he needs to do for me while behind bars, now can he?"

His eyebrows lift expectantly and I nod my understanding before he looks to Rat. "You, on the other hand, while you're fully able to control yourself, cannot seem to pull your head out of your ass and make good decisions to save your life. Tonight's a prime example." He dips his head in Rat's direction. "Once you prove yourself in that capacity, I will happily hand over a Glock."

A knock alerts us to Juan's presence. Silas jerks his chin toward the door, dismissing us with the gesture. Rising out of his seat, Rat extends his arm and shakes Silas's hand. I too begin to stand, but before my ass even leaves the cushion, I'm halted by *The Hand*.

"Dalton, I need to discuss something with you. Please stay seated."

Rat looks as though he's about to speak, but before he has the chance, I interrupt. "Meet you at the car, brother."

He hesitates, but soon makes his exit, gently clapping me on the shoulder as he passes. As soon as the door closes behind him, my eyes meet Silas's. His face is no longer hard and cold.

"Do you know why I let him go? Unpunished?"

I shake my head because I really don't know.

Leaving the question unanswered, he asks more. "How long have you two been working for me? Since you were what? Twelve? Thirteen?"

"Twelve."

The memory of the day I met Silas takes me from the present straight to one of the worst days in my life.

It hurts to breathe.

I'm trying to hurry because I know that while Deena, my latest foster mother, is too loaded to notice my absence, Bill will be home soon, and after last night I need to lie low. My entire body aches as I try to make my way to the snack aisle, but my legs aren't moving as fast as they usually do. This is going to be more difficult than I thought.

I suck in a breath, the pain almost too much to bear, and tears fill my eyes. Bill's not stupid. It seems he's had a lot of practice on where exactly to punch and kick so it's hidden from sight. And while my body has been conditioned to handle a lot, it's no match for steel-toed boots.

I unzip my coat and lift my shirt to look at my ribs. Angry black and purple splotches cover every inch of my stomach clear to my sides, and I know my back looks the same. I also know, based on previous experience, he broke a lower rib or two during my latest lesson.

A lady in purple pajama pants and matching slippers enters the same aisle as me, so I quickly lower my dirty T-shirt and zip my coat back up. As she passes, I remain still, suddenly feeling as though she's watching me.

You always get paranoid. Just do it, I think to myself.

My eyes graze slowly over my choices. Once she turns the corner, I quickly grab everything I can get my hands on—chips, cookies, gum, a pickle for me, and of course, a candy bar to give to Rat later. I look to the left, then the right, and once I'm sure I'm in the clear, I turn and head toward the door.

Trying to move as quickly as I can, I make it about two feet before a burst of pain shoots up my back, so agonizing, my legs stop moving. Every muscle in my body tightens, and I'm forced to hold my breath to keep from screaming.

"Hey, you little thief. Get over here," the store clerk yells.

Before I know it, the pain dulls as my brain takes over, forcing my body into flight mode. I jump toward the open door and begin to run as fast as my body will allow.

But I don't make it far because instead of running outside, I run smack-dab into a man's chest.

"Whoa there, boy," he calmly states. I fight to get around him, but he's got a fistful of my coat.

The clerk runs over, and there's no mistaking the fear in his voice when he speaks. "Thank you, Mr. Kincaid."

"What's going on here?" the man asks.

The clerk stutters. "Um . . . this boy, uh, he stole some things from the snack aisle."

"Oh, really?"

The man extends the arm holding my coat, positioning me so I'm forced to look at him. The green eyes study my appearance, then tighten. Another crippling pain explodes along my back and I wince, my legs buckling beneath me. I would have hit the floor had the man not tightened his grip.

Then his gaze falls to the arm wrapped around my stomach. They narrow further, almost as though calculating something. After a few seconds, his expression clears.

"I'll pay for whatever the boy has taken," he states, eyes still on me.

"Mr. Kincaid . . ."

The man's face hardens, silencing the clerk immediately. Satisfied, he once again looks to me. "Well, boy, let's see what you've got in there."

He releases me and waits patiently as I slowly unzip the coat. I close my eyes so I don't have to watch everything spill onto the floor, but open them when I hear a surprising chuckle. The pickle rolling across the floor almost distracts me, but I manage to keep my attention focused on the amused green eyes above me. The clerk drops to his knees and snags the items off the floor, then disappears behind the counter.

The man then bends at the waist, centering his face with mine. "I don't think your parents would be very happy if they knew their son was stealing from the corner store, do you?" he asks with a hint of a grin.

My face goes tight. "I don't have any parents."

His eyebrows draw together. "Is that so?"

"Yes, sir."

He gestures toward my stomach. "Fight at school?"

"Something like that."

His grin widens as he nods. "I see. What's your name, boy?"

"Dalton."

He nods again. "How long has it been since you've had a decent meal, Dalton?"

"A while." I angle my head in question. "Mister, do you only ever ask questions?"

And for the first time in a long time, I find myself smiling as he bursts into laughter. After a few seconds, he wipes his eyes and then glances back down at me.

"Silas. You can call me Silas."

He sighs deeply before speaking again. "Well, Dalton, why don't we go grab something to eat? I have a business proposition for you that we can discuss over a good dinner."

My head jerks and I try not to focus on the burning sensation the movement brings. "Business proposition? I'm only twelve."

The corners of his mouth tip upward. "Well, that may be true, but you seem like a very resourceful young man. I need someone like that, like you, working for me. Someone to run errands, to pick up some things around town that I just don't have the time to do. And in return, I will make sure you always have money and food when you need it." He gestures toward my stomach. "I can also teach you how to protect yourself, from anyone," he adds, an eyebrow lifted.

The way he stresses the word "anyone" tells me he's no stranger to my situation, and for that reason, I find myself trusting this man. Something I've never allowed myself to do before in my life.

"Well, Silas. I have a friend named Rat who would also be good at running your errands. You bring him on board too, and you've got a deal."

Reaching out my hand, I offer him a solid handshake, relief flooding me for the first time in a very long time.

He took me to dinner and it was the best meal I'd ever eaten in my life. He also made good on his promises. I never had to steal to eat again, and I always had a pocketful of cash. And the protection he taught me? Well, eight months later I beat Bill to within nearly an inch of his life. It was the last time he ever laid a hand on me. I was escorted out of his house—for *his* safety—and straight to emergency foster care with Spencer's mom.

The past fades as I'm brought back to the present by Silas's voice.

"Yes, twelve," he nods thoughtfully. He grins slightly before continuing. "And who was it that made sure you two always had what you needed?"

"You did, 'Caid," I answer honestly.

"Yes, I did. And all I ask for in return is loyalty and trust. To know when I ask you to do something for me, it will be done without hesitation and the job completed successfully. And regardless of the . . . *hiccup* this evening, Rat completed the job."

Clearing my throat, I reposition myself in my seat and nod.

"You are too good to let what happened tonight ever happen again. You're the best in my entire crew. You're far more lethal and experienced, and moreover, you're smart. That's what gives you the edge."

He stands and motions for me to do the same. As soon as I've risen, he places his hand on my shoulder and peers into my eyes. "I called in a favor tonight and had the charges against you dropped. I need you on the streets, not behind bars." His hand squeezes in warning. "Tonight was your one free pass, Dalton. You rein in that fucking temper of yours because if this happens again, you *will* owe me. And you know better than anyone that owing me is a very dangerous debt to acquire."

"I understand," I answer immediately. "It won't happen again."

"I know it won't." He releases my shoulder and gestures toward the door. "Now, go home and get some rest."

I turn to leave, only to twist back around when he states, "Allegiances will be tested soon for both you and Rat. As you grow older, I need to know that your loyalties lie with me and no one else. You will soon enter the smallest, most elite circle within my organization, and eventually, you'll lead your own crew underneath me. You will have your pick—drugs, guns, prostitution. Wherever you choose to go, my world will become yours to reign, and everything you've ever wanted will be at your fingertips. But before that happens, I need to know that no one comes before my business or me. *No one.* Got me?"

His eyes bore into mine and I suppress a shiver at the ominous words. Another wordless dip of my head is given before I finally turn and head to the door. I'm fully aware my path has already been decided. It was decided the day I joined forces with Silas Kincaid. And regardless of what Lawson believes me capable of doing, there's no way out of this life other than being buried six feet underground.

After closing the door, I head to Rat's car. Once in the main warehouse, I spot him leaning against his trunk, arms folded leisurely across his chest.

As soon as I'm within hearing distance, Rat presses his body off of his car. "Everything solid?"

"Yeah." I head to the passenger-side door. "Our loyalties will be tested, just in case you were wondering," I recap.

His snicker fills the air. I fold myself into the car as Rat does the same. "I'm getting my own fucking Glock. Fuck that shit. We need more protection out there."

I say nothing in response because I'm too goddamn worn out. I lean back and rest my head on the seat, the evening's events finally taking their toll. My entire body aches and my fucking head hurts from dealing with Silas. I stare out the window as Rat puts the car in reverse.

"You'd better call Spencer as soon as you get your phone replaced."

Shit. My phone.

Right on cue, Rat adds, "Yeah. You're gonna need to lie low, brother. There's no way she's going to believe all that damage was done to your face at the *garage*. I would contact her as soon as possible. Otherwise, she'll make a surprise visit, and if she sees you, she's going to lose her shit, which isn't good for either of us."

My good eye closes in frustration, leaving me in complete darkness. Although my entire body is clenched in pain, the only sensation I'm able to feel is that of asphyxiation. Silas's expectations saturate my mind and clog my lungs, making it impossible to breathe. And my only relief from the suffocation, from the absolute agony burning within my chest, is the one person who I'm forced to deny myself.

Fuck.

It's going to be a long week.

Chapter 6

Spencer

To: Dalton Greer
Subject: Where the hell are you???????
Date: Friday, March 26, 2010 9:29 PM

Dalton,

Four days. It has been *FOUR* days, Dalton. Where the hell are you?

I have always respected your privacy and your need to be on your own sometimes. But this is just a pure assholish move on your part because I know for a fact you are just sitting there in your apartment, hiding out and avoiding me. I know this because I saw you Wednesday when I was forced to bribe Cassie with a pint of Ben & Jerry's to do a psychotic, spur-of-the-moment drive-by, leaving both of us nothing short of surprised when we spotted your Camaro in the driveway. Giving you the benefit of the doubt, I instructed her to keep driving, thinking I would hear from you later that day. Yet, my calls and texts continue to be unanswered.

So I'm writing you as a courtesy to let you know that if you do not reply to this email, I will be at your door first thing in the morning, banging it down like one of your crazed ex-girlfriends. And I know how much you like to be woken up early, so when I say first thing in the morning, I mean the ass-crack of dawn. You have been warned.

Your extremely pissed-off friend,
Spencer

I press send and recline in my chair, staring at the computer screen until my message has been successfully delivered. Once it disappears out of my drafts, I shut my laptop and head to the bathroom to take a much-needed shower.

As the warm water cascades down my body, relieving the tension in my muscles, my mind drifts to the increasing amount of Dalton disappearances as of late.

Am I worried about him? Of course.

Do I wish he would just tell me what the hell is going on? Duh.

Am I going to force him to tell me? Not in a million years.

Because here's the thing about Dalton: I know I absolutely cannot push him about his private life, no matter how frustrated I become. I can ask all I want, but I will never force his disclosure because if I press too hard, I know without a doubt he will completely shut down. Just like everything with Dalton, it needs to be on his own terms.

With that being said, I am not above forcing my way into his home to make sure he's all right. I just cushion the blow by announcing my arrival beforehand. And since I don't have a car, *yet*, he knows I will be showing up with Mom or Cassie, either of which should prompt a reply to my email sooner rather than later.

Wickedly, I laugh to myself as I climb out of the shower.

As soon as I'm dressed in my pajamas, I amble over to my desk, disappointed to find I have nothing in my inbox. In fact, it's not until the ass-crack of dawn, primed and ready, that I get my answer.

To: Spencer Locke
Re: Where the hell are you???????
Date: Saturday, March 27, 2010 5:47 AM

Assholish isn't even a word, Pencil. You are maiming the English language.

A goofy smile crosses my face, as I'm sure he intended.

I, however, refuse to succumb to his little game. So I quickly dismiss the grin and blank my face, then hit reply.

To: Dalton Greer
Re: Where the hell are you???????
Date: Saturday, March 27, 2010 5:53 AM

Don't be cute. It's not going to work. I'm still pissed at you.

His answer is instantaneous.

To: Spencer Locke
Re: Where the hell are you???????
Date: Saturday, March 27, 2010 5:55 AM

Unless you still plan on banging on the door like one of my crazed ex-girlfriends at the ass-crack of dawn this morning, you might want to let Cassie know her services won't be needed.

Shit.

Jumping out of my seat, I run to my bed and snatch my phone from underneath my pillow to shoot a quick text to Cassie.

ME: Got hold of Dalton. Abort the mission. Repeat. Abort the mission.
CASSIE: Are you kidding me?!
C: You still owe me another pint of Cherry Garcia.
C: And be up by 10. We're going shopping.
ME: Doesn't shopping negate the required ice cream payment?
C: Am I up at almost six on a Saturday morning? No, it does not. Not even close.
ME: Fiiiiiiiiiine. See you at 10.
C: Love you ;)
ME: Love you, times two.

I toss the phone onto my bed and turn my attention back to the computer.

To: Dalton Greer
Re: Where the hell are you???????
Date: Saturday, March 27, 2010 6:05 AM

Stop trying to thwart my anger.

Where the hell have you been and why haven't you answered
my calls or texts? And why are we communicating via email?

Five minutes later . . .

To: Spencer Locke
Re: Where the hell are you???????
Date: Saturday, March 27, 2010 6:10 AM

Thwart. Nice.
My phone was broken earlier this week and I won't get it back
until this afternoon. Therefore, I wasn't able to call you to
tell you that I was out all week on a project for the garage.
It was last minute and I arrived back in town just last night. Rat
drove, which is why my car was in the driveway. I think that
answers all of your questions.
Listen, I'm really sorry you were worried for FOUR long days.
I'd like to come over tonight and make it up to you ;)

The thought of Dalton making *anything* up to me sends a fiery
blush across my cheeks, which reminds me why he can't come over
tonight. Cassie's plan has already been set in motion.

To: Dalton Greer
Re: Where the hell are you???????
Date: Saturday, March 27, 2010 6:17 AM

Yes, I believe that answers all of my questions. Thank you.
Consider yourself forgiven.
And regarding tonight, I would love for you to come over, but
I have plans. Sunday?

It takes a couple minutes before I receive his response. My adrenaline spikes as soon as it hits my inbox, and my hand trembles as I
open his reply.

To: Spencer Locke
Re: Where the hell are you???????
Date: Saturday, March 27, 2010 6:22 AM

Daisy Mae can wait. You see her every day.

My eyes narrow at the screen. Is it really that inconceivable that Spencer Locke could have a date on a Saturday night? With a person of the opposite sex? In a romantic capacity? And when did Spencer Locke begin referring to herself in the third person? I hate it when people do that.

I shake my head and refocus on the issue at hand.

I guess when you've vowed to kill any possible offenders by cutting off their testicles and letting them bleed out on the school parking lot (I confirmed Cassie's vendetta allegation), a false sense of confidence is to be expected.

Fueled by this knowledge, I type my response and hit send.

To: Dalton Greer
Re: Where the hell are you???????
Date: Saturday, March 27, 2010 6:35 AM

It's not that easy, actually. CASSIE will be accompanying me tonight on a date. Well, not by herself. It's a double date.

I hit send, my heart thrashing beneath my chest. This is it. The defining moment in our relationship. Either Dalton feels nothing for me and this date will spur no further reaction from him, or he does and the idea of my being with someone other than him will force him to admit it.

An email pops up in my inbox, and my finger hovers over the touchpad of my laptop, unsure if I'm ready to read his reply. I swallow deeply, trying to calm my nerves, and after a couple of agonizing minutes, I finally click on the message.

To: Spencer Locke
Re: Where the hell are you???????
Date: Saturday, March 27, 2010 6:43 AM

What time?
And with who?

I bark a laugh. Right. As if I would put my date's life in danger by answering that loaded question. It wouldn't be proper first-date etiquette.

To: Dalton Greer
Re: Where the hell are you???????
Date: Saturday, March 27, 2010 6:52 AM

None of your beeswax, buddy. Assuming you will have your
phone by tonight, I will CALL you afterward so you know I made
it home safely. You know, so you don't worry unnecessarily.
See how that works?

Snickering to myself, I send the email and await his response,
which takes longer than the others. When it hits my inbox, I open it
quickly, but his words diminish all foolish hope I had been clinging to.

To: Spencer Locke
Re: Where the hell are you???????
Date: Saturday, March 27, 2010 7:15 AM

I guess you'd better get back to your beauty sleep.

My forehead creases and my mouth curves toward the floor.
Well, there's his answer.
No need for a reply.
In fact, I'm still staring blankly at the screen when my phone
buzzes. I dejectedly slide off my chair to retrieve it, only to see Cassie's missed call flash across the screen. A couple seconds later, it
vibrates again.

CASSIE: Bitch. I can't go back to sleep. I'm trading my ice cream
in for breakfast. Then shopping. So put on some clothes
and meet me in your kitchen in 20.

I roll my eyes and breathe out a deep, resigned sigh. I know I
will lose this battle, but make a half-assed attempt to discourage her
anyway.

ME: I don't feel like it, Cass. Really.
C: You owe me. It's your fault I have been up since 5:30 ON A
SATURDAY mORNING!!!!! Now stop rolling your eyes and
get ready.
ME: Grrrrrrrrrrrrr. Fine.

After sliding on a pair of snug flare jeans that hug my hips, I throw on my favorite vintage navy-blue peasant top and toe on my flip-flops. Once my blonde hair is piled into a messy bun, I clear the loose tendrils away from my face, then exit my room when Cassie barrels her way into my house. The crash of her entrance fills the hallway, and in full-on zombie mode, I continue my trek to where cabinets slam and pans begin to clink from within the walls of my kitchen. With each step in her direction, I force myself to accept that Dalton just doesn't feel that way about me. I get it. It's hard to swallow, but I understand. I don't know why I allowed myself to think it was anything more.

I turn the corner and shove my sorrow back into its secret place. It burrows itself safely within the familiar confines of my chest, and I ignore the burn it leaves behind. The hurt I refuse to admit is there . . .

But always remains.

Chapter 7

Spencer

"HEY!"

I'm harshly roused by the familiar snap of two now blood-red-painted fingernails jutting in front of my face, way too freaking close to my eyeballs. Startled, I flinch and my face scrunches as I swat wildly at the hand in front of it. My attacker, however, remains unfazed and continues snapping.

"Hooker. Wake up."

I blink with each click of her fingers, and it's not until I land a good, hard smack on Cassie's hand that she stops. Aghast, she draws her arm to her chest. "Ouch, Spencer. That hurt."

If I wasn't still half-asleep, I would laugh at how pathetic she looks. Instead, I stretch a lazy stretch and yawn exaggeratedly, addressing her only when I've finished with my theatrics. "Well, you deserved it. Your nonstop snapping was completely ridiculous. And unnecessary. And *annoying as hell*." I blink again. "I have a headache now, actually."

She narrows her dark-brown eyes and stomps her foot. "Spencer. This is important. This is *prom* we're preparing for."

"For you," I correct. "For me, it's payback for making you wake up early this morning." I glance at her attire. "I'm sorry. I must have zoned out around option forty-two." And I must have because there is no way in hell I would have let the toga dress draped over her body pass without some sort of snide commentary. It's the same color as the sun and just as bright.

"*Forty-two?*" she screeches, her tone bordering the ability to shatter glass.

I giggle.

Cassie releases a frustrated huff and shakes her head in obvious protest, her long, dark ponytail swinging with it. "I have shown you"—she lifts her hand and displays her fingers—"three dresses, Spencer. *Three*."

My nose crinkles in disbelief. "Are you sure? It seems like a hell of a lot more than that." Another laugh works its way up my throat when the shade of her face turns angry red, but I choke it back down. My eyes water in objection.

Bringing my knees up to my chest, I kick off my flip-flops and recline into the cushions of my chair. With a resigned sigh, I wave my hand as an indication for her to continue. Cassie's dark eyes tighten before she raises her even darker brow. "Are you going to pay attention now?"

"Of course, Cass. My life revolves around you. You know that. Now please, let's see the next dress. The first *three* were absolute rubbish," I yell, slapping my palm loudly on the arm of my chair. I'm pretty sure I've finally reached delirium.

Or maybe I'm overcompensating for this nagging burn that I can't seem to shake today.

The passing store clerk clutches her chest and gasps, giving me a stern look before tsking and walking away. Feeling genuinely rewarded for my efforts, I smile widely back at her. Cassie, however, just glares at me, paying the clerk no attention.

"Oh my God. You totally were *not* paying attention because the first one was *tha shit*."

"Then why, may I ask, are we still here?" The boredom in my voice cannot be denied.

Much like the store clerk, she gasps and clutches her chest, horrified. "Because shopping is fun, Spencer. It's not every day that we get to peruse for prom dresses with our parents' credit cards. Come on! What is *wrong* with you?"

Mockingly, I lift my hand, palm out while presenting her with three fingers. "One, *you* are shopping for a prom dress, not me. And two, *you* are the only one with a credit card here. For obvious reason." I tilt my head. "So, please excuse my lack of enthusiasm. But"—I sigh for dramatic effect—"I shall suffer through this for you because that's what best friends are for." At that, two fingers fold downward and I rotate my wrist approximately one hundred eighty degrees, effectively demonstrating how I really feel about shopping with the sole finger left on display.

Cassie's glare tightens as she eyes my gesture, but I'm convinced she finds my aversion to shopping nothing short of hilarious, which is why she insists on dragging me along on every single trip.

"Killjoy," she growls and whips around, the rustle of the yellow taffeta monstrosity filling the air with her movement.

Just as the tiniest bit of guilt begins to surface, my previous suspicions are confirmed when I see a full smile break across her face in the mirror as she heads back to the dressing room.

I grin openly as she closes the door.

She loves me.

After mere seconds, the door flies open with what has to be the fastest wardrobe change like, ever, and Cassie exits in our school uniform.

I shake my head disapprovingly.

The plaid skirt is rolled up at least three times at the waist, barely covering her ass, while the knee-high socks and Mary Janes give the ensemble a contradictive air of innocence.

It's disturbing.

It's also Saturday, so I have no idea why she's wearing it.

Okay, I lied.

I totally know why she's wearing it.

I say a quick, silent prayer to the god of good little Catholic girls everywhere that she's at least wearing panties today. And as catcalls and whistles from a herd of guys sound from across the store, I find myself praying harder.

She flashes them a devious smile (thankfully nothing more) and waves before turning back to me. "It's cool. I was done torturing you anyway."

I laugh, my eyes falling to her forearm, which is draped with a gorgeous, shimmering navy-blue number. I assume this to be option number one because it is, indeed, *tha shit*.

"The dress is beautiful. Glad my expert advice helped you with your decision." But as I eye it more closely, I amend, "Although, it's not as formal, *or short*, as I thought it would be."

Cassie gives me a warm, genuine smile before extending her arm and placing her free hand on my shoulder. "My dear, *dear* friend." She shakes her head. "Who do you take me for? This dress does not go at all with my coloring, and as you so cleverly stated, this length will do nothing for me in the least. It's too long."

And to think I was actually going to commend her on her choice.

She glances at the dress and pats it lovingly before looking back at me. "No, this is for you. For your date tonight."

My eyes widen in shock.

"What?" I exclaim. "Cassie, I can't let you do that. No way."

She squeezes my shoulder with her fingers. "I refuse to let you ruin my brilliant plan with your single-variety, bohemian wardrobe choices." She gestures at my apparel. "No flare jeans with worn, frayed hems. No loose-ass peasant tops that hide your fantastic body. You need to be Monroe tonight, not Joplin."

My brows pinch as I glance down, tugging the sides of my peasant top while debating whether or not to explain that her brilliant plan is actually a complete bust. Lost in thought, I continue to stare until my sight is obstructed by the navy dress as Cassie shoves it into my ribcage. With the look of excitement blazing in her eyes, I know that even if I tell her about Dalton's response, there is absolutely no way I'm getting out of tonight or allowing her to buy me this dress.

Right on cue, she states forcefully, "I *need* you to take this dress. Please for the love of all that is holy." She proceeds to bless herself with the sign of the cross, and I step to the left in preparation for lightning to strike.

She eyes my movement. "I'm going to assume that was to get away from the dress, and not because of my blessing."

My lips curl into themselves and I say nothing. Her expression tightens and she stares until I can't help but laugh. After a couple of stubborn seconds, she relents and giggles with me before once again falling silent. With warm eyes, she steps forward and presses the dress into my arms.

"Take it, Spence. Please. You do so much for me, let me do something for you for once."

Knowing she will afford me no other choice, I accept the dress. "I don't know what you're talking about."

She holds my gaze and her eyes glisten as she quietly states, "Of course you don't, and that's why I love you." After a deep intake of air, she wipes the corner of her eye then smiles widely before adding, "Plus, I already paid for it while you were comatose, hooker."

I shake my head but grin, holding the dress in front of me for better inspection. The top is a blue bodice covered in navy Chantilly lace, joined with the solid navy satin sheath bottom by a black-velvet-banded waistline. The V-neckline and V-back are connected at the shoulders with three black velvet bands that match the ones lining my waist. It's exquisite. And it's also retro 1950s.

Therefore, it's absolutely perfect.

My smile widens as I meet Cassie's eyes.

"I know," she states with confidence. "You don't have to tell me." She glances down at my feet. "And I have the perfect heels to go with it." Resolute, she nods her head and drapes her arm over my shoulder.

"Now let's go make you Monroe."

Five hours later, I'm still staring at the dress, but this time it's in the reflection of my mirror. My nerves are at an all-time high, and although I'm about to go on my first date ever, I'm still hung up on the last words Dalton wrote this morning.

A loud clap next to my ear jars me from my musing. Cassie glares at me over my shoulder in the mirror. Scandalously clad in what has to be the shortest black minidress I've ever seen, she warns sternly, "Stop thinking." Her dark six-inch stiletto heel taps the floor.

My eyes widen, proclaiming my innocence. "What? I'm just looking at the dress."

Cassie shakes her head. "No, you're thinking about something. I don't like it." She fluffs her loose curls around her shoulders and smacks her lips at her reflection before bringing her eyes back to me. "*That* Jase Williams will be here in twenty minutes. We need to get our game faces on, and right now, you look like you've just lost your best friend. Which I know is not the case because I'm standing right here."

I give her another patented fake smile in return and she narrows her eyes. "Something's going on. What happened?"

The corners of my mouth descend and I swallow deeply. "Nothing, really. It's just, well, it's . . ." I gather my composure before continuing. "Dalton pretty much made it abundantly clear that his feelings do not extend past friendship. This morning, I told him about my date and his only response was to"—I pause to add finger quotes—"'let me get back to my beauty sleep.' Nothing else. I mean, that pretty much solidifies the fact that he doesn't feel the same way I do, right?"

Cassie holds my eyes in the mirror, then breaks into laughter. "Have I taught you nothing?" she inquires. When I don't respond, she quickly schools her features and adds, "No, I suppose I haven't."

Placing her hands on my shoulders, she smiles and her dimples deepen with her chuckle. "He's pissed. Trust me."

When I begin to protest, she presses her fingers into my shoulders. "Let's not focus on Dalton right now. Instead, let's focus on the fact that you're about to go on a date with *that* Jase Williams. If Dalton wants to play games, he can do so while you are getting a proper dating education by *moi*."

I snicker. As much as I love Cassie, something tells me I should definitely steer clear of her dating advice. Case in point, her busted-ass plan. Or maybe it's the number of meaningless sexual encounters she's had within the last month alone.

Either way.

At my laughter, she whips my body around, forcing me to face her. "Look. You are absolutely gorgeous. You have the perfect dress, the perfect shoes, your hair is perfectly tousled, and your makeup is perfectly applied. Let's not waste all of this perfection worrying about Dalton. Let's use it to our advantage because I know you don't believe me, but you need to trust me. This plan will work."

My mind wanders, pondering her words, and guilt begins to set in. "Don't you think this is wrong, though? I mean, going on a date with one person just to garner someone else's attention?"

Cassie's lips pucker in thought. "No, I don't think so." She places her hands on her hips. "*That* Jase Williams has his own motives, I think. When he started showing interest in you, I asked around a bit, and I happened upon some very interesting information."

My head jerks back in surprise. "*What* information?"

She hesitates before answering. "Well, it seems that he and Dalton have history. I'm not sure what happened, but there is definitely no love lost between the two of them. I personally believe, while he's genuinely interested in you, his motivation also lies in giving Dalton a big 'fuck you,' since everyone knows there will be hell to pay when it comes to dating you. It makes sense. He's been the only one to step up to the plate."

She shrugs her shoulders. "So, I wouldn't feel too guilty. I would just look at it as the opportunity to go out with *that* Jase Williams and to have fun on an actual date. Stop worrying about the underlying circumstances and just go with it."

Cassie grins widely, and my guilt is replaced by sudden apprehension. "You don't think he will try to pressure me, do you? To like, have sex?" My throat constricts just thinking about the possibility.

Her lips curve into a sympathetic smile before she pulls me into an embrace. Squeezing me tightly, she states, "That is exactly why I'm not going to leave your side tonight. Don't you worry your pretty little inexperienced head. I am officially on guard duty and will throat-punch him if he attempts anything other than a friendly handshake."

So that's why she insisted on a double date. It all makes sense now. My throat clogs with unshed tears. "Thank you, Cass."

She squeezes me tightly. Just as I release her, the door to my bedroom opens and my mother enters, wearing black yoga pants and a Pink Floyd tank top.

My Pink Floyd tank top.

She smiles innocently before giving me a once-over. Her gaze moves along my face, down the length of my dress, and lands on the Mary Jane heels covering my feet. The smile slowly disappears, and as she makes her way back up to my face, her chin begins to tremble.

"Oh, honey. You look . . . *gosh*." She reaches up to wipe her eye. "Jim would have been so proud to see his little girl become such a beautiful young woman."

At the mention of Jim, the tears I tried so hard to avoid spring into my eyes. Her husband, my father, James William Locke III, passed away when I was eight years old from a sudden heart attack. He was only thirty-two.

I wish I'd had more time with him. Mom always makes sure I know how much he loved me, and I'm well aware that that kind of love doesn't come along often. And in times like these, I'm really sad I missed out on it.

After another swipe along her cheek, she takes the few necessary steps to close the distance between us. She folds her arms around my neck, enveloping me in my second embrace of the night. Cassie smiles warmly at me over Mom's shoulder, only to glance toward my door when the doorbell rings. Her eyes are wide with excitement when she looks back at me and her lips form an enthusiastic grin.

"Let the games commence."

Mom releases me to glance at Cassie, but I distract her with a quick kiss on the cheek before announcing, "We'll be back by ten. Don't worry."

I step away from her and snag my purse while Cassie jets to my mother, giving her a quick hug before exiting my room. Mom follows in her footsteps, but turns and stops in the doorway, twisting back to face me.

"Do you have your phone?"

I nod.

"And it's on?"

Internally, I roll my eyes. Outwardly, I smile and answer, "Yes, ma'am."

She watches me briefly before her face breaks into a satisfied grin. "Good girl. I've stocked the freezer with ice cream just for tonight. When you get home, we'll grab a couple of bowls and you can tell me all about your date."

I smile as past ice-cream-filled moments with Mom flood my mind. She winks before finally leaving me alone in my room. Inhaling deeply, I face my mirror for a final once-over.

Hair? *Tousled*.

Makeup? *Smokey*.

Dress? *Extremely fitted*.

Heels? *Scary high*.

I smooth my hands over my fluttering stomach in an effort to calm my nerves. As voices from the living room begin to filter into the air around me, I find myself no longer looking at my reflection in the mirror but at the window across the room. Disappointment threatens as I think about Dalton, his whereabouts, and his indifference to my plans this evening. Frustrated, I shake my head.

I know he's lonely.

I know because I've been there.

I know the need to push everyone around you away in order to keep your secrets safe.

I know how tiring it is to remain on guard, watching, waiting for the monsters to make their reappearance.

I guess I just wish *he* knew that he's not alone.

I feel his heartbreak.

I understand his actions.

I harbor the same anger.

The truth is, regardless of the secrets that he keeps, no matter how hard he pushes, I will always be connected to him in a way few people can understand.

But that's as far as I can allow it to go.

I need to banish this ridiculous idea that we will ever be more than friends. Which means vetoing this already floundering plan of Cassie's and just going out with *that* Jase Williams to go out with *that* Jase Williams, and for no other reason.

Laughter from the other room disrupts my thoughts, and I break my stare from the window.

Closing my eyes, I take another deep breath, then refocus on my reflection. Determination sets in as I give myself a final *internal* once-over.

Any and all romantic notions about Dalton Greer?

Releasing the breath, I give myself a stern look and dip my head in resolve.

Gone.

Chapter 8 ✦
Dalton

DOUBLE DATE.

Those two words sliced open a gaping wound I didn't even realize existed. Panic seized my insides with the realization that Spencer would be with someone else tonight. Her contagious laughter, the sincerity of her smile, the innocence in her eyes . . .

All the things I love about her, she will be sharing with someone else. *Tonight.*

Bitter anger laces itself around my grief.

She's mine.

For hours, I tried everything I could think of to mute the chanting of those two words in my head. To quiet them with the admission that she *needs* someone else, someone who knows how to love in the way she deserves, someone far better than me. To silence them with my reality, my lies, my path. But nothing would censor the hum of my fury.

She's mine.

All day long the words taunted me.

Finally I gave up the fight, jumped in my car, and drove until finally parking three houses down from hers, lying to myself the entire way. Over and over, I repeated that this reconnaissance was nothing more than the act of providing myself the security of knowing she's safe. *Nothing more.*

But now, being this close to her, I'm overwhelmed with the urge to sling her over my shoulder, to steal her away and keep her all to myself. And as I watch four people pour through her front door onto her porch, *our* fucking porch, I find the impulse far more difficult to contain.

My eyes lock onto one of the parties in question and my fury begins to flare. "Tha fuck?"

The fingers curled around my steering wheel clench tightly and I squint my eyes, straining to see through the pitch-black air concealing my car.

Cassie, Spencer, Jonathon Hawkins, and a blond guy who I pray isn't who I think it is are huddled together, speaking with Mrs. Locke as she escorts them outside.

I disengage my stare from the blond guy and redirect it to Spencer. Once it locks onto her, I'm unable to focus on anything else. The humming magically ceases and the anger squanders because, in this moment, there is just *her*.

Her wide smile graces her face, almost as bright as the porch light highlighting her long blonde hair. My gaze drops and I continue to watch as she nervously runs the palms of her hands along the dress hugging her body. I stare at her muscular legs, accented by a pair of high heels, longer than I know I should. I didn't even know she owned shoes like that. *She should wear them more often*. But as my mind is slammed with images of those long legs circling my waist, I quickly banish the thought.

Shifting in my seat, I notice she turns her attention and laughs at something blondie says, and I refocus on the mission at hand. Leaning to the side, I reach for the glove compartment, grabbing the binoculars from inside before slamming it shut. Just as I'm upright, a hand slams against my passenger-side window.

I roll my eyes, settling in my seat.

This is exactly why I'm in charge of our surveillance activities. It's impossible to be stealth when you've just pulled up right behind the person you're trying to scare with your fucking brights on.

I hit the unlock button, then lift the binoculars into my line of sight, seeking my person of interest. The extremely short fuse of my rage lights once again when I spot him.

Motherfucker.

"Got the tacos." A warm gust of seasoned ground beef and fresh-fried shells engulfs my car as Rat slides into the seat next to me. "We can't surveille without Mama Rosa's. It just wouldn't be right."

I fight the urge to knock him upside the head with a dictionary, choosing instead to focus my energy on what's happening in front of me. Rat wordlessly opens the bag and rummages through it as though he hasn't eaten in four days.

"Rat," I whisper, my patience waning. "Please, brother."

A snicker sounds, followed by a loud crunch. With his mouth completely full, Rat responds, "They aren't going to hear us all the way over here, dumbshit."

I inhale deeply. "I know. But I need to concentrate, and in order to concentrate, I need you to stop fucking chewing at a decibel that makes my head want to explode."

Another laugh followed by a massive swallow. "Decimal? That doesn't even make sense."

Peeling the binoculars away from my eyes, I glare at him.

Rat's eyes widen. "What?"

I give no response other than shaking my head, then glance back to Spencer's porch just in time to watch her lean in to give her mother a hug.

The binoculars are torn from my hand and I release them willingly. I've already obtained the information I need to know. The idea of watching any more already makes my stomach turn, so I'm pretty positive experiencing it at ten times magnification wouldn't end well.

For me or my leather upholstery.

"Double date," Rat announces from behind the binoculars, then lifts his free hand to shove the remainder of the taco into his mouth. "Who's with who?"

"I'm not sure. Neither one of them have come close enough for me to tell. Cassie's blocking either of them from getting within three feet of Spencer."

Right on cue, Cassie steps in front of Spencer as Motherfucker extends his hand in her direction.

Good girl, Cass.

But the relief quickly dissipates as Spencer steps right around Cassie and hesitantly slides her hand into his. Cassie's mouth drops wide open and mine slams shut. My teeth grind and I yank the binoculars away from Rat to zoom in on her face. Spencer's lips form a tight, feigned smile as she's led to the BMW coupe parked on the street.

My hands tighten their grip.

Something's going on.

I don't know what it is, but I know Spencer, and the look on her face tells me she's extremely nervous.

Dipping the binoculars, I readjust the focus. My eyes hone in on their interlaced fingers and remain there until he finally releases her, but only to place his hand on the small of her back, guiding her toward the car.

Motherfucker is *touching* her.

Uninvited.

My jaw tightens and flames lick the inside of my chest. I force myself to breathe before asking, "You remember when we busted up Chaz Caldwell's party last year?"

"That kid who distributed 50K-worth of 'Caid's blaze and never paid for it?" Rat laughs. "Yeah, I remember that stupid motherfucker and his party. Everyone was wrecked, man. We did them a favor that night."

"Well"—I jerk my chin in the direction of the BMW—"the blond one next to Spencer? That's Jase Williams. He was there that night."

Cassie and Jonathon climb into the back seat and I slide my keys into the ignition, my eyes never leaving the BMW. Fury rises, but it remains contained with the placating promise that I will be releasing it from its confines soon.

"While I was looking for Chaz, I caught Jase with a fucking *freshman* who was putting up one hell of a fight while he was forcing his hands down her pants."

One scream from her was all I needed.

I glance quickly at Rat, expression stern. "He missed school for two weeks."

After shutting Spencer inside, Jase rounds the car and deposits himself in the driver's seat. "She's not safe with him, especially if this is some form of retribution against me."

The lights from the BMW filter into my car, and Rat and I slide down in our seats until it passes us by. When obscured again by darkness, Rat chucks the tacos onto the floorboard and presses himself into a sitting position. "Well, what the fuck are we waiting for then?"

I watch in the rearview mirror until the car turns the corner, then flip the key. As soon as my engine roars to life, I press the gas pedal and execute an illegal U-turn right in the middle of the street.

Rat shakes his head as we gain speed. "This wouldn't be happening if you would just ask her out instead of stalking her like a fucking creeper, brother."

Gaze locked on the road in front of me, I turn the corner and tag the Beamer. "I just needed to make sure she was okay. That's all. I wasn't planning on following her anywhere until I saw Jase. That changed everything."

I look again to Rat, who eyes me, unconvinced.

"Shut the fuck up," I snap, tearing my stare away from his and signal left.

Rat's shoulders shake as he chuckles under his breath. "I didn't say anything. I don't have to because you sure as shit know I'm right."

He points when the BMW swerves into the right-hand lane. My knuckles turn pure white when the person behind them is forced to slam on their brakes. I stay in my lane, privately declaring that Spencer will *not* be getting back into that car.

Rat releases a breath. "Mark my words, shit's going to hit the fan tonight, and I'm not even gonna bother with the I-told-you-so later because I'm calling it right the fuck now." He grips his door handle as we veer into the left lane before taking a sharp left turn. My foot hits the floorboard just as he concludes, "Keep your temper in check, D. That's all I'm going to say."

I don't respond. I just ease off the pedal when the BMW pulls into the legendary Indigo Lounge, where nothing good ever happens and bouncers are paid to look the other way. I'm sure whoever's on duty tonight will be making a shit-ton, seeing as all occupants within the BMW are well below the required entry age of twenty-one.

Purposely, I pass the entrance to the parking lot, deciding it's less likely we will be seen if we circle the block first. On the next pass, I pull in and park a couple spots away from the entrance. The engine dies, and I reach behind my seat to grab my trusty NY Yankees cap. Pulling it onto my head, I lower the bill enough to shield my eyes.

After tugging my hood over the cap, I throw a quick glance at Rat, then we both exit the vehicle.

I don't bother pulling out my ID as we approach the front of the club. "Moose."

Moose's meaty fingers give me a salute before he opens the door. "Greer." The light reflects off his shaved head as he dips his head in Rat's direction. "Cherry."

"How many times do we have to go over this?" Rat bites. "It's Marchione, asswipe. As in Italian, not the fucking *maraschino* cherry."

The sides of Moose's light-blue eyes crinkle and the scar on the right side of his cheek dips into his dimple with his smile. He shrugs. "Eh, semantics."

Rat looks to me, cross and confused. "What the fuck did he just say to me?"

Regardless of my foul mood, I find it impossible not to laugh at his baffled expression. A chuckle escapes and I grin. "We really need to look into getting you a dictionary, man. Or maybe just subscribe to one of those 'Word of the Day' email lists or something."

His eyes narrow on me as I turn, clapping Moose on the shoulder when we pass to enter the club. The door slams shut behind us, and the light dims along with my previous amusement. My eyes strain, swiftly scanning the smoke-filled air for Spencer. The bass of the music pounds through the speakers, the sound reverberating in my chest as I search.

After a few seconds, my vision finally adjusts and I spot all four in a circular booth tucked into an unlit corner. Jase slings his arm around Spencer's shoulder, forcing her into his body, her own tensing with unease.

I curl my hands into fists, watching as she gently presses him away, offering him a slight smile while shyly tucking her hair behind her ear.

"D, you're going to have to chill," Rat shouts above the music as he struts up beside me. "You're staring at her like a fucking psychopath, man."

He shoves my shoulder, breaking my attention from their table. I tear my glare away and pin it on him. "I'm not staring at her. I'm staring at *him* and his fucking hands on her."

His brows rise in response, then he leans in close, his voice low in my ear. "All the more reason for us to take a seat, brother. You don't need an up-close-and-personal view to make sure she's okay. We can do that sitting over there." He gestures toward a distant table. "Plus, we should probably stay outside of reaching distance. Otherwise you're going to clock him for no reason and shit will go south real quick."

Frustration mounting, I reach up and curl my hands around the bill of my cap, bending the sides before relenting with a nod. Rat steps in front of me, and I look nowhere but at the heels of his Nikes until we arrive at the table of his choosing . . . clear across the fucking bar.

I move to take a chair opposite Spencer's location, but Rat knocks me away and takes the seat for himself.

With a huge grin on his face, he jerks his chin toward the chair across from him. "I'll watch. You pout."

I scowl, but when he doesn't budge, I reluctantly take the seat as directed. My knee bounces nervously as a result of having absolutely no control over this situation.

Glancing at Rat, I try to gauge what's going on by his reaction. He maintains a blank face but offers random commentary as the time painfully drags along.

"They're getting drinks. Those crazy kids."

"Man, I forgot how fucking hot Cassie is."

"Since when does Spencer wear heels?"

"More drinks."

"And shots. They should probably slow down. Amateurs."

"Okay, now they're dancing."

My body seizes and I pinch my bill with the palms of my hands. Rat disengages his attention and redirects it to me. "Spencer and Cass. Boys are still at the table."

He looks again over my shoulder, and I watch as his mouth draws tight.

"Cancel that. Fuckers are on the move."

I twist in my seat, my eyes frantically seeking out any one of the four. The dance floor is packed, the crowd having increased exponentially since we arrived.

After a couple seconds, my eyes find Spencer, whose face is nothing short of panic-stricken as she searches for Cassie. I then locate Cassie about five feet away, pushing against Jonathon's chest as he forces her through the mass of people, separating her from Spencer. My stare darts back to Spencer pressed against the wall, shoving desperately as Jase buries his head in the crook of her neck. Our eyes lock over his shoulder and my entire body trembles uncontrollably as I hear her silent call.

Help me.

The flame in my chest explodes into a raging inferno and I leap to my feet, already on my way before the chair even hits the ground.

Fire.

It's everywhere.

"Shit," is the last thing I hear from Rat before the blood roaring in my ears prevents all other sound.

I have no idea how many people are physically removed out of my path on my way to Spencer. I push, I prod, I sling, I manhandle.

Bodies fly until I get to the one person upon whom I fully intend to release my wrath. I will its blaze to surface and the corners of my vision blacken in preparation for *that* place. The deep, dark place in my mind where rage soothes and conscience ceases to exist.

Spencer's frantic eyes meet mine right as I reach forward and fist the back of Jase's shirt, wrenching his body upward before slamming him to the ground.

"Dalton. No!"

Spencer's voice is muffled, barely filtering through the thunder in my head. My fists clamp shut and my knuckles snap in succession. I inhale deeply, reveling in the solace of this place, temporarily relieved from the constant ache in my chest as I make good on my promise, allowing my rage its freedom. Once I've released the reins and allow it to flow freely, unconfined . . .

I see nothing.

I'm bound securely within the comfort of my darkness. Everything fades to black, with the exception of the motherfucker in front of me.

A malicious smile spreads across his face, instigating me further as I rear back, ready to knock him and his smug grin into fucking oblivion. Just before I strike, two gentle hands wrap around my bicep and Spencer's voice breaks through my trance.

"Dalton, please. Don't. He's not worth it."

I glance over my shoulder, plucked from the hollows of my mind. Her beautiful blue eyes shimmer with unshed tears as she moves her head from side to side. Hesitantly, she unlatches her grip then reaches forward, cupping my cheek in the palm of her hand. Her touch is warm and soft, full of unspoken sorrow with her whispered breath. "*This* isn't worth it."

Her chin quivers slightly as she mouths, *I'm sorry.*

"She's right."

My neck twists in the direction of *fucking* Jase Williams, whose eyes fill with loathing as he presses himself off the floor. Our traded glares remain unbroken while he tugs at the hem of his shirt. "Neither of you is fucking worth this shit."

I lower my arm and curl it around Spencer's petite waist, trying to gently usher her behind me, but she remains rooted where she stands. After another failed attempt to move her, I give up and square my shoulders in his direction. Cocking my head, I inquire with brows raised, "Come again?"

My voice is harsh and my tone daring. My shirt is drawn taut as it's fisted inside Spencer's hand, a silent warning, but my eyes remain trained on him.

Watching.

Waiting.

He snickers before answering, "You don't scare me, Greer. I know what you do and who you do it for. I also know why you were there that night, who you were looking for, and what you were planning on doing to him once you found him."

My jaw clenches and my hands ball into fists. His eyes temporarily break from mine, glancing downward before his face splits into another wide, vindictive grin. "That's right. One word from me and your precious *Spencer* will never look at you the same again." He tsks. "And wouldn't that be a shame? To ruin your fucking superhuman status in her eyes?"

I feel Spencer turn to look at me, but I don't dare break my stare. I know without a doubt that the questions in her eyes would absolutely break me.

Jase's voice rises in anger. "You think you can just waltz into Chaz's and humiliate me over some fucking *freshman*? Ruin *my* reputation over some whore you probably already fucked six ways from Sunday? Well," he gestures to Spencer, "I guess it's time for you to know how that feels."

I step forward, but Spencer's hold tightens and she draws me back.

Jase, in turn, just scoffs. "You two are fucking pathetic." His eyes narrow on Spencer. "You reek of his filth, you know that? Of hand-me-downs and shelter meals. Of deprivation, of poverty, of trash." He shakes his head. "It's a shame really, that he's purposely marked you with his stench so no one will come near you. I really think I deserve some kind of reward for being the first person in four long years brave enough to endure it."

He licks his lips and his eyes scour her body from head to toe. As he does, the air tangibly heats and swelters all around us, but it's not stemming from me. It seeps from Spencer like molten lava. Her cheeks enflame and her eyes burn before she steps directly in front of me. I reach to grab her, but with absolutely no warning, she launches a closed fist across her body, clocking Jase right in his jaw and snapping his head clear to the side.

"Well, you reek of assholishness," she shrieks at the top of her lungs. "Don't talk about Dalton like that." Just as he regains his bearings, she expertly slams her knee right into his groin and concludes, "And don't you *ever* put your hands on me again."

His body knifes toward the floor and I almost shed a tear, it's that fucking beautiful. Unfortunately, Rat and Cassie break through the crowd right at that moment. Without thinking, I rip my gaze away from Spencer's magnificence to glance their way. Cassie's eyes widen before Rat grips her around the waist, then lifts her off the ground and slams the back of her body into his chest. Frantically, she points and screams, "Dalton!"

My eyes fly back to Spencer, then all the commotion is silenced and everything pauses.

The image of Jase's arm crossing his body in preparation to backhand Spencer's face is the last thing I see before my vision fades once again and I disappear into that peaceful place in my mind.

And that's the last thing I remember.

Chapter 9

Spencer

"So, uh, interesting night?" I remark to no one in particular from the passenger's seat of Dalton's car.

Dalton's reply? The same forward brooding stare that's been present on his face since we began this lovely drive home.

Rat's reply? "Fuck yeah, it was," shouted from the back seat, followed by a beckoning high-five in Cassie's direction.

Cassie's reply? Giggling and answering Rat's high-five request while taking another long draw from the flask of whiskey previously stashed in her purse.

I turn, my eyes grazing over Dalton's swollen knuckles before taking in the damage done to my own. I wince, curling my fingers then straightening them, relieved nothing is broken.

Dalton inhales next to me and I glance back to him, mesmerized by the rapid tick of his jaw. My lips scrunch to the side, deciding on another tactic.

"Moose seemed nice," I state, again to no one in particular.

"Fucker," Rat growls, and Dalton's mouth barely lifts at the corners.

"You know, I didn't even realize that club ran underground until he led us down there," I continue. "I don't even want to know what happened in that room where they took Jase and Jonathon."

Dalton finally looks at me, eyes fierce with his broken silence. "No, you don't."

He turns away, my lips drawing taut with his stern tone.

Rat laughs. "Whatever. They can't do much more than we already did, D. I took that other fucker out right before we found you, and well, we all saw that Jase kid when you were through with him. Plus, Moose gets paid to handle all that stuff, so I'd be more worried about Sila—"

"Rat," Dalton interrupts, his voice full of warning.

Rat clears his throat, but remains silent.

"Look," Dalton continues, breaking his stare from the road to meet mine, "that part of the club doesn't exist. Understand?"

"It does." My voice is firm, challenging. "I saw it."

Dalton's expression hardens. "Then unsee it."

I clamp down on my teeth and tighten my stare, thinking I don't much like brooding Dalton.

Cassie, however, breaks into another drunken giggle. She pokes her head between the space separating us, then apparently deciding it's too heavy to hold up on her own, perches it on the edge of my seat. Her unfocused stare slides slowly from me to Dalton, a hiccup escaping as she gestures between the both of us.

"I don't know why you guys can't just screw each other and get it over with. It would definitely relieve the sexual tension making this car ride incredibly uncomfortable for those of us in the back seat."

"Preach," Rat exclaims.

Blood rushes to my face and I return Cassie's innocent stare.

Another hiccup. "What?"

Even if I could find the words, I still wouldn't be able to reply. Utter mortification has lodged itself in my throat. After a few seconds of nothing but speechless gawking between Cassie and me, I finally find the courage to peek at Dalton, seemingly unaffected with his menacing stare focused on the road.

I glance back at Cassie, whose eyelids have become too heavy for her to manage. She blinks sleepily a couple of times, then tears begin to surface.

Her chin quivers with her whisper. "I'm so sorry, Spence. Tonight was my fault. I promised I would stay by you and I didn't. And that asshole cornered you . . ."

Her words become an unintelligible string of curses and sobs. I place my hand gently on her cheek, smile, and whisper, "There was nothing you could have done, Cass. Don't blame yourself. Shit happens sometimes."

Then, I lean forward, adding a wink, "Plus, that Jase Williams got exactly what he deserved. *Twice.*"

She nods, giving me a weak, drunken smile in return. "Love you."

I grin back. "Love you, times two."

Her eyelids finally lose their battle, the sound of her flask hitting the floorboard announcing that sleep has finally found her. Rat leans forward, gently eases her back, and curls her into his body. With her cheek on his chest, she smiles peacefully before wrapping her arm around his waist. He inhales, then lifts his hand to stroke her hair, the tenderness of the gesture both genuine and intimate.

My eyes meet Rat's and tighten into a threatening glare, just in case. He laughs quietly but flashes me the thumbs-up sign to let me know he gets the message.

Facing forward, I straighten just in time to see my house as Dalton slowly eases us alongside the curb. Once the engine is cut, he turns to me, announcing, "I'm walking you in. Rat . . ." He throws a glance over his shoulder, and the hardness that often dominates his features softens at the sight. Jerking his head in their direction, he instructs before opening his door, "Make sure she gets home safe."

Rat nods, then Dalton's feet hit the ground and the driver's seat collapses forward, giving Rat the room he needs to exit. As Rat moves to leave, I add in a whisper, "Use her window. It's the only one on the far side of her house."

A wide smile breaks across his face as he tucks his free arm under Cassie's knees and lifts her onto his lap. After curling her into his chest, he leans to grip her purse from the floorboard, then rises as though she weighs nothing.

I watch until they're safely across the street before bringing my eyes to Dalton, who has fallen back into his seat. I know we need to talk about everything that happened tonight, but I just can't do it right now. I'm emotionally exhausted.

Ready to just end the night, I raise my brows in question. "You know you don't have to walk me in, right? I mean, I'm pretty sure I can make it the remaining ten feet to my door on my own."

"I highly doubt it."

Anger pricks my skin and I inhale deeply. "Fine. Suit yourself."

Remembering Cassie's flask, I turn toward the back of the car, get onto my knees, and lean to retrieve it. The dress rides up my thighs, barely covering my backside as it shoots up into the air, but I don't care. I'm too pissed to think of anything other than getting into my house and downing an entire pint of ice cream in mourning for the absolute disaster that was my first date.

"Shit," I mutter, hand screaming with pain. I press my right elbow into the console and attempt to reach the flask with my left arm, straining my fingers to full capacity. Once they've locked onto the flask, I put all my weight on my resting arm and press upward. As I rise, my shoulder grazes Dalton's and I twist my neck just as my face passes his. I stop midmovement, halted by his pained expression. He swallows deeply, his blue eyes piercing mine as his warm breaths fan my face. I inhale, breathing in his familiar scent as it invades my senses and revel in the sugary smell. Musky yet sweet, like amaretto or almonds. I can never really put my finger on what it is. It's just . . .

Dalton.

Stares fused, our breaths mingle, quickening in sync. I tuck the section of my forward-falling hair behind my ear, and as I do, my tongue brushes my bottom lip.

His eyes fall to my mouth, the heat of their scrutiny launching an unfamiliar chill over my entire body. And when they darken with intensity, a fresh surge of goosebumps pricks every inch of my skin. Hesitantly, Dalton raises his arm, gently cradles my cheek, then gingerly runs his thumb along my bottom lip. Tears well in my eyes, clogging my throat, as I witness Dalton experience this moment of connection he so desperately needs, with no inhibition, no reservation, and no walls between us.

His gaze moves deliberately along my mouth, then my face, finally settling on my unshed tears. "You're so fucking beautiful, Spence." His head moves back and forth almost indiscernibly. "I just . . . *can't*. Not with you. Not *to* you."

The tears finally break free, their heat trailing down my cheeks as I watch his walls strategically brick back into place one by one. And with each reconstruction, another piece of *my* Dalton disappears, replaced with cold distance and lifeless eyes. His warmth vanishes and he throws open his door, leaving me alone to grieve the loss as he slams it shut behind him.

He leans his body against the hood of his car, furiously manipulating the bill of his cap before pulling it low on his forehead. Wiping my cheeks, I slowly ease off my knees and slide back into my seat, suddenly unable to breathe. The disappointment is just too much, too heavy. I know better than to let my mind wander, to seek emotion from him that just doesn't exist. Because no matter how much I believe in Dalton, if he doesn't believe himself capable of feeling, there's nothing I can do to convince him otherwise.

After chucking Cassie's flask into my purse and snaking her borrowed Mary Janes from the floorboard, I climb out of Dalton's car. My bare feet pad along the cold cement of my driveway and I say nothing when I pass him on the way to my front door. My purse dangles from the wrist of my injured hand while I drop the heels and begin to search for my key. Anger and frustration escape the corners of my eyes and trail my cheeks. Ignoring the tears, I blindly finger through my purse until I find what I'm looking for. Snatching the key between my fingers, I pin the screen door open with my hip. Dalton's presence looms next to me as he bends to retrieve my shoes. His eyes land on my bare feet and slowly make their way up my body. He says nothing once he's upright but he extends his hand, requesting my key.

My chin trembles as I hand it over. Dalton watches me in silence, then turns away, pushing the key into the lock.

He pauses to stare at the door, his voice thick. "I'm sorry, Spence. I know I hurt you—"

"You didn't hurt me. I'm just tired." I shake my head dismissively.

The corners of his mouth dip downward and he frowns at the door, taking a few seconds before finally facing me. As his apologetic eyes meet mine, he lifts his hand, swiping the moisture from my cheek with his thumb. Typically, my heart would melt at the tenderness of the gesture, but now I find it only aggravates me. I narrow my eyes and slap his hand away from my face. "Don't do that. Don't do something you don't mean."

My sorrow begins to burn as it's churned into anger. I step away and turn my back to him, my bare feet carrying me to the wooden rail that lines my porch. I brace my good hand against it, leaning forward and inhaling deeply.

Dalton growls with frustration. "What the fuck? Of course I mean it. The last thing I want to do is hurt you, Spence. I'm trying to apologize here."

I laugh humorlessly, turning back in his direction. "For what, exactly? For stalking me on my date tonight?"

His eyes darken, narrowing as they slice to mine. "The date in which you were being manhandled by some fucking loser who asked you out for no other reason than to get back at me?" He scoffs openly. "You should be thanking me."

Any fight I had left in me is gone. I allow the tears free rein, permitting them to flow freely as I respond. "I handled it, did I not? I don't need you to protect me, Dalton. I can take care of myself."

He chuckles, unsmiling, as he removes his cap and throws it to the ground, dragging his fingers through his hair. My glare hardens, and I continue my rant. "And yes, he asked me out to get back at you. Are you apologizing for *that*? Or are you apologizing for the fact that because of your stupid crusade against anyone asking me on a date EVER, I was so excited to be asked out that I accepted a date with said fucking loser? Or are you apologizing for robbing me of any hope of romance or feeling desired over the past four years? Of being wanted?"

My breaths are heavy and my pulse thrums madly through my entire body. I angrily swipe away the tears, asking the one question that has been suffocating me since Cassie informed me of his actions. "Why is that, Dalton? Why is it that you don't want me, but no one else is allowed to have me?"

Frustrated, I shake my head, stumbling on my words. "I just . . . I don't understand." My voice trembles with the admission.

Dalton's heavy boots sound as he stalks across the porch. I avert my gaze, but once he's in front of me, his fingers curl around my chin, pulling my face into his line of sight. His furious stare bores into mine. "You think I don't want you? Goddamn it, Spencer," he bites. "I want you so much I can't fucking breathe when I'm without you. Every single time I walk away from you, there is nothing but agony as the anger that simmers here"—he breaks to pound his closed fist on his chest—"chars my insides. With each step I take, the farther I am from the relief just being near you provides."

His eyes glisten and his jaw tightens with a stern shake of his head. "I can't fucking breathe without you, don't you get it? I want you so much that being without you is absolute torture."

He swallows hard, and moisture seeps from my eyes as I witness the sight of true emotion as it's freed from Dalton Greer. "I want you, Spence, but I can't have you. I won't allow it. You're too good, too pure, too innocent. And just as your presence soothes me, mine will eventually flaw you. It's inevitable, and I care too much for you to let that happen."

A lone tear escapes from the corner of his eye with his conclusion. "But you're right. Even thinking about you with someone else, with someone else's arms around you as you look into their eyes the same way you're looking into mine right now, I just—"

He looks down and shakes his head. "I can't. So I guess I'm a selfish, heartless prick because where does that leave you?"

The tear finally falls free from his chin and I step forward, placing my hands on either side of his face, forcing his rueful eyes to meet mine. My voice trembles as I speak. "I know you like to control things, Dalton. That's how you've learned to cope and I understand that, but you *don't* control me. My feelings. My heart. And even though you feel you don't deserve those things, that they're not yours to have, you're mistaken."

Dalton tries to look away, but I tighten my grip and say with emphasis, "You ask where that leaves me? Well, it leaves me right here in the same place, on the same porch I was five years ago when I first met you. The day I willingly handed over all those pieces of me you feel you can't have without question."

Releasing him, I turn away to speak into the night air, knowing his refusal will absolutely destroy me. "I have always belonged to you. I *will always* belong to you. Regardless of what you've done, what you do, even what you will do, I will forever be yours. And that's *my* choice to make, whether you choose me or not."

I stand there waiting in silence, and after what feels like an eternity, I finally get my response.

Crickets.

I *literally* hear crickets as I stand with my back to Dalton. And if I hadn't just poured my heart out to the only person I will probably ever truly love in this lifetime, I would laugh at the cliché of unrequited love and cricket-filled silence playing out in front of me.

But instead, as I hear his footsteps begin to recede, I find my only reaction to this pathetic situation is to cry.

So that's what I do.

Chapter 10 ✦
Dalton

You reek of his filth, you know that? Of hand-me-downs and shelter meals. Of deprivation, of poverty, of trash. He's purposely marked you with his stench so no one will come near you . . .

That motherfucker's speech wages a bloody war inside my mind. His lethal words fulfill their purpose as they continue to strike deep, reminding me that Spencer deserves so much better than anything that I could possibly offer. She deserves more than the haunting memories of my past, more than the fraudulent version of myself in the present, and most importantly, far more than the corrupt future to which I'm bound. His truths pillage all hope of experiencing Spencer's love as those words circle my mind, leaving me completely hollow.

I turn and begin to walk away. To do the one thing I always promised myself I would do, which is to protect her, *especially* if it's from me.

I will always belong to you. Regardless of what you've done, what you do, even what you will do, I will forever be yours . . .

Spencer's heartfelt words follow, frantically gathering the carnage Williams's truths leave behind, melding the fragments back together as she willingly offers the one thing I never thought possible in this life. In *my* life.

The gift of unconditional love.

And as the sound of her gentle sobs filter through my internal battle, I halt where I stand, her sorrow seizing my movement as it washes over me. I close my eyes and inhale deeply, allowing her emotion to cleanse my mind, her tears to mend my wounds.

Her essence blossoms within me, permeating my hollow voids. The constant ache in my chest dwindles as it's replaced with the fervor of renewed hope. Of the promise of love and acceptance with absolutely no expectation other than receiving mine in return.

The *only* thing I've ever wanted is being offered to me by the *one* person who means the most to me in this world. And I'm about to walk away.

I shake my head.

I don't fucking think so.

My eyes fly open and I pivot on my heel. I'm met with the sight of Spencer's blonde hair cascading over the cradled face in her hands. My heart lurches, crying out for her.

So close, yet so far.

My feet can't carry me there fast enough.

I stride with purpose, closing the distance between us, and with absolutely no hesitation or doubt, I reach forward, curl my fingers around her upper arm, and whirl her around to face me. Her shocked expression barely registers as I crash my mouth down onto hers. Every single ounce of emotion I've suppressed over the years barrels itself into this kiss.

It's not gentle. It's not slow. It's not composed.

It's frantic.

It's demanding.

It's savage.

It's unrestrained.

It's every uncontrollable, innate desire I've withheld since meeting her on this porch as they rise to the surface, finally freed from constraint.

And she gives it back just as hard as I give it.

Teeth gnash, tongues spar, fingers clutch, and bodies press.

The need to breathe escapes us, and with my mouth sealed over hers, I guide her to the porch railing, then lift her onto its wooden surface. My tongue sweeps deeply and her dress inches upward as her legs wrap around my waist, drawing me into her body. I grip her hips, my fingers digging into the fabric, and pull her as close as I physically can. Firmly, I press my hardness between her legs, drawing her soft whimper into my throat. She squeezes her thighs, the warmth from her body seeping through my jeans, and the friction between our bodies spurs an animalistic, hungry growl from deep within my chest.

In response, she threads her fingers into my hair and tugs my head to the side, claiming my mouth with her own. And as she does, I open myself completely and give her all that I have—all that I am—and pray that it's enough.

Moments later, just as our lips part, a hoot comes from across the street and a familiar voice shouts, "It's about motherfucking time."

I settle my forehead against hers, our breaths heavy and our eyes locked as we listen to the sound of Rat's engine coming to life. It's not until he's long gone that I dare move, for fear of losing this moment.

Gently, I place my palms on her cheeks and lean forward one more time, just to savor her. My mouth brushes tenderly across her swollen lips, then I run my nose leisurely down the length of hers, inhaling her sweet, citrus scent before finally releasing her.

Her legs fall away, her warmth vanishing, and I grip the wooden ledge on either side of them and attempt to slow my breathing. My eyes fall to her bare feet, crossed at the ankle and dangling in front of me, the memories of the many summers we've spent together racing through my mind.

Spencer in her favorite cut-offs running barefoot in the grass. Her face full of light and joy with the sun shining all around her and the innocence of her laughter as her long blonde hair trails behind. Her big blue eyes radiating their warmth and the freckles on the reddened bridge of her nose as she scrunches it at something I said.

She's mine.

As my mind resolutely affirms those words, my heart is filled with pure joy, and for the first time in as long as I can remember, I'm glad to be alive.

Because in her . . . I find purpose.

I want to *be* for her.

I want to *exist* just so I can experience her.

I want to *live*, to *feel*, to *laugh*, and to *love* with her.

"Teach me."

The words escape me without thought, and I lift my pleading eyes to meet her puzzled expression. "I don't know how to do this, Spence. How to love like you do. To *live* like you do."

I pause briefly, trying to figure a way to explain so she will understand. "Emotions such as trust and compassion, feelings of patience and empathy—those gifts that come so naturally for you—I've never been able to understand, much less exercise. I need you to teach me because I want to be able to give you everything you deserve. And you deserve someone as flawless as you."

Her features soften and a compassionate smile tugs at her lips. She gestures with a subtle motion of her head. "Come here."

Gradually, I lean into her, my forearms falling in line with the sides of her thighs. She places a lingering kiss on the corner of my mouth, her lips warm and soft as they remain pressed against mine.

When she disengages the kiss, I find it impossible to do anything other than foil her attempt. My face follows hers as she rises, but it's her giggle that finally gives her victory. My mouth breaks into a wide smile at the sound, and as I finally resign, I'm nothing short of amazed at the newfound reality that I can kiss her whenever I like.

Reaching forward, I tuck a section of her hair behind her ear, taking a moment to relish the silkiness of the texture. Beautiful grin on her face, she gazes down at me, her eyes full of reassurance.

"There is so much more to you than you believe, Dalton. You think yourself incapable of trust and compassion, of patience and empathy, but I know better." She flattens her palm on her chest. "I know because I feel you *here*. The *real* you, not the concocted version you want everyone else to see. And I know with absolute certainty that you are every bit as compassionate and patient as I am. You just keep all those qualities hidden so deeply within yourself that even you don't know they're there. But I feel them, every time my heart beats."

She runs her fingers through my hair, and I burn the image of this moment into my mind. The conviction in her eyes and her unyielding confidence in the words she's just spoken fuel me to believe I can do anything.

I drop my stare to her lap, where her hand sits swollen and bruised. My jaw tenses. "Shit. Your hand."

I glance back up just in time to see her nose crinkle. "It doesn't really hurt anymore."

A disbelieving smirk crosses my face and she throws her head back in laughter. "I promise, Dalton. It doesn't hurt." She gestures at my hand. "How 'bout yours?"

I shrug my response, long since numb to the pain. Her smile falls and she draws her bottom lip between her teeth.

"I'm sorry about tonight," she states, her voice timid.

"Spence—"

"It was my fault, the whole thing with Jase. I shouldn't have gone out with him." She shakes her head and the guilty expression on her face sparks my anger.

"You did nothing to warrant his fucking hands all over you."

Images of her helplessness while his hands stroked her bare thighs flash through my mind. My hands clench tightly, and her eyes fall to my fists before she shyly glances back to my face.

"I know. It's just . . . well, I only went out with him to . . . uh . . . well, to get your attention, so to speak."

My eyes widen and my head jerks back. "What?"

She nervously nibbles at her lip before deflecting, "It was Cassie's idea."

Her lips pucker while she struggles for some semblance of an explanation. "She . . . well, *we* wanted to . . ."

As she flounders, the pieces finally click, and I whisper a silent thank you to Daisy Mae while my lips strain against an emerging grin. Her gaze tightens as she eyes my twitching mouth. I cock my head to the side and arch my brows expectantly.

"You're going to make me say it, aren't you?"

While answering with a slow, patient nod, the grin breaks free and her eyes narrow further into a hardened stare.

"We were testing a theory."

My smile widens. "And what theory was that, may I ask?"

"No, you may not ask." Her face relaxes and the corners of her mouth lift slightly. "But I will say the theory proved to be true, and while I'm extremely happy about that," she pauses, her brows knitted together in thought, "I'm just sorry it got out of hand. You could have been hurt. I could have been hurt. It just wasn't a good situation and I'm really, *really* sorry."

I reach forward and take her hands into mine, careful not to squeeze too tightly. "No more apologies. Not tonight. My being able to hold you, to touch you, to kiss you . . ." I shake my head for emphasis. "I won't apologize for anything that had to happen to get us to this moment, and neither should you."

She nods, her eyes filling with tears. Just as I lean forward to steal yet another kiss, the screen door opens and Mrs. Locke steps out onto the porch. One look at us and her brows shoot skyward. She glances between the both of us, revealing a shrewd smile as she makes her way to where we stand. Once in front of us, she focuses her amusement solely on Spencer.

"I think we're definitely going to need some ice cream."

Spencer giggles, nodding eagerly before hopping off the railing. Her feet hit the wood beneath us, then she asks, "Can you give us another sec? Then I'll come in."

Mrs. Locke reaches forward and grazes the tip of her finger down Spencer's cheek. "Sure thing, honey."

Then she turns in my direction. Her grin widens, then she steps to embrace me. Always uncomfortable with the gesture, I awkwardly pat her back. Her entire body shakes with laughter and she squeezes me even tighter before whispering, "Believe it or not, your hugs are getting better."

A smile tugs at my lips and I give her one more tentative pat before she releases me. Mrs. Locke gives me a wink then turns away, pressing a kiss on Spencer's forehead before entering the house.

Spencer watches the door close before bringing her eyes back to mine. She grins and wraps her arms around my waist, resting her cheek on my chest. My arms fold around her and I press my lips to the top of her head, inhaling contently.

"Your hugs *are* getting better." She giggles.

I grin into her hair. "Well, with adults, not so much. But with you, it's as natural as breathing."

She sighs. "What now? Where do we go from here?"

My arms tighten around her shoulders. "Well, I think I should probably ask you out on an official date. Your first one was kind of a bust."

Her cheek presses into my shirt with her smile. "You sure? I mean, it would kind of defeat the whole purpose of your no-one-dates-Spencer-Locke crusade if you broke your own rules."

I smile, and with my arms still around her, I lean away to better see her face. "It would, but I've never really been one to follow the rules anyway. As you well know."

She giggles again and the sound filters straight to my heart.

"Plus," I add, "I will have the image of you bent over my seat, your ass in that dress, etched forever in my mind. You had no idea what you were doing, but it was sexy as hell. Trust me." My brows rise as I inquire, "You think I'm gonna let you go anywhere near another dude's car after that sight in my rearview mirror? Nope. Never."

Her mouth stretches into a wide smile, and unable to resist, I lean and brush my own against it. She parts her lips and my tongue darts between them, sweeping deeply as I bask in her taste. She smiles against my mouth.

"Your kisses definitely don't need work," she states with a devilish grin, releasing me from her hold. "See you tomorrow?"

"It's a date," I respond, once again gifted with the sound of her laughter.

My body immediately misses her warmth as she turns away and heads to her door. Before entering, she offers me a warm, contented smile over her shoulder. I grin back, watching until the door shuts and locks behind her, then reach down, grab my cap, and turn my boots in the direction of my car. The night air is brisk and I breathe it in deeply, my lungs inhaling a full breath for the first time in what feels like forever.

Sliding into my car, I fit the cap snugly back on my head. Glancing to Spencer's window, I grin inwardly as joy and innocence combine, creating soothing warmth as they flare to life within me. Leaning back, I place my palm flat on my chest and soak in the feeling.

I feel you too, Spence.

Right where I need it the most.

Chapter 11

Spencer

Closing my calculus book, I toss it beside me just as the front door opens. I twist to look over the back of the couch and watch my mother enter, eyeing her troubled expression as she chucks her bag on the dining room table. Various college applications and random pamphlets from school peek out from the top of the canvas, reminding me that I should probably start looking into college soon.

"What's wrong?"

She turns to face me, hand resting on her hip, anxiously nibbling on the inside of her mouth, the telltale sign of worry. Her light-brown eyes find mine and her features soften. "Claudia called. Michelle Owen left with her daughter and we think she may have gone back home." She shakes her head. "She's been increasingly agitated over the past couple of days. I knew something was going on when she didn't show up in court after the temporary restraining order expired. She has absolutely no protection now, so if she goes back to him . . ."

I nod in understanding. Leaving an already established life behind isn't easy. Starting over somewhere new, trying to support your children on your own, always looking over your shoulder . . . Sadly, sometimes victims feel it's just easier to go back home. I've seen this happen quite a few times with women at the shelter.

Mom breathes in deeply and looks to the ceiling. "I just hope wherever they are, they're safe."

My mouth curves downward while I recall Michelle's sweet daughter, Penny, and I say a quick prayer for their safety as well.

"Are you going up there?" I inquire.

She kicks her heels off onto the floor and her expression dips in apology. "Yeah, I'm sorry, honey. I need to file some paperwork and check up on a few things."

I rise from the couch, giving her a small smile. My steps are soft as I walk to where she stands and wrap my arms around her waist, breathing in her crisp apple scent before stating, "And to make sure you're there in case anything happens with Michelle."

Her arms tighten around my shoulders and I listen as she draws in a long breath. After a light kiss to my forehead, she releases me, then smiles as she grazes my cheek with her knuckle. "How did I get so lucky with you?"

I match her grin with one of my own and shrug. As she steps away, she asks, "Plans with Dalton tonight?"

The smile on my face widens and I eagerly nod. "Yeah, he should be here within the hour."

She eyes my joyful expression before taking my hand into hers and pulling me toward the couch. After placing my calculus book on the coffee table, she sits and pats the cushion. I hesitantly take a seat, drawing my legs underneath me, then turn to face her.

With my hand still enveloped in hers, she smiles tenderly. "You and Dalton have been friends for a long time. I know from experience when you start a relationship that stems from that close of a friendship, things can progress rather *quickly*."

Her mouth broadens into a brilliant smile and her shoulders shake as she laughs. "Jim and I were the best of friends for years before we became high school sweethearts. But you already knew that, didn't you?"

I give her a subtle nod. My mother's love for her husband is still so very obvious by the way she keeps him alive in our day-to-day conversations.

She squeezes my hand. "Well, when you enter into a relationship with someone with whom you're already familiar, with no barriers of awkwardness or uncertainty, it's easy to bypass the time it typically takes to get to know someone before you feel comfortable . . . physically."

Blood rushes my face, fanning its warmth as it spreads across the tops of my cheeks. She eyes my reaction, then smiles. "I know we've already had *the talk*, so I'm not going to subject you to it again, but I just want to make sure you're careful, and not just in the physical aspect. You and Dalton . . . well, there's something magnetic between the two of you, and it will be easy for you to get wrapped up in those feelings and lose sight of the fact that even though you're close, there are certain things you still don't know about each other. Things that need to be discussed in order to build a stable, lasting relationship. Things necessary to acknowledge about your pasts before taking that next step."

Her eyes narrow. "You need to tell him, Spencer."

I nibble my bottom lip and nod once again. Her features relax, then she continues. "You'll be eighteen next month, a legal adult, free to do what you choose. I trust you, your decisions, and I know you've seen the consequences of what happens when poor choices are made. You see them every day. So, just be careful. Be smart. But most importantly . . ." she pauses, sucking in a breath, and moisture begins to build along the base of her dark lashes, "be true to who you are. Be honest. Because I think Dalton's reaction to your past will only serve to strengthen the bond you two already share. And yours to his, just the same."

Tears prick my eyes and my chin trembles slightly as I reach forward to wrap my arms around her neck. "I love you so much," I whisper, my chin perched on her shoulder.

She sniffles then tightens her hold. "I love you too, my sweet Spencer. I thank God every single day for bringing you into my life. I hope you know Jim would have been so proud of you. Of the beautiful, intelligent, caring young lady you've become."

She releases me, then adds, "And I also thank God I had to put you on birth control when you were thirteen."

My mouth flies open.

"Mom!" I squeak.

She gives me a wink before heading to her room, leaving me alone in my semimortification.

Once my face returns to its normal shade, I glance to the clock and hop off the couch to shower before Dalton arrives.

Thirty minutes later, I'm scrubbed clean and fully dressed. Just as I slide the daisy flower crown headband over the top of my hair, the doorbell sounds. My heart jumps clear into my throat and my face burns. I take a final look in the mirror to make sure my cheeks aren't as blood red as I imagine them.

My hair is curled in loose waves and my makeup is minimal. With just a light-brown eye shadow and mascara on my eyes, a nude gloss coating my lips, and my natural blush reddening my cheeks, I nod in satisfaction, then grab my phone and shove it into the back pocket of my trusty flare jeans. Smoothing my hands over my Jimi Hendrix tee, I take in a breath to calm my nerves, then slide my feet into my favorite canvas flip-flops before finally opening my door.

Voices filter through the air as I make my way to the living room, and I pray my mother isn't giving Dalton the same lecture she just gave me. But as laughter hits my ears, I feel fairly certain their conversation has nothing to do with birth control or the physicality of relationships.

Dalton turns at the sound of my arrival, and I momentarily forget how to breathe. You would think, after all these years, that my reaction to seeing him would change, but it never does. The air is sucked right out from my lungs as I mentally catalogue his appearance. His charcoal-gray V-neck T-shirt is drawn taut across his entire upper body, his dark-blue jeans ride low on his hips and bunch slightly around the tops of his black Docs, and pieces of his blond hair peek out at me from underneath the bill of yet another Yankees baseball cap. His mouth glides into an easy grin when his blue-gray stare lands on the top of my head, displaying his approval for the daisies crowning it.

I return the expression with a giddy smile of my own, and it's not until my mother clears her throat that we disengage. With her hair piled into a loose bun, she looks to Dalton then to me, her mouth working to hide her own grin. Now dressed in an oversized sweatshirt and a pair of jeans, her Nikes pad softly across our wood floors as she moves to embrace Dalton before doing the same to me. When finished, she lifts her brows, silently reiterating our conversation from earlier. I dip my head in response, and watch her face as her grin breaks free.

"So lucky."

She presses one last kiss to my forehead before leaving. The door shuts behind her and I twist back to face Dalton, whose eyes remain trained on me, the intensity in his gaze spurring another warm flush across my cheeks.

"I like the daisies."

With just three strides, he's in front of me, and the sweet musk scent of his presence saturates the air as he swipes the hair off my shoulder, then curls his fingers at the base of my neck. With his thumb, he strokes my cheek gently, then leans to brush his full lips over mine.

I press up on my toes and wrap my arms around his neck. His free arm folds around my waist, pulling me firmly against his body. Angling my head, I part my lips, and am rewarded with a tender caress of his tongue as it enters my mouth. My body remains flush against his and our breathing quickens as he guides us to the back of the couch. Fingers still entwined in my hair, he pulls me with him as he widens his stance, securing our weight against the plaid upholstery. His teeth nip my bottom lip and a current of electricity surges through my entire body. A moan escapes me and I tighten my hold, only for him to break the kiss with a wide grin against my lips. After running his nose along mine and giving me a light peck on the tip, he releases his grip from my hair.

He drops his arms, both thumbs hooking into my belt loops. "I could do that all night."

Trying to calm my own breathing, I place my palms against his rapidly rising chest. His heart beats wildly in sync with mine as we stare deeply into each other's eyes.

A mischievous grin crosses my lips. "Why don't you then?"

The whites of his teeth flash before he shakes his head. "I need a sunset, Pencil. Let's take a ride."

In this moment, I'm completely mesmerized by how youthful and carefree he seems, very much a rare version of Dalton Greer.

Removing my hands from his chest, he places a gentle kiss on each palm before threading our fingers together, then kisses the top of my head before leading us to the door. Our hands remain joined until I'm tucked safely into the passenger seat of his Camaro, and even then I find myself not wanting to let go.

I don't think I will ever be close enough to Dalton. That feeling, that *need* . . . it's overwhelming at times. I've never experienced anything like it.

I want to inhale him. To taste him on my tongue. To feel him course through my bloodstream. To consume every bit of his essence. Only then do I think my craving for him would be satisfied.

And as he slides into the seat next to me and I greedily inhale in his scent, I know my mother is right. There is no barrier, no awkwardness, no uncertainty between us. There is only this unseen magnetism that draws us to each other. *As it always has.*

An unbreakable force that will continue its pull until we finally become one.

Chapter 12

Dalton

With our backs resting against my windshield and our legs stretched along the hood of my car, I thread my fingers between Spencer's. Our eyes are glued to the sky. Slowly, she scoots closer and nestles her face against my shoulder. I inhale contentedly, then break my forward stare to press my lips against the top of her head. *I love that I can do that.*

Peace and serenity settle into my chest, calming the singe of yet another day of corruption under the reign of Silas Kincaid. I breathe her in and allow her citrus fragrance, her innocence, to bathe the filth from my soul.

Gone is the transport of 500K-worth of ice to a local meth dealer.

Disappeared is the guilt of threatening the family of Jenson Biggs, 40K-deep into Silas's debt. Now 10K.

Erased are the Glock 9mms Rat picked up for us, against Silas's wishes, clean and freshly filed.

All that remains is the orange in the sky and the sweet scent of the angel lying next to me. Nothing else.

We watch in silence until the sun finally sets, then both breathe out a long sigh. I turn to her and clear my throat, nervous smile on my face. "I have something for you. It's not much, but I saw it and thought of you."

Her eyes widen and a joy-filled smile spreads across her beautiful features. I reach into my pocket and pull out the item I spied just a couple days ago. I bought it as a gift for her upcoming birthday, but as it turns out, I really suck at surprises. Who knew?

Dangling the strand of black beads in front of her face, an unexpected rush of anxiety races through my system. I've never given anyone anything. Ever. It's extremely unnerving.

Her grin broadens as she extends her hand, uncurling her fingers in my direction. I lower the bracelet and watch as it coils on the surface of her flattened palm. I look up at her and swallow deeply, trying to rid the nerves constricting my throat. "It's . . . uh, they're onyx—the beads. I read that they offer protection for the person who wears them. I just . . ." I clear my throat again. "I wanted you to be protected, even when I'm not around."

Her teeth graze her bottom lip, hindering her smile. I fight the urge to take that pouty lip in between mine and tear my stare from her mouth, briefly glancing at the bracelet before meeting her sky-blue eyes.

She grips the bracelet tightly, then turns to fully face me. "Put it on me?"

I nod and slowly uncurl her fingers, allowing my touch to linger on the soft pads with each one drawn away. She shivers in response and I breathe a light chuckle, still amazed each time I elicit that reaction from her. Once the bracelet is pinched between my fingers, she turns her wrist and patiently waits while the ends are hooked together. I watch, mesmerized as it slides gracefully down her arm and settles across the bones of her delicate wrist. Instinctively, my fingers glide along the soft skin just traveled, then I curl her hand in mine, pressing a soft kiss in the center of her palm.

She releases a shuddering breath. "I love it, Dalton. It's perfect. Thank you."

My face warms with her compliment, so I look away and focus on the stars. After a couple moments of peace-filled silence, I inquire, "If you were a color, what color would you be?"

She giggles beside me, eyes locked on the bracelet. "What *color* would I be?"

I nod. "Yeah . . ." I stall, hesitant with my admission. "It's just, sometimes I feel like a chameleon, you know? Forced to change my colors based on where I am in my life."

I release a heavy breath. "Lately it feels as though I change them so often, I'm nothing more than a fucked-up version of an impressionist painting."

Glancing to the side, my heart lurches as she crinkles her nose, my absolute favorite of her expressions. My eyes linger on the freckles lining her nose before once again seeking obscurity in the night sky. "To those far away, I project a solid, recognizable image. But in reality, I'm composed of nothing but a series of angry, incoherent strokes brushed in every color imaginable. Disjointed."

I pin her with my stare. "Broken."

Her mouth dips at the corners in thought. Then she turns on her side and tucks her hands under her cheek, the sincerity of her stare relentless as she looks at me. "Do you think Renoir and Monet didn't know what they were doing? That they didn't purposely place each stroke of their paintbrush in order to create their envisioned masterpiece?"

She tightens her gaze. "You are a work of art, Dalton. Your *own* masterpiece, regardless of whether you choose to acknowledge it or not. Every experience that paints your picture is a stroke made just for you. Each one of them is essential in order for you to grow, to learn, and to teach."

She shrugs her shoulders. "You ask me what color I would be? Well, I would be every single color I could because to me, they're more than just colors, Dalton. They're emotions. Feelings. Reminders of *our* journey. Life would mean absolutely nothing without every single color, every single stroke, every single experience that molds us into who we are meant to become. Broken or not."

My skin pricks with irritation as it floods me. I try to ignore it, to push away the animosity, but expectation and accusation ring loudly in my ears. I shake my head.

Not from her. I can't.

Breathing fails me, crippled by growing fury as every single muscle in my body goes rigid. I open my mouth to tell her how much I *feel*. What exactly I've experienced—shit that I wouldn't wish on anyone. To finally explain to her why remaining numb is so much easier than reopening the ever-present scars of my past.

But before I can speak, my phone vibrates on the hood of the car, sliding down the black metal until it falls directly into my hand. My fingers sweep it up and as I glance down, a phone number flashes along the screen. No name, just unfamiliar numbers as they cross.

Pressing off the windshield, I sit up straight and debate answering, unsure if it's Silas-related. Spencer sits up with me and her eyes fall to the screen as it vibrates again. She looks at me with curiosity, and I swallow deeply before swiping my finger across the glass.

Every single hair on my body stands on end as the high-pitch wails of a child cross the line. The sounds threaten to steal me from the present, the screams too familiar as they continue. I jump to my feet and as soon as my boots hit the ground, the yelling stops, followed by the muffled sounds of panting and tiny footsteps on the move.

"Hello? Who is this?" My voice is thick when I finally speak, and the monsters from my past make their presence known when I jump in response to Spencer's delicate touch to my shoulder.

My entire body pulsates with each rapid beat of my heart. I force myself to breathe, only to lose the ability when a familiar voice finally makes its way to my ear.

"Dalton? Can you"—*sniffle*—"come save me?" Penny's sweet but terrified voice filters through the whooshing in my ears. I tighten my hold on the phone, making my way to the driver's side of my car. Spencer follows suit, and we both land in our seats at the same time. I turn the key already in the ignition, revving my engine.

"Where are you, Penny? I can't come to you unless I know where you are."

At the mention of Penny's name, Spencer reaches down, grabs her purse, and lifts her own phone to her ear. Her hands tremble as she waits for an answer, and as much as I would like to comfort her, I can't. Fear and anger are the only emotions I'm capable of as I throw my car in reverse, then rapidly turn the wheel, righting the direction of the car as we spin to face forward.

"I'm at home. We came back home."

My eyes dart to Spencer. "Do you know her address?"

She shakes her head. "No, they're not required to provide that information at the center. I have no idea—Mom! Mom, it's Spencer . . ."

Her voice fades as I turn my focus back to Penny. "Penny, sweetheart, I need you to tell me your address. You know your address, right?"

"I live on East Street. I don't know the numbers. Do you want me to go see?"

More muffling sounds through my phone. I turn onto Lamar Boulevard, thankful that I'm heading in the right direction. As I picture her hand on the doorknob, I yell, "No!" then soften my tone. "No, Penny. I need you to stay where you are."

"Okay." She sniffles.

I take a strong left onto Palm and mouth *East Street* to Spencer, who frantically relays the information to her mother. She nods then disconnects the call, chucking the phone into my empty cup holder. "Her mom drives an older Accord. Black. Look for it in the driveway. Mom's on her way."

I nod, then focus on the road as the East Street exit comes into view. Spencer yanks the daisy crown off her head and snags an elastic band from her purse, haphazardly throwing her hair into a ponytail as I veer right. Just as I take the exit, my heart stalls in my chest.

"I'm scared, Dalton."

I clench my teeth and my nostrils flare in effort to leash my fury. "We're almost there, Penny. Just stay on the line with me, sweetheart. And try to be as quiet as you can until we get there."

A female shriek followed by a loud crash and a soft whimper from Penny results in my foot hitting the floor. We pick up speed, swerving in and out of traffic until we take a left onto East Street. I slow the car, glancing to the left and right as I continue to drive.

"There!" Spencer shouts, bounding upward in her seat. "There. I see it." She points to the right. As soon as I see the Accord, I pick up speed and don't stop until we fly into their driveway, using the black Harley to absorb the full impact of my bumper. It ricochets off the garage door, then falls on its side, and I grin internally. I know without a doubt the now crumpled piece of machinery was some fucker's pride and joy.

Just as my door flies open, Spencer's fingers wrap around my arm. "No. Mom said to wait."

Glass breaking and another loud scream fill the air. I glance back at her. "Fuck that."

My boots hit the ground and my chest implodes. Fury heats my blood, circulating, firing life into every faculty I need for this fight.

Spencer's cries mix with those of Penny's as I kick the front door open. I'm met with the sight of Penny's mother bloodied and lying unconscious on the floor, Penny's reddened, swollen, tear-stricken face as she's held midair by a meaty palm fisting her shirt, and the absolute terror on Ed Jamieson's face as he twists to face me.

The same Ed Jamieson who had me jumped not even a month ago.

Oh, the irony.

His fear radiates across the room.

I crack my neck in preparation, permitting a menacing laugh to escape my lips. It's then that my fire ignites, relinquishing the absolute evil that thrives within me.

Chapter 13

Spencer

I fly into the house with abandon. Just as I enter the ransacked living room, the hairs on my arms raise and I stop dead in my tracks. I watch in silence, my eyes glued to Dalton's predatory mannerisms. The expression in his eyes is lethal as he steps closer to where a man stands, holding Penny by her Minnie Mouse pajama top. She is dangling about three feet from the ground and looks terrified.

"Put her down, Jamieson." Dalton's voice is cold, hard, and void of any emotion.

I have no idea how Dalton knows this man, but his tone seems to work because soon after, Penny is slowly lowered to the ground. Once her feet are planted, she runs to where her mother lies on the floor, crying out as she folds herself over her mother's body. I carefully make my way over to them, and slowly crouching down beside Penny's sobbing frame, I reach forward, relieved when my fingers find her mother's pulse beating weakly at the base of her neck.

My throat is raw as I whisper, "She's okay, sweetie. She's just sleeping." Penny's puffy eyes rise to meet mine and I sweep my hand along her long blonde hair to reassure her. "I need you to stay right here in case she wakes up, okay? I'm going to go check on Dalton." Her head dips as she nods, then it falls to her mother's chest, tears still leaking from her eyes.

I press off the balls of my feet, gradually standing, my stare trained on Dalton. The look in his eyes is like nothing I've ever seen before. Not even with Jase.

It's as though he's completely disappeared. No humanity is housed within them as he continues to approach Penny's father with deliberate movements. A viper ready to strike at any moment.

"Dalton," I whisper. "Let's wait for Mom. She's bringing the police."

My tone is soft, soothing even, in an attempt to distract him, but my request falls on deaf ears. He continues to stalk his prey. Only when he draws his fist back do I make my move, the knowledge that the police are coming spurring me into action. I launch myself forward and grab hold of his arm, digging my heels in as his strength drags me across the floor with the attempted delivery of his punch.

"Spencer," he growls, "let go."

"The police are on their way. They can handle this." My hold remains as I narrow my eyes onto his flushed face.

Penny's father chuckles, the stench of alcohol permeating the air between us. His taunting eyes latch onto Dalton's, refusing to let go as he speaks. "That's two. Two times you've missed your mark. First we beat your ass to a pulp, and now you have to sit there like some pussy-whipped motherfucker while your girl tells you what to do. It's embarrassing really. Something tells me Silas won't be happy about your new reins." He leans forward, breaching Dalton's personal space, and smiles, his rotting teeth made evident with his grin. "Be sure to tell him hello, by the way."

Dalton displays no emotion, but inhales deeply, taking in a long breath. When he finally turns to face me, he says nothing, but dips his chin. I assess him for a couple of seconds, taking in his calm manner, and watch his face return to its normal coloring. Relieved, I drop my hold on his arm.

He moves toward me and I step back to give him room, only for his scowl to return. He twists his body opposite me, and with the momentum gained, slams his fist into the side of the man's face.

The man falls to the floor upon impact and I watch in horror as Dalton swings his booted foot and kicks him in the stomach. The man curls into himself, releasing a loud wail, and I raise my hand to stifle my own scream. Tears gather in my eyes and my entire body trembles as Dalton leans over, reaches forward to pull the man up by his hair, and centers his head not even two inches away from his face.

"You lay one motherfucking hand on *either* of them again, I will hunt you down. And once I find you, the pain you're experiencing now will feel like ecstasy in comparison. That's a fucking promise."

The head within his grasp remains suspended until he slams it against the floor, knocking the man unconscious.

Only two feet away from where he stands, my heart races beneath my ribcage. Fearfully, I watch his controlled movements, his lifeless eyes as he tugs at the hem of his shirt, clearly unaffected by the violence. Several silent minutes pass, then he finally glances up at me. His eyes blink rapidly, finally finding focus on something other than the slaughter of the man on the floor.

He scans my body, my face, then my eyes. His vacant expression softens before disengaging to survey the room. Once his stare finds Penny and her mother, an audible intake of air breaks the heavy silence. Tears clog my throat as his eyes begin to glisten, taking in the sight of Penny's body hovered over her mother's.

My chest, my *heart*, is consumed with fire, and I know without a doubt that this is Dalton's pain, not mine, searing my chest. I bite my bottom lip as he strides over to where Penny lies. Her head rises, and as soon as she sees Dalton's crouched presence, she jumps into his arms, burying her head in the crook of his neck and sobbing uncontrollably.

"Shh, shh . . ."

His hand strokes gently along her back as he soothes her. Once the whimpers soften, he leans away and presses the sections of her hair clinging to her tear-soaked cheeks away to better assess her injuries.

A scab forming on her bottom lip and the bruises lining her cheeks show she took quite a beating. My chest flares and I unconsciously begin to rub my palm along my sternum to ease the burn, watching from afar as Dalton's jaw muscles tick steadily.

Her eyes still wet with tears, Penny watches his reaction before reaching forward with her hand and placing it on his chest. The burning subsides within my own as she whispers, "I knew you would save us." Her stare meets mine over his shoulder and a dimple dents the surface of her cheek. "And *she* will save *you*."

My breath catches as he twists in my direction. *My* Dalton stares back at me, his features no longer hardened in anger but relaxed as he continues to hold the little girl in his arms.

Commotion in the doorway interrupts the moment as my mother enters the house. Frantic and distraught, she quickly scans the room. Her search is stalled when her eyes hesitate on the image of Penny's father lying on the floor, but eventually she finds me.

"I'm okay," I reassure her.

She expels a relieved breath, redirecting her attention to Dalton and Penny before it falls to Penny's mother still on the floor.

She snaps out of her haze. "Penny, baby, are you okay?" Her tone is shaky as she tries to maintain a hold on her composure.

Penny nods. "Dalton took care of it."

My mother's eyes widen, pride flashing across her features before she clears her throat. "Yes, I can see that." Mom turns to Dalton. "I need you to take Spencer and get out of here. She doesn't need to see any more than she already has, and you . . . well, the cops are on their way."

Dalton glances at me before affirming with a slight jerk of his head. He turns back to Penny, whispers something in her ear, and I watch her nod gently before climbing off his lap. Just as her feet hit the floor, Michelle Owen's eyes flutter open, only to close again when her baby girl is in her arms.

Dalton stands, towering over me with his approach. With the loss of Penny, his features have solidified with returning rage, and his eyes are as hard and cold as steel. My mother wastes no time, turning both of us in the direction of the door before shoving us lightly. "I'll handle it from here."

Just as we step outside the house, she calls from behind us, "Thank you, Dalton. For *everything*."

His eyes hit the ground and his expression tightens, but he raises his hand, giving my mother a two-finger salute in acknowledgment.

Just as we arrive at the side of the car, a police cruiser slows and pulls into the driveway.

"Fuuuuck," Dalton growls.

A uniformed policeman and another man in dark dress pants and a light-blue polo step out onto the pavement. The man in the polo instructs the other to go on ahead while he stays back, eye-ing Dalton as he leans back against the cruiser. Once the policeman disappears, the man addresses Dalton with a knowing tone. "Fancy meeting you at Ed Jamieson's house, Greer."

Dalton's muscles tense, but his tone is relaxed with his response. "Just came by to take the girl home, at the request of her mother, due to the *circumstances* involved. Haven't stepped foot inside the house, Lawson."

Lawson's stare flits downward, taking in Dalton's noticeably swollen knuckles. "Is that so?" After a beat, he lifts his gaze, his expression filled with unspoken satisfaction. "Two counts of domes-tic assault within the past six months. Jamieson will be going away for a while."

Dalton nods then opens the passenger-side door and gestures for me to get inside. I remain where I stand, eyeing Lawson warily.

Lawson watches our interaction, then chuckles to himself and presses away from the cruiser. "She suits you."

Frustrated with my forced anonymity, I step in front of Dalton and extend my hand. "Spencer Locke, and *you* are?"

Dalton releases a ragged growl, which only serves to widen Law-son's grin. His kind brown eyes crinkle at the sides with silent laugh-ter, and I can't help but notice that he's quite handsome for an older man. I fight my own grin as he takes my hand.

"Kirk. Kirk Lawson." His smile remains intact as he glances to Dalton. "Stubborn. She *definitely* suits you."

Dalton remains silent and I take the cue. "Well, it was nice to meet you, Kirk. We'll just be leaving now."

He dips his head in my direction and I avoid Dalton's stare while climbing into the car. Just as Dalton moves to shut the door behind me, Lawson leans in and states, "Off the record, I hope you taught the prick a fucking unforgettable lesson." Dalton's face remains blank as Lawson rises. "On the record, I have officially noted that you did *not* enter the house, and your presence here was merely in response to a request made by the girl's . . . ," he breaks to glance down at me, "*Spencer's* mother."

I smile at him and he grins in return, before stepping in the direction of Penny's house. "Well, it was good to see you, Greer.

Make sure Spencer here gets home safe." His smile widens. "And I would ice that hand if I were you. Looks like you bashed it against something pretty hard."

Lawson winks at me, then turns on his heel, leaving both of us in stunned silence.

And in silence we remain until we arrive at my house.

An eerie, uncomfortable silence.

A silence known as the calm before the storm.

Chapter 14 ✳

Dalton

The second we enter Spencer's house, I head directly to the freezer. After grabbing a bag of frozen peas, I slam the door, then toss the bag on the island in the center of the kitchen. My entire body breaks into a cold sweat and I brace the heels of my hands against the island's lip, trying to harness my anger.

My mind is reeling and the voices inside are screaming for me to hit something. *Anything.*

Visions of Penny's swollen cheek, her mother's contorted body lying on the floor, the fucking grin on Jamieson's face as it morphs into Bill's, laughing as he strikes me over and over . . .

And then I'm gone, disappeared, transported to my past. No longer eighteen years old, but twelve, then nine, then six, then four, then . . .

The faces blur but the laughter continues with the beatings. Each punch, each kick, each slash, each whip . . . each strike is felt, and my body clenches so tightly, I feel myself shaking, but there's nothing I can do. I'm lost in my past . . . consumed by the humiliation and pain dealt to me by my many abusers. Vanished into the memories of each new home entered, none bringing the security of family that I craved, but fresh forms of evil. Evil I didn't even know could exist in this world. Evil that should be found only in books . . . in Dante's visions of hell. Not here on this earth.

Evil that should definitely not be inflicted upon fucking helpless children who only seek love and acceptance, who cry themselves to sleep at night because they want so desperately to be wanted, who have their dreams demolished over and over again with each new "family."

I wince as another belt strikes my back and I fight the urge to cry out. I've never cried in front of them. I've never given them the fucking satisfaction. I endured beatings that left me rendered completely immobile for days, but I never . . . fucking . . . cried.

Fuck them. Fuck all of them.

Another kick to the ribs. My body jolts upon impact, leaving me breathless.

"Dalton?"

A familiar voice filters through the heinous laughter, somehow breaching the crowd surrounding me. Light and warmth break with it, and my muscles protest as I reach for it just as it begins to encompass me. Soft skin presses against my cheek and I cling to the feeling, leaning into the touch.

"Dalton, I'm here." A tremble rakes through my body at the sound. Warm arms wrap around my neck, enveloping me securely and silencing the demons of my past, now merely clouds of smoke as they dissipate around me. My ribs scream in agony as I fold myself around the angel who has taken pity on me and hold on as tight as my bruised body will allow.

Silken tresses caress my face and I breathe in deeply, the pain finally subsiding. My body quakes within the embrace, but I'm too fucking exhausted to ward it off. I allow it to continue as warmth permeates me, soothes me, calms me.

I have no idea how long I remain within the salve of her hold, but eventually, I find myself back in the present. My eyes open hesitantly, and as the light seeps in, I blink rapidly until they finally adjust. I unclench my arms and lean away, met with Spencer's tear-drenched face.

My skin is coated in a cold sheen of sweat as I fully release her, stepping away before the pollution of my past can be transferred to her. I shake my head when she attempts to close the distance I've created, holding my hand up and signaling for her to remain where she stands.

And just as I've found relief, it disappears, replaced by bitter repugnance. A fiery discharge detonates in my chest, an explosion of savage fury that chars any serenity her presence momentarily provided.

"I need some time," I choke out.

Spencer releases a sob, and my heart suffers the blunt impact of the sound, but I ignore it.

"Dalton, you need to talk about it. It's not *healthy* for you to keep it bottled up. I feel what it does to you."

Still seething in hatred and loathing, I snicker, uncaring about what my words will do to her.

"Why? So you can pity me? Feel sorry for me? Fucking *weep* for me?" My lips curl and my nostrils flare. "You want to know me? To really know me? To be let in on the big secret of my fucked-up past so it gives your perfect life some sort of twisted purpose?"

Her eyes narrow and I feel her anger brewing from where she remains rooted to the floor. Fresh tears spring into her eyes as she states barely above a whisper, "My life is far from perfect."

I scoff and shake my head. "Seems pretty perfect to me. Your perfect house. Your perfect mother. The both of you, and your perfect crusade to change the world. Where the fuck were you when *I* needed you, huh?"

My eyes prick with moisture and my throat narrows, forcing me to swallow back the sorrow so I can continue my rage. "Where were the two of you when I was born a bastard child to a crack-whore mother, only to be abandoned in the hospital the day after she gave birth—unwanted? Where were you when I was shuffled from one shit home to an even shittier home, forced to endure situations your untainted mind wouldn't even be able to comprehend—completely helpless? Where were you then?" Emotion overwhelms me. "WHERE THE FUCK WERE YOU THEN?"

Her body jolts with my scream, but anger continues to drive me. "By the time you two found me, I was already too far gone. While your mother did her job because the Housemans were a good family, I didn't need them. I didn't even fucking want them. In fact, I *loathed* them. I hated the idea of their very existence because every day spent with them forced me to face the reality that there were actually caring families out there that I just happened to miss out on for the first twelve years of my life. Twelve long years in which absolutely no one helped me. *No one.* Not until I found Silas Kincaid did anyone bother to pay any attention to me. To feed me. To protect me."

My mouth puckers in distaste. "And because of that, I am indebted to him. Stuck in a life of crime in which there is no escape. I'm involved in drug trafficking, Spencer. Loan sharking. Gambling rings. I beat the shit out of people who owe Silas Kincaid, my boss, money. One day soon, I will be forced up the hierarchy to *kill* people who owe Silas Kincaid money. And then, shortly after that, I will be required to assume my role as the rightful heir to part of his organization since I've been ordained the adopted son of a crime lord."

I expel a long, deep breath, exhausted and defeated. "Is that what you want to hear? My sad, pitiful life saturated with lies and deceit. Do you still think you can help me? Save me from a life in which there is absolutely no way out, other than death?"

Tears spill from my eyes as I fist my shirt, pulling it away from my chest. "I'm coated in filth, Spencer. Other people's blood. Unforgivable corruption. Not even you can rescue me from what I've done. From the person I've become."

Spencer eyes me cautiously, her tears flowing as freely as mine. Our gazes remain locked until she finally wipes them away and inhales deeply. "I was lucky. I *am* lucky. I would give anything to trade places with you, Dalton. I would give my life to do that, to lessen the agony burdening you. To alleviate the guilt that so clearly plagues you. I understand doing what you need to do in order to survive. I don't, and will never, fault you for that."

She tightens her stare. "But I *will* fault you for assumptions. For your belief that my life is perfect, because it is anything but."

Just as quickly as the moisture was cleared from her face, it's replaced as she speaks. "I'm seventeen, Dalton. One month away from eighteen. Did you know I still sleep with the light on? I can't . . ." Her head moves back and forth adamantly. "I can't sleep in the dark. I haven't been able to since I was six years old, when Deborah, my *adoptive* mother, found me locked in a room about the size of our pantry—soiled, starved, and terrified. I had been locked in there by my biological parents for . . . well, I don't know how long. But it was long enough for every single indention in the walls surrounding me to be burned into my mind forever. For the putrid smell of my own excrement to be permanently singed into my nostrils. Long enough for the agony of my completely shredded fingernails, for the burn of my skin as it was torn from my hands, and for the torment of my own screaming to haunt my dreams. Every. Single. Night, Dalton."

Just when I think I couldn't feel any more pain, my heart rips wide open as I envision each horror she describes. I open my mouth to speak, but she pounds her fist on her chest, silencing me. "Do you think I don't know how it feels to be abandoned, to be betrayed by those who are supposed to love you? To care for you? To continually wonder what you did to deserve the life you were born into as you remain locked in your past by the ever-present question—*why me?*"

Her chin quivers uncontrollably and the sight cripples me. "I feel everything you do. Your pain. Your rage. Your hatred. Everything. I'm no better than you. We are one in the same, Dalton, don't you see that?" My feet remain planted by her insistent eyes as she places her palm gently on my chest. "Don't you *feel* that?"

I cover her fingers with mine, clutching them tightly, before lifting her hand away and bringing it to my mouth. My lips relish in the heat of her skin as I press them into the center of her palm, inhaling deeply as my forsaken tears continue to flow, refusing to be harnessed.

She closes her eyes, and a tremor works its way through her body before they open again. Her stare is locked with mine as she cups my cheek, then tenderly runs her thumb along my tear-soaked skin. "I was broken too, Dalton. Shattered. Unsalvageable."

My gaze falls to her lips, watching as they curl upward into a timid smile. "Until the day I met you, that is. The day that every single one of my fractured pieces permanently fused with yours, rebuilding me with renewed strength so I could stand strong and fight for you." She shakes her head. "I won't give up on you. I will never stop believing in you. And I will continue to fight for you until the day I die because without you here"—she brings my palm to her chest—"I do not exist."

Eyes brimming with absolute ferocity, her belief in me douses the inferno burning within my chest, and my shattered pieces slowly begin to combine.

Anger no longer suffocates me.

Fear no longer stifles me.

Pain no longer asphyxiates me.

I brush my mouth against hers, and as soon as our lips touch, her strength floods me, binding together the fragments of my past.

I put all that I am into this kiss, wordlessly expressing my everlasting gratitude as I allow her to heal me. To fuse my brokenness. And once mended and whole, I willingly give her the only gift I have to offer in return.

My heart.

Chapter 15

Silas

"Boss?"

Sweet smoke is expelled from my lungs, and I enjoy the burn before stabbing the blunt out in the ashtray in front of me. My jaw tightens in irritation at the complete fucking obliteration of the one and only free moment I've managed to acquire in the past week. I close my tired eyes and inhale deeply before setting my elbows on the desk and threading my fingers together. "Come in."

Juan's bulky frame fills the doorway, obstructing the majority of the light behind him. His black eyes consider my annoyed expression and he hesitates marginally before finally stepping into my office. I smell his fear and it makes me sick, but what I actually find even more revolting than his anxiety is his need to please, to pacify. His body may depict strength and power, but his mind is feeble and weak—both absolute travesties in my eyes.

But he remains my second-in-command because I do not question his loyalty. I do not question his intention. And I do not question his ability to fulfill my requests.

He's a killer. *My* killer. My guarantee that these hands will never be bloodied, therefore never implicated when the only option available to me is disposal of the problem. And he does so without question.

So I will forgive him his weakness, but he is the only one. Anyone else in my organization, I will not stand for such foolishness. And I have a feeling there will be some spring cleaning going on pretty fucking soon to weed out potential . . . *problems*.

I gesture at the leather chair in front of me, then recline into my seat. Juan, as usual, does as he's told before clearing his throat.

"Jamieson was released on a technicality. I figured you'd want to know."

Of course I know. I fucking arranged it.

Waiting four weeks for his trial has not been easy, and cops are never cheap, especially when you have to pay them to lie under oath. The local police never fail to astound me with their greed. I shake my head internally at the irony. And people think *I'm* fucking corrupt?

"Yes," I respond, my tone terse. "We will seize him while we can. Set a very important precedent in response to his organized assault on my boys. Naturally his being in and out of jail the past few months has delayed my reaction, but the time has come."

Juan nods and I lean forward, speaking through gritted teeth. "The rules, *my* rules, need to be effectively communicated to everyone we do business with and, more importantly, to those we may potentially do business with." I slam my palm flat against the wood of my desk. "Everyone needs to understand . . . you do not *fuck* with me. You do not *fuck* with my crew. Or you *will* suffer the consequences."

Juan says nothing, but dips his head in understanding. I adjust my tie, buying time while gathering my composure. Once calm, I get up and move to stand in front of him. Ignoring the flinch of his muscles, I settle against the desk behind me, crossing my arms over my chest before I continue. "That being said, this will not be your job to complete."

Confused by the announcement, he opens his mouth to speak, but I quickly silence him with my hand. "The time has also come for the boys' initiation into the higher levels of this organization. Before they can advance, I need to be convinced that their loyalties lie with me, and *only* me. So this will be Rat's kill. We both know the first one tends to be the most challenging. If we find he cannot complete the job, we will need to persuade him, which means we will need to have someone in our pocket to sway his decision. He will have to choose. Watch them die. Or kill for me."

Juan's eyes light up with recognition. "His sister."

"Yes. I need you to tag her as soon as we get Jamieson."

Another dip of his head as he rises. "On it, Boss."

"Thank you, Juan." I offer him a firm handshake before he turns to leave. Just as his hand curls around the knob, I add, "And keep an eye on Greer. His time is coming soon, and with no family, I need to find the person who means the most to him. It's the only way I can be certain that his devotion comes before everything and everyone else. And judging by his unusually distracted demeanor as of late, I'm willing to bet it won't be hard to find that certain *special* someone."

Juan's eyes meet mine, cruel mischief lining his features with the wicked smile displayed. "Yes, sir," he responds, grinning fully before closing the door behind him.

I, however, remain perched against my desk, lost in thought as I watch him leave.

Do I feel guilty that I have to force my allegiances? No. Not at all.

I rescue them. I nurture them. I teach them.

And then, I force their hand.

Because once they kill for me, they're mine. I will always have death by those hands to hold over their head. They will forever remain beholden to me, and in return, I offer them absolution.

Plus if they can't perform that one simple function, they display nothing but weakness. And if that's the case, honestly . . .

They deserve to fucking die anyway.

Chapter 16

Spencer

"You two are totally doing it tonight, you realize that, right?" Lying on my bed, head propped on her elbow, Cassie's excited eyes are charged with anticipation. Her burgundy off-the-shoulder Henley falls to the side, revealing a black bra strap, expertly coordinated with the black tights on her legs.

"You do *realize* you say that every time we go out, right?"

She narrows her gaze and I grin while tugging a light-blue Aerosmith tank top over my head. After pulling it taut over my dark-blue flares, I glance back in her direction, declaring, "What? You do. It's been weeks of constant speculation regarding which date with Dalton will result in the loss of my virginity."

And it has.

She presses herself up, features resolute. "Tonight's the night. I can feel it. You guys are all over each other every time I see you together, obviously incapable of keeping your hands to yourselves. Plus . . ." She bends at the waist and searches under my bed. When she finally gets up, she's holding a large hat box, chocolate-brown with light-pink polka dots and a matching pink bow in the center of the lid.

Her face breaks into a playful grin. "It's your birthday."

"Cassie . . ." I say, stuck somewhere between thanks for her kindness and wonder at how long that box has been underneath my bed.

She winks. "I brought it up while you were in the shower."

I bite my bottom lip to curb my smile, but laughter works its way through my throat. You know you're truly best friends when you share a brain. Not even your innermost thoughts are safe.

I take a seat next to her on the bed, allowing the grin to break free before graciously accepting the gift. Her eyes widen and her cheeks flush with excitement. "Open it, hooker."

More laughter bubbles through my nose. I slowly remove the lid, then dig through the tissue paper until my fingers find what is at the bottom. Lifting it carefully, my heart catches as I see what must have taken her days to complete.

Within my grasp, a framed, heart-shaped collage of hand-trimmed pictures captures every single one of my favorite moments spent with Cassie over our twelve-year friendship.

The time my mom took us to the zoo when we were eight, smiling widely in front of the orangutan mother and baby, right before a bird pooped in her hair. I don't think I'd ever laughed so hard until that day.

At our very first campout in my backyard, tent and tiny fire in the background as we each bite into homemade s'mores. Chocolate oozing out the sides of our mouths, we're caught in a candid moment of the giggles.

Last year at the science fair, when Cassie almost deafened the entire student body with some whacked-out version of a volcano eruption. Toilet cleaner and aluminum foil mixed in a two-liter bottle is a small bomb. Not an eruption. Just in case you were wondering.

Each memory displayed brings laughter and joy to my heart, but when I read the inscription lining the bottom of the scrapbook paper below the collage, I'm overwhelmed with emotion.

"A friend is one that knows you as you are, understands where you have been, accepts what you have become, and still, gently allows you to grow."

~Unknown

I turn to face Cassie, her eyes brimming with tears. A modest smile plays on her lips as she states, "Thank you, Spencer. For accepting and loving me, no matter the choices I make. For your willingness to look past the bad and seek out the good. You have a way of making people actually believe they can become what you see in them. It's a gift you have given to me so many times over the course of our friendship, one I'll never be able to fully repay. I just . . . well,

I wanted to capture all those moments that made a difference in my life and give those to you as a way of thanks for just being *you*."

I set the collage to the side, and with both of us a blubbering mess, we wrap our arms around each other tightly. "I love you, Cassie," I whisper through my tears.

She sniffles. "Love you, times a million."

Giggles fill the air until we're finally broken apart by a knock at my door. Quickly, we wipe away all evidence of our emotion, but our puffy eyes give us away.

Mom pokes her towel-covered head into my room and smiles knowingly. Cassie pops off the bed, her black, patterned tights and Doc-covered feet hitting the floor. She tugs the frayed jean shorts down onto her hips before smiling brightly back at my mother.

"What a coincidence. I was just on my way out."

In typical Cassie fashion, she heads over to the window, unlatching it and pressing it upward. Warm April air rushes my bedroom as she climbs out, but as soon as she lands, she pokes her head back into my room, index finger pointed in my direction.

"I expect a call and full report this evening."

Her brow lifts with a stern warning and I giggle before saluting her in return. "Sir, yes sir."

She waggles her eyebrows, blows a kiss, then she's gone.

I twist to face Mom, who has taken Cassie's seat on my bed, her pink terrycloth bathrobe still damp from a recent shower.

"Happy birthday, sweetheart."

Whipping out a small box from behind her back, her grin broadens as she sets it on my lap. My gaze falls on the square black box, then as I look up, I know my expression is etched with unease. I know for a fact we don't have a lot of extra money, and I really hate the idea of her spending anything on me.

Seeing my response, she laughs. "It's nothing extravagant. I promise."

Relieved, I release a breath and return my attention to the box. Slowly, I pull the white ribbon and lift off the top to find a brass, circular object lying at the bottom.

A large letter "J" and a smaller "W" and "L" on either side are engraved in fancy script in the center of an antique pocket compass. Recognizing the initials, tears once again fill my eyes.

"Is this . . ."

Mom nods. "It was, yes." She smiles and pushes in the knob at the top, releasing the cover. It flips open to reveal the exquisitely designed face hidden inside. A needle sits in the center of a copper-colored sun, and the circular casing is lined in tiny garnets, giving it a sophisticated brilliance. She runs her finger delicately over the glass.

"It was Jim's great-grandfather's and has been passed down throughout the years. It's over one hundred years old." Her glistening eyes return to mine. "And it's your first official family heirloom."

I take it from the box and hold it tenderly, shifting it slowly within the palm of my hand. Awed by its beauty, I watch in silence as the needle dances with the movement. After a few seconds, Mom cups her hand over mine, covering the compass and expertly redirecting my attention back to her.

"You're eighteen now, Spencer, and as you begin this exciting new journey, there will be times during your travels when life seems to come at you from every direction possible. It's very easy to lose your way when trying to discover your own path into adulthood. This"—she looks to our joined hands, then lifts hers away to reveal the compass—"well, if you ever find yourself lost, this will help you find your way as it serves to remind you of the importance of family, of love, of laughter, and most importantly, of *second chances*."

Tears spill onto her cheeks. "A second chance is a gift that many, many people long to receive, yet sadly, few are given. Never forget that, sweetie. Be appreciative, return kindness, forgive openly, and love completely. Practice these traits that flourish inside of you because of your second chance, and you'll always find yourself pointed in the right direction."

Overwhelmed with emotion and unable to speak, I nod, then look to the compass in my hand.

James and Deborah Locke. My saviors as they took me in and gave me a life I never believed possible. And even though I didn't have nearly enough time with him, held safely inside my grip is the one thing that will forever tie me to my father.

Warm arms envelop me and I sniffle, the scent of apples marking what will forever be one of my most treasured memories. With both of my parents.

The doorbell rings, my heart seizing with the sound. My mother's laughter fills my ears as she squeezes one more time. After a few moments, she releases me, wiping her cheeks before rising from the bed.

"Happy birthday, Spencer. I love you more than you will ever know."

I smile and run my fingers underneath my eyes. "I love you too, Mom."

She gives me a wink and turns on her heel, announcing over her shoulder, "I'll grab the door. *You* grab a jacket."

I look down at my tank top and chuckle, then head to the closet to grab my favorite vintage army jacket. Shrugging it on, I hurriedly exit my room, only to slow at the sight of Dalton. My cheeks ignite, and suddenly shy, I clear my throat, tucking a loose strand of my tousled hair behind my ear. He grins back at me and I can do nothing but sigh.

As always, his shaggy blond hair is covered by a Yankees baseball cap, which matches the blue thermal stretching across his chest. My eyes fall to his jeans, my absolute favorite, worn and frayed as they cover the tops of his booted feet. He steps toward me, the familiar sweet smell that always accompanies his presence blanketing me with his approach.

"Happy birthday, beautiful."

His gorgeous eyes crinkle at the sides with his easy smile, reminding me of how at peace he seems to be these days. No longer do I feel the burn of anger that has afflicted him for so long. There is only soothing warmth as it exudes from within. *My* Dalton as he was meant to be.

He leans, brushing his lips lightly against mine, then presses them against my forehead. Involuntarily, my body shivers, and I feel his smile against my skin before he turns to address my mother, watching us from behind a cup of coffee with a goofy grin on her face.

"I'll have her back by ten, Mrs. Locke."

She shakes her head. "No need. It's Friday night, she's eighteen, and most importantly, I trust you implicitly with my daughter."

Dalton's cheeks flush, prompting a light chuckle from my mother as she strides forward to give him a chaste kiss on the cheek. Dalton's face reddens, and I curb my laughter as she leans to do the same to me. After another grin, she turns, leaving us alone in the living room.

Just as the bedroom door shuts behind her, I glance up at Dalton's blush. "You're cute when you're embarrassed."

His brows lift along with the corner of his mouth. "Cute?"

I nod my answer just before he hooks his thumbs through my belt loops and pulls me into him, lowering his face and crushing his mouth against mine. His tongue parts my lips and I willingly concede, giving him the access he seeks. My legs weaken and I sink into him as he tenderly explores my mouth, sweeping deeply before caressing my tongue with his own. I inhale him, enjoying the soft touch of his fingers working their way under my tank top and across my lower back. Goosebumps rise in their wake, prompting his grin against my lips.

He presses his forehead against mine. "How's that for cute?"

Breathing heavily, I state, "That wasn't cute. That was *sexy*. Do it again." My lips curve into a playful smile.

Dalton chuckles under his breath, placing a quick peck on my cheek before stepping away. "Later, Pencil."

He grins, lacing his fingers with mine and leading me to the door while I give him my best pout in return. My fight doesn't last long. Mere seconds after we're shut into his Camaro with his engine growling to life, an eager smile crosses my face. "Where are we going?"

He shrugs playfully, reaching down and turning on the radio. "It's a surprise."

As he backs out of my driveway, Stevie Nick's rendition of Fleetwood Mac's "Crystal" filters through the speakers. Dalton reaches, taking my hand in his and I smile as the chorus hits my ears. No song could be more perfect to describe the way I feel. The magnetism that draws me to him, fueled by my innate need for this *very* feeling—the narcotic sensation of pure tranquility as his love, the torrential downpour, crashes down and drowns out everything in existence besides us. Because with him, there's nothing else I need. There is no one. Just Dalton.

I'm hopelessly addicted, and I wouldn't have it any other way.

We pick up speed and with the windows down, giddiness floods me. Hand in hand, the breeze tugs my hair in every direction as he drives. When his fingers tighten around mine, I face him, and my breath stalls at the magnificence of his candid smile. I grin back, my mind wandering to how different he is now.

No longer is his reaction harsh and cold.

No longer is his demeanor nervous and reserved.

His carefully guarded walls have disintegrated, and the sight of *my* Dalton completely uninhibited is nothing short of breathtaking.

Seeing my stare, he lifts my hand, pressing his lips to my skin. I can do nothing other than lean my head against my headrest, helplessly enthralled with his beauty.

In fact, my eyes are unable to leave him until about twenty minutes later when we turn into a secluded field. Only then do I disengage them to survey the meadow in front of us. Wildflowers of every color are scattered as far as my eyes can see. Purples, pinks, and yellows cover the ground, and with the coral-and-blush sky tinted by the setting sun, the scene is picturesque.

"Dalton, it's beautiful," I whisper, lost in admiration.

He chuckles under his breath before pressing his lips against my temple. His eyes are warm as they survey my face. "It's nothing compared to my view."

A heated flush creeps across my cheeks and his lips jerk upward. After leaning in to touch his mouth to mine, he breaks the kiss then opens his door. Ridiculous grin still on my face, I step out onto the ground and close my eyes, inhaling the floral scent of the wildflowers surrounding us. I listen to his movements, and it's not until I hear the trunk shut that I finally open my eyes.

Oversized picnic basket in one hand, he tosses a huge blanket over his shoulder, making his way to where I stand. He offers me the crook of his elbow and I loop my arm around his, nestling into his shoulder. Together, we walk to the top of the hill, only for me to stop suddenly at its crest.

A huge tree rests at the bottom, its trunk and branches illuminated by the twinkle of white lights, swaying and dancing with the breeze. Peeling my gaze away, I glance sideways, met with yet another dazzling smile. I break into one of my own while shaking my head in disbelief.

"How did you . . ."

He tsks in response. "A magician never reveals his secrets."

A giggle escapes me and I smile coyly before gesturing with an open hand. "What is this sorcery you weave? There are no outlets in nature."

He breaks into laughter and takes a step forward, pulling me along with him. "Batteries."

I gasp and clutch my chest in mock surprise. "I thought you said a magician never reveals his secrets?"

He grins. "I also remember saying that I've never really been one to follow the rules. Case in point."

Another laugh passes through my lips as we approach the tree, the lights bright against the settling darkness. I release my hold, watching as he sets the basket down and tugs the blanket off his shoulder, whipping it open and laying it on the ground in front of us. Once situated, he sets the basket in the center, pulling the contents out and distributing them onto the knitted surface.

First, a vase filled to the brim with daisies. Next, four jar candles, each lit as they're removed and placed on the corners of the blanket. Then a Crock-Pot, two champagne flutes and an illegal bottle of champagne, paper plates, napkins, and plastic utensils are all set out before he extracts the final item—yet another blanket. This one, however, is slightly less sophisticated. I giggle at the worn sleeping bag, its entirety covered with Spiderman striking numerous attack positions.

He glances over his shoulder, raising his brows. "You dare laugh at Peter Parker?"

"No." I mirror his wide-eyed gesture, stifling laughter. "Never."

His chin dips in satisfaction before he pats the blanket beneath him. I kick off my flip-flops and take a seat next to him. He pulls me close, draping his arm over my shoulder, and I snuggle into his warmth. After a couple of seconds of silent bliss, he leans forward, bringing me with him to move the picnic basket onto the other side of his body.

Once it's out of view, he grandly gestures at the arrangement in front of us. "For your birthday dinner this evening—because you deserve nothing less than the best—I have made for you . . . mac and cheese."

I bite my lip to contain my laughter while he continues his demonstration, moving from the Crock-Pot to the champagne. "Cheap champagne and"—his hand is still in motion as he speaks—"plasticware, of course."

"Of course," I repeat with a nod, my smile refusing to be concealed.

The setting sun highlights his features as he glances to the basket at his side. The length of his nose, the curve of his jaw, the golden locks of hair that peek out from underneath his cap—they're all I see as he pulls out a large black box, then places it on the blanket beside me.

His expression is suddenly full of subdued eagerness. "But first, your present."

Grin still intact, I reach and drag it in front of me, surprised by its weight. My fingers curl underneath the lid and I lift it off slowly, digging through the tissue paper before finally landing on its contents.

Lying on the bottom is a silver heart composed of several intricately etched puzzle pieces, all linked together to form the roughly six-inch tall, three-inch wide structure in my hand. The glint of the metallic surface reflects off the candlelight, and as my gaze trails along the joined lines, my nervous breaths pause in recognition of the meaning.

"The day that every single one of my fractured pieces permanently fused with yours . . ."

All previous amusement is gone as he watches my reaction, his eyes brimming with unspoken emotion. "That's us, Spence. All separate pieces of you and me. But together, we're whole. We're *us*."

He jerks his chin at the heart in my hands. "Those are some of the strongest magnets I could find. Made with neodymium. The pieces are practically impossible to break apart, just as we are, as we've *always* been."

Sentiment constricts my throat and I swallow deeply, fully embracing his words. And although I find myself rendered completely speechless, my eyes convey every ounce of emotion bursting inside me. After giving him a nod of understanding, I place the heart to the side then kneel before him, fully resolved.

I tug off his cap and press my lips to his, my silent reward for the brazen gesture so openly displayed in this uncharted vulnerability. As our mouths slowly meld, I willingly concede that this moment will forever change both our lives.

Damn, I guess Cassie was right . . .

Because as I break the kiss only to become lost in the depths of the piercing blue eyes staring back at me, I know without a doubt . . .

Dalton Greer is not going to be the only one breaking rules tonight.

Chapter 17

Dalton

"Spence," I force myself to speak, which proves difficult because everything within my entire being wants to continue getting lost in her.

Her warmth.

Her eyes.

Her mouth.

Her taste.

But I can't be selfish. Not with this. I need to know with full certainty that she's ready to take this step, to know there will be no regrets.

So I force my head to overrule my lower brain and press her away. "Spence," I try again between heavy breaths, "we need to stop."

She stills at my words, her heavy lids fluttering open as sounds of our rapid breaths fill the air. Her features morph from that of pure pleasure to those of embarrassment and incomprehension, completely shattering the heart pounding within my chest. I swallow deeply, then clear my throat before trying to reassure her. "I want to take it slow. I don't want to mess this up by moving too fast."

She nods, inhaling deeply and tucking a disheveled lock of her hair behind her ear. My fingers curl into themselves with the need to thread through those thick tresses again, to feel their softness brush lightly against the skin of my hand, to tug them with frenzied impatience as I position her mouth right where I want it. Unable to fight it, I twist a section of her hair around my grip, then pull her mouth to mine, sweeping my tongue along her swollen lips for just one more greedy taste.

She moans into my mouth and I swallow it ravenously as my need to feel her, to consume her, to become one with her, slowly begins to dominate my already waning conscience. With my war continuing to wage, I drag my parted lips along her neck, noting the thrum of her heartbeat as they make their pass. Arriving at the edge of her jaw, my tongue laps at the sensitive area behind her ear before finally taking the lobe into my mouth and nipping ever so gently.

Her needy whimper fills the air as she tugs me closer. We both rise onto our knees, our mouths remaining perfectly aligned. I curl my hand around the back of her neck and wrap my other arm around her waist, pulling our bodies flush. Just as she angles her head, I release my hold on her neck and ease her back, allowing our weight to be absorbed by my arm as it's braced beneath us. I slide the weight of my upper thigh ever so slowly over the seam of her jeans, the area I know will provoke the exact response I'm looking for. She gasps, parting her lips, and I selfishly use it to my advantage, diving in deeply and claiming her mouth for my own. Her entire body shudders, the movement bringing my pathetic excuse for a conscience to the forefront with the knowledge that I'm about two seconds away from ripping her clothes to shreds.

The need to feel her bare skin against mine drives me, but guilt and remorse finally claim victory, forcing me to break away. My lips yearn with the loss of her warmth, but I ignore the feeling. Once a safe distance away, I place my elbows on either side of her head, trying to calm the whirling frenzy inside me. The passion between us fuses our eyes, making it impossible to look away, and I'm lost again, mesmerized by the unadulterated beauty below me. Her dark lashes sweeping the tops of her cheeks as she blinks. Her wavy hair fanned out underneath her shoulders. Her perfect, plump lips curving into a barely there grin.

"Why are you staring at me?" she asks, holding my heated gaze as her heart pounds beneath mine. Her nose creases, obscuring the freckles lining it, and my heart practically explodes with the sight.

"Because I can't seem to take my eyes off you, no matter how hard I try."

With her stare locked onto mine, her voice husky, she responds, "Well, it seems we have the same problem. What are we going do about it?"

I graze my knuckles along the soft skin of her cheek. "Not a goddamn thing."

She clears her throat, then draws her tongue slowly across her lips and shakes her head. "I don't want to stop, Dalton. I know what you're doing. You feel the need to protect me, to guard my innocence, but I want this. I want *you* . . . In this field, on top of this blanket, under the light of the moon, and for the stars to be our only witnesses. I can't think of a more perfect place, a more perfect night, than this. Please don't take that away from me."

She curls her fingers around the nape of my neck and strokes my cheek with her thumb. "Don't stop, Dalton." Her plea completely annihilates whatever semblance of a conscience I conjured in my mind.

She tenses when I lift away, breaking only to pull the Spiderman sleeping bag securely over us, but relaxes again with the realignment of our bodies. I watch in awe as she curls her fingers underneath the hem of her blue tank top and lifts her body to remove it, the white lace of her bra the only thing covering her chest when she reclines onto the blanket beneath us. My heart races and I stare open-mouthed at the pure magnificence of the gift lying in front of me, dumbfounded as to what good I must have done at some point in my life to deserve this moment.

I marvel at the vulnerability in her eyes with her offering, uninhibited and without hesitation. She grins up at me, reaching forward to run her fingers delicately over my lips. I take her index finger fully into my mouth, her eyes darkening with the swirl of my tongue around the tip just before my teeth nip the pad. She shifts her body underneath me and the friction of the movement sets me ablaze.

Fueled with heated desire, I hook my arm over my back and peel off my thermal in one fell swoop. My skin aches to feel hers, so much so that when her arms curl around my shoulders, the heat of her bare skin scorches mine as she pulls my body to cover hers. Sheer ecstasy.

Greedy for more, I slide my hand beneath her body. She arches her back in response, giving me the permission I need. I unclasp her bra, my mouth finding its way to the hollow of her neck, savoring her taste between my parted lips. Placing my weight on my bent elbow, I lean to the side and slowly drag the strap over her shoulder.

My tongue traces its way across her body while I deliberately pull the other strap down her arm. Once both are removed, I tug the remaining material away. My teeth clench and I instinctively hiss at the contact of her breasts on my skin as she does the same.

Her fingers weave tightly into my hair, tugging and pulling, directing me downward and placing me completely under her control. Our moans fill the air as I caress the curve of her breast with my lips, stroking lengthy trails along her skin with my tongue, until she reasserts her authority by guiding me unhurriedly to her nipple. I take it into my mouth and almost explode when it hardens with just a flick of my tongue. She whimpers, her back curving off the ground, her body pressing into me as I grind myself shamelessly into her center. We begin to move in sync and my cock throbs mercilessly with the need to feel her, aching as it searches for its release with each pass of her body.

"Goddamn, Spencer."

My words are strained, unintelligible, and muffled against her naked skin. I release her breast from my mouth just as she unclenches her hold on my hair, moving her hands down the skin of my back and sliding them into the back pockets of my jeans. Her fingers dig deeply as she wraps her legs tightly around my waist, continuing to massage my cock with her steady movements.

The heat between us builds underneath the weight of the sleeping bag. With ease, my chest glides along her slick skin until my mouth finds hers. Our kisses become frantic as we become lost in each other. My tongue sweeps deeply and hers strokes mine, our breaths becoming heady pants and needy whimpers with our continued rhythm. After one last squeeze, she removes her hands and directs one up my back while the other falls between our bodies. Her legs draw me tighter and as her palm presses into the front of my jeans, she curls her fingers, gripping my length. Indescribable pleasure flares throughout my entire body.

"Jesus . . . Spence," I moan. "You're incredible."

Driven by the need for her to experience the same euphoric sensations, I turn my focus to her. I trail my fingers along the side of her breast before they veer onto her flattened stomach, and continue downward until my palm grazes the seam of her jeans. Applying pressure, I circle once and she cries into my mouth before tipping her head and arching her neck, breaking our kiss. The sight alone sends a tremor to my already throbbing groin, threatening to end this before it's even started.

She's mine.

The whispered thought echoes in my brain. I watch her reaction to my touch, and the truth of that statement drives me to show her how thankful I am to have her.

My lips drag down her sweat-laden neck, the soft area between her breasts, and the hollow of her ribcage until my tongue is gifted the trembling of her stomach muscles with its touch. Once again, her fingers are gripping my hair and I smile against her skin, contented that I'm affecting her just as much as she's always affected me.

My mouth continues to trail its scorching path downward, not stopping until it hits the waistline of her jeans. I dip my tongue just underneath, drawing a leisurely line from hip to hip, inhaling her deeply before lifting my head to watch her response. With her neck still curved toward the night sky, her tongue darts across her lips and the column of her throat moves slowly with her swallow. My eyes remain locked on her face as I make another pass along her skin.

"Dalton," she whimpers, imploring for more, which I am more than fucking happy to give her.

My fingers make fast work of her buttons before I finally remove my hand from between her legs to slowly tug the jeans over her hips and down her long, smooth legs. The sensation of her soft skin grazing my knuckles spurs an animalistic growl from deep within my chest.

Flinging the jeans to the side, I hungrily run my palms along her bare thighs. Her muscles tremble as I skim the tips of my fingers over the sensitive flesh of her inner leg. Leaning forward, I permit my tongue to trace the same path along both thighs. Her scent fills my nostrils and I breathe it in greedily, tasting her sweet skin with my open mouth until I hit the silk line of her panties. The mewling sound that escapes her causes me to cease any and all movement. An intoxicating shudder rolls through my body and my jeans tighten painfully with each of the pulsations. I rise to my knees in an attempt to relieve the mounting pressure before finally hooking my fingers into the sides of her panties and removing them from her body.

Leaning forward, I part her legs and lower my head, my mouth watering for the chance to taste her essence, her innocence. Enveloped in darkness, I disappear below the top of the sleeping bag, sliding downward until my lips find the apex between her thighs. I take her into my mouth, suckling the budded skin gently, taking time to enjoy each throb against the edge of my tongue. Her hips buck in response and her taste floods me.

Insatiable, my mouth releases her and I trace lower, dipping my tongue deep inside her. The sensations of her clenched muscles and quivering thighs urge me to continue. I completely devour her. Lapping and sucking, I'm further driven by the sounds of her pants as they transform into needy whines. She tugs my head, pulling me closer, and I continue to consume as much of her as I can while her rhythm increases, falling into sync with my working mouth.

"Oh my God, Dalton . . ." she moans. Her thighs clench and her body tenses as she cries out breathlessly with her climax. I guide her through the waves, gently caressing her with my mouth until her legs finally relax. Then, with a long stroke of my tongue, I take one last indulgent taste before rising above her body to witness the most beautiful sight I've ever seen.

Her eyes are darkened with desire, her face flushed and her lips parted, panting with each rise and fall of her chest. As she continues her heavy breaths, I notice a bead of sweat teetering on her skin, then watch as it rolls down the curve of her breast. I lower myself, capturing it with the tip of my tongue, only to instigate another shudder of her body. My gaze is unbreakable as I take in the vision of her lying in front of me, exposed and unabashed. Her hooded stare lingering on mine, she grazes her bottom lip with her teeth and I sear the memory of this moment into my mind.

Because just as the lion in Aesop's "The Lion in Love" so carelessly allowed the removal of his claws and teeth, or as Samson became so blindly infatuated that he remained utterly defenseless in Delilah's lap as he slept, I would give *anything*, sacrifice *everything*, for even the smallest of chances to experience the love that only Spencer can provide.

I would die for it.

I would die for her.

And with the acknowledgement of that potential cost, I lock my eyes onto hers, fusing our stares with purpose and resolve. My mouth opens to readily form the words, words I have *never* before spoken. Without an ounce of reluctance, I willingly equip her with the ability to completely destroy me as I whisper . . .

"I love you, Spencer."

Chapter 18

Spencer

"I love you, Spencer."

My breathing ceases with those poignantly spoken words. Tears prick my eyes as I stare back into the light-blue irises hovering above me, no longer obscured by the ever-present storms brewing within them. Eyes that are now clear and lucid, filled with vigor as courage and conviction illuminate his gaze.

Mesmerized by the sight, I lightly brush his hair away so I can better see them. My lips curve into a satisfied smile as I run the tips of my fingers down his cheek, inhaling deeply. "I love you too, Dalton. I will only ever love *you.*"

His mouth tips up at its edges before he dips his head, leisurely brushing his lips against mine. Our mouths fuse and our breaths mingle with the tender caress of my tongue with his kiss. A kiss much different from the frantic, frenzied ones just experienced. It's soft and tender, sweet and affectionate, as he communicates his love silently with deliberate movements.

I curl my arms around his neck and wordlessly respond, sweeping my tongue just as delicately along his. My fingers weave into the length of his hair just as he toes off his boots, kicking them to the side. Our lips remain joined as I release my grip, slowly tracing my fingers across the soft skin of his exposed chest, smiling when his nipples harden with my touch. My thumbs skim lightly over their firmly raised surfaces, producing a throaty growl. Greedy for more, I lower my hands and just as my fingers hit the top of his jeans, he leans to the side, freeing the space I need to unbutton them.

As soon as they're open, I graze my fingers along his lower back before dipping them into his boxers, the bare skin of his backside molding against my palms. I curl my fingers inward, massaging as I explore. His masculine groan fills my mouth, only to turn into a deep rumble when I press his jeans and boxers over his hips, releasing him from their constriction. Together they hit his knees. Unable to maneuver them any lower with my hands, I hook them with my foot and push them the rest of the way. Once removed, he leans to reach into the back pocket, revealing the silver glint of the condom wrapper pinched between his fingers.

I shake my head. "No condom necessary. I'm on the pill and you've been tested, right?"

He nods. "Never been without one."

A light giggle passes through my lips. "Well, this is a first for us both, then."

His eyes are warm with sincerity, as is his smile. "You're my first everything, Spence. First smile. First laugh. First *love*." All humor is slowly lost between us, brute honesty replacing it as he adds, "My life didn't begin until the day I met you."

I swallow the growing knot in my throat and dip my head, my gaze never leaving his. Relenting, he lowers his body and realigns it with mine, nerves pricking my skin as his hardness skims the top of my thigh. It lands between my legs, positioned right at my entrance. Our stares remain cemented with the knowledge of what's about to happen, and my heart thuds in my chest, pounding furiously in my ears.

He centers his face with mine, and his eyes taper at the sides. "We can stop, Spence. We don't have to do this. Not until you're ready."

My eyes latch onto his and root deeply in their conviction. I take in a deep breath and my muscles relax with knowledge that this is Dalton. *My* Dalton. And there's nothing I want more in this world than to share this experience with him. Nothing I want to give him more than this one gift. To relinquish all of me as we come together, fusing our pieces as we become solidified in one another.

Unbreakable.

One.

And with my lessening tension, a comforted smile crosses my face as I nod gently. "I'm ready. *More* than ready."

Reaching forward, I pass my thumb across his lips, then shift my body in preparation as I maneuver him right where he needs to be. The head of his length barely skims my sensitive skin and the heat from its passing warms my insides. I look into his eyes and state with absolute honesty, "You claimed my heart years ago, Dalton, but now I want you to have all of me. Every single piece, together in body and soul, I offer freely because they *already* belong to you. All you have to do is accept them as you take me."

His features soften, then the corner of his mouth lifts into a subtle smile. He shakes his head as though in shock, then releases a light breath through his nose.

"My life hasn't been one that I would wish on anyone. But *you* . . . God, Spencer. I would live this shitty life ten times over just be guaranteed I'd have you in it. You are the reason I *keep* living. And to see you lying here, in front of me, *asking* me to take you?" His head moves back and forth. "It should be the other way around. I should be begging *you* to take *me*, for *you* to accept *me*, but I don't have to because you do so without hesitation. With absolutely no judgment. For you, it's simply inherent. And it just . . . it blows my fucking mind. It's the reason I love you, and it's the reason I will continue to love you until the day I cease to exist."

Unable to speak, I join our hands, interlocking our fingers and settling them on either side of my head. His eyes hold mine one last time before he tightens his grip and bends his neck, lowering himself to touch his mouth against mine just before gently pressing his hardened erection into my body.

My fingers burrow into his skin and I bite my lip to keep from crying out. His body stills and he lifts, his concerned expression suspended above my face.

"Are you okay?"

With my teeth digging into my bottom lip, I lift my eyes and train my gaze on the crystalline orbs peering down at me. His expression is raw with vulnerability as he roams my features, assessing me. Once his eyes land on mine, I'm lost, helplessly fixed into their depths. Pain is no longer present. Warmth and the strength of his love encompass me, blanketing my apprehension as it solidifies the bond between us. They infuse and permeate my soul, resolving my strength.

"Yes. I'm okay."

In affirmation, I tenderly squeeze his hands and prompt, "Keep going."

I rock my hips forward, the pressure mounting with his forward movement. And with our stares joined, I'm suddenly overwhelmed with the knowledge that we are indeed one in this moment. Physically. Emotionally. Fused in every way possible.

"Goddamn, Spence. You feel so good. So perfect."

Taking his time, he withdraws unhurriedly, then reenters just as slowly. A hiss passes through his teeth and as I watch from below, my body starts to relax. My heart releases, completely surrendered to him as we begin to move in unison. His hands press mine into the ground beneath us with each smooth stroke of my insides, and my body tightens in attempt to consume him. My muscles ravenously clench around his length, the hardened flesh growing with each entry.

He inhales sharply through his nose, his heavy lids shutting completely. Lips parted, his eyes remain closed with each thrust and I find myself emboldened by his reaction. My tongue draws across my lips, wetting them with unquenchable need, and I lift to capture his mouth with mine. Another moan passes as I selfishly invade the inside, my tongue plunging deeply as our bodies maintain our rhythm. The moan changes into a deep, guttural growl when I rake my teeth across his bottom lip. Greedily, he presses his weight forward, forcing me back as his tongue battles mine. His hips thrust harder and I lift my legs, wrapping them tightly around his waist as he buries himself deeply inside me.

Our movements begin to turn desperate, needy as our pace quickens.

Kisses become impatient.

Tongues and teeth wage war.

Grips tighten for leverage as we rock our bodies.

"Spencer . . . I . . . I'm not going to be able to hold off much longer . . ." he pants into the skin of my neck.

I purposely tighten around him as he thrusts again. Completely lost in the moment, lost in *him*, all my inhibitions seem to vanish. I moan into his ear, "Then don't. I want to feel you come inside me."

Dalton stills and goosebumps rise along my glistening skin. Centering his face with mine, his eyes narrow.

"Say it again."

I meet his thrust and a wicked grin tugs at my lips. "I want to feel . . ." I break to stifle my groan as he fills me. My legs squeeze tightly to hold him in place while I circle my hips. "I want to feel you come inside me. Please, Dalton," I whimper.

His eyes roll into his head, and my smile breaks free as I watch. I continue to stare, mesmerized by his reaction to my movements. Finally, he opens his eyes and focuses his gaze on me. His mouth quirks up at the edges as he breathes, "You're so beautiful, Spence."

He lowers his head, kissing me deeply before nestling into my neck. The warmth of his rapid breaths elicits an involuntary shiver, and the softness of his dampened hair tickles my skin as he begins to move. Our fingers remain interlaced, their hold tightening with each new thrust until he draws his hips back and rises, pressing his weight onto our clutched hands and training his gaze on my face.

"So. Fucking. Beautiful."

With one lengthy stroke, he drives his arousal forward until it's fully embedded in my body. Upon impact, my back arches off the ground, and with my legs still circled around his waist, I pull my hips flush with his so I can receive him in his entirety. His fingers dig into my hands, but his eyes never leave mine as his body shudders with his release.

I hold his gaze, the intensity of the moment robbing me of my breath. Because as he continues to stare, his eyes silently communicate what he cannot say. But I know.

He has just willingly given me all that he is.

Tears blur my vision and I breathe in deeply, absorbing every piece he offers. I consume his anger, his heartbreak, his revulsion, even his agony—taking each and every broken shard into my heart so I may cleanse them from his soul.

Still hovering above me, his chest expands with a long breath before he lowers his head and brushes his lips over mine. I taste the salt of his skin as our mouths are sealed, and with his deepening kiss, I know he is thanking me. I stroke his tongue with mine, comforting him. His relief floods my chest and the feeling overwhelms me. I break the kiss to survey his reaction. A contented grin crosses his face before he places a gentle kiss on the naked skin above my heart, lips lingering with his deep inhale.

Disjoining our hands, he strokes my cheek with the tip of his finger before leaning to the side and sliding out of me. The movement is unhurried with his gentle withdrawal from my body. After a lingering gaze, he leans and snatches his boxers, passing the soft cotton tenderly over the sensitive area between my legs. I wince and suck in a breath. Immediately, his brows dip and concern flashes in his eyes.

"I'm okay, Dalton." I smile reassuringly. "I'm not going to break. I'm just sore." Pulling the sleeping bag over my shoulder, I curl onto his chest and chuckle under my breath. "It looks like the stars weren't the only witnesses tonight. Spiderman got a good show as well."

Dalton's body shakes with silent laughter as he wraps his fingers over my shoulder. "Pervert."

My cheek presses into his heated skin with my grin. We remain quiet, the intermittent sound of the light breeze the only noise breaking the silence around us. His fingers trace lightly along my skin before moving to my hair and stroking it softly. Minutes pass before he finally speaks.

"Why didn't you tell me about . . . *before*? Your past, I mean." His voice is low, barely above a whisper.

I take his hand, weaving our fingers together. The strength of his grip as his hand encases mine gives me the courage I need to answer. "I don't know, really. I guess it's just easier to pretend my fears remain in the past. That they no longer affect me. That I no longer dream about that room, and that I no longer need the security of a nightlight to help me sleep."

I move off his chest, my head braced by my elbow. Dalton faces me, his expression dipping downward as I continue. "I never wanted you to see that part of me. I wanted to be strong for you, and I guess I felt if you knew about my past, you would see me differently."

"I *do* see you differently," he responds immediately. I remain expressionless, but my heart stammers in my chest. He tightens his hold on my hand. "But not the way you think. I underestimated you with my need to protect you all the time. I mistook your kindness and generosity for weakness that needed defense. But knowing you, *all* of you . . . well, your strength is undeniable, Spence."

He pauses, swallowing deeply. "I know firsthand how abuse can break a person. How damaging the effects can be as they whittle away at your will to live. How they carve away your humanity, completely hollowing you out to leave you a shell of your former self when they're finally done. But you"—he narrows his eyes on mine—"you are far from broken. Even though you still have your struggles, you find the strength to try to help others, to guide them through their own issues as you lead the way. Your positivity radiates to everyone around you, and those who are lucky enough to be in your presence will forever be changed by your ability to heal with something as simple as a touch or a smile."

His lips form a shy grin. He releases my hand to stroke my cheek with his fingers. "And being given the opportunity to experience you is something for which I will forever be thankful. You've changed me, altered my perception of a life I loathed, and given me the strength to try to change it."

He tightens his gaze, gingerly cupping my face with the palm of his hand. "I will find a way to get out from under Silas. Please know that. You are everything to me, Spence. Your safety means *everything*. And in order to guarantee that safety, I need to sever those ties. I *will* sever those ties. It's the only way we can be together."

I nod, but my throat constricts as the words he so angrily spoke not too long ago race to the forefront of my mind . . .

"Do you still think you can help me? Save me from a life in which there is absolutely no way out, other than death?"

I hold his eyes and lean forward, placing a kiss on his mouth. As I breathe him in, I try to shake the nagging feeling lodged in the pit of my stomach. He curls his arm around my neck to draw me closer, and as he does, all my supposed strength withers away, my gut churning with unmistakable fear.

And for the first time since knowing him, I find myself consumed with foreboding worry that a situation has finally presented itself in which not even Dalton Greer can survive.

Chapter 19

Dalton

An hour and a half later, we've packed up everything and painstakingly make our way back to my car. Not wanting to end our time together, I relive the absolute best night of my life as Spencer and I walk hand in hand.

After eating a blissful meal of lukewarm mac and cheese, for which I apologized profusely, and downing a glass of champagne, we lay on our backs, staring in silence at the darkened sky. With our hands joined, my thumb stroking along the softness of Spencer's skin, I allowed myself to become lost in the sight above me, disappearing into the darkness as though I was seeing the glimmer of every single star for the very first time.

The feeling, the astonishment of *experiencing* the beauty around us, completely captivated me. Things that seemed so dull and trite before seemed so alive. The gleam of the stars in the night sky, the fragrance of the flowers surrounding us, the hint of chill in the breeze cooling our heated bodies . . . I *felt* all of them for the first time in almost nineteen years. And in that moment, I opened my heart and my mind, allowing Spencer's essence to invade my senses—the sweet scent of her hair fanning my face, the delicious taste of her skin as my mouth ravaged hers, the soothing feel of her velvet skin skimming mine.

With the memories stirred, my cock hardens within the confines of my jeans and I adjust myself as we walk, the denim scraping against my bare skin due to the loss of my boxers. The same boxers I used to gently wipe away the loss of Spencer's innocence, the memory alone reminding me of the resounding trust she places in me. A trust that remains a complete enigma, but one I will forever honor. Because with the gift of that trust, I find meaning as I'm driven to become a better person. To be the man she believes me to be. The man I can become.

I know that now.

As we arrive at my Camaro, I release her hand, throwing everything into the trunk before meeting her by the passenger's door. Her hair moves softly, taken by the breeze, and I tuck a piece behind her ear before curling my fingers around the back of her neck. My thumb lightly skims her cheek and I grin when she gifts me a shy smile in return. Her blue eyes are practically childlike, exuding pure joy and happiness as she gazes back at me. Again, I shake my head in disbelief at this angel standing in front of me, watching me with distinct adoration, as though I could take on the entire world.

Simply amazing.

My mouth aches for just one more taste, so I lower my head and lightly sweep my tongue across the seam of her lips. They part upon the touch, and my grip tightens, pulling her flush against my body. Our tongues meld, and as a light whimper escapes her, I'm forced to break the kiss with a smile.

Spencer sinks her teeth into her bottom lip, then grins back. "Thank you, Dalton. It was the perfect night. Everything was just *perfect.*"

The apples of her cheeks take on a pinkish hue as a blush creeps across her face. I smile with its appearance, then press my lips gently on the warming skin before opening her door. The silver of the puzzle heart held carefully within her grasp catches my eye. I grin with its representation, knowing tonight both our hearts and bodies fit perfectly together just as the giant magnet she holds in between her hands. And just like the heart she clutches so closely, mine is also nestled safely within her possession, exactly where it should be.

As she slides into my seat, I offer meekly, "You're welcome, Pencil. But in all honesty, it should be me thanking you."

Her face crinkles and I bend, stroking her nose from base to tip. "*You* are an extraordinary gift."

A humble smile lifts the corners of her mouth and I give her a wink before shutting her in safely.

Once we arrive at her house, silence fills the car, neither of us ready to say good-bye. With my head resting against the back of my seat, my eyes fall to her mouth, where a wide grin forms.

"What?" I inquire.

"Did you know Cassie asked Rat to prom?"

An involuntary chuckle works its way into my throat at the thought of Rat attending any occasion where an undershirt and ripped jeans aren't acceptable dress code. I swallow deeply, grin still present on my face.

"Is that so?"

She nods. "Yeah, just as friends though. She was supposed to go with Jonathon Hawkins, but . . . well, after the night at Indigo, Cassie told him to fuck off."

My eyes widen with her use of the expletive. In all the years I've known her, I've never heard that word come out of her mouth. *Come* and *fuck* in one night. Call me a bastard, but I kind of like it.

She giggles at my stunned expression. "Cassie's words, not mine."

"Definitely sounds more Cassie than Spencer," I concede. "Is he going?"

She laughs again. "Well, I hope so because she bought a killer dress last weekend. I think . . . I think she really likes him. It's kind of hard to tell with her, but considering she hasn't slept with him yet and they've seen each other a couple of times over the past few weeks, I think it's different with him."

I make a mental note to bust his balls about it, then return my attention to Spencer. "Are you going?"

Her shoulders lift slightly before she states, "No. I don't know. Maybe?"

The bridge of her nose creases with uncertainty and it's my turn to laugh. I reach over to take her hand in mine, then clear my throat, my tone surprisingly tentative. "Would you like to go *with me?*"

Wide-eyed, she holds my gaze before responding, "With you?"

I dip my head and she narrows her eyes before turning them upward in deliberation. My heart rate skyrockets with her hesitation until after a few seconds, when she looks back at me with a full smile on her face.

"Of course, you dope."

Relieved, I chuckle and lean to kiss her mouth before reclining back into my seat. "Well, then. It's a date."

Spencer grins, then glances at the clock on my dashboard. "It's late. I'd better get going."

My smile falls, but I relent. We meet at the front of the car and I place my hand on the small of her back, guiding her to the front porch. As soon as we're at the door, she turns and lifts up on her toes, placing a small kiss on the corner of my mouth. As she lowers, I graze her cheek with my knuckles.

"See you tomorrow?"

Uncertainty flashes in her eyes and I angle my head in question. "Tomorrow?" I prompt.

Her mouth curves downward, then suddenly, she wraps her arms around my neck. "I don't want to let you go."

The tremor in her voice pummels my chest. I fold both arms securely around her waist, drawing her tightly against me as I whisper, "I'm not going anywhere, Spence." With one arm still holding her, I lean away and place my palm over her heart. "I will always be here. Even when I'm not around." I wink. "So that will just have to hold you over until tomorrow."

Her expression softens, and she nods her head.

"Tomorrow then," she responds.

Grinning back, I open the screen door, holding it in place with my body while she unlocks the lock. I place my hand on the knob and press my lips against her forehead before shoving it open. After stepping inside, she turns to face me, and the smile on her face renders me breathless.

"I love you," she whispers.

My heart lurches as I state with ease, "Love you too, Pencil."

The sound of her giggle is the last thing I hear before she shuts the door. I wait until the lock sounds, then pivot around and head to my car. As soon as I'm inside, I inhale deeply, her scent still saturating the air around me. Reaching behind my seat, I grab my Yankees cap and slide it over my mussed hair.

My eyes fall to the floorboard, where a clear bottle with amber liquid catches my attention. I lean over and snag it between my fingers. Once upright, I twist the cap off, then sniff the contents.

Spencer's citrus scent fills my nostrils and I breathe it in deeply before twisting the bottle to look at the front. The words "Love and Happiness" prompt my laughter because if I could bottle a fragrance that *is* Spencer, that's exactly what I would call it. Selfishly, I place the bottle in my console, promising myself I will give it back tomorrow as I start the car.

With the engine idling, I eye her bedroom window, surprised the light hasn't already been switched on. Although she's probably talking her mother, part of me hopes that after time, she will never have to sleep with the lights on again. That I will be enough to protect her from her fears, from the monsters that haunt her sleep.

Once I've pulled out of her driveway, my car idles alongside the curb as I open my glove box to retrieve my phone. The 9mm Rat gave me is right beside it, and the sight sickens me. Shaking my head in disgust, I grab my cell and close the hatch, my mind already churning with ways to get myself out of this fucking mess. I have to. I refuse to drag Spencer through my mud.

After a quick look in the rearview mirror, I shift into drive. Powering on my phone, I set it on my console, my attention alerted when I hear three dings next to me. I look to the phone, surprised to see Rat's name flash across the screen. Knowing that he only texts when something's going down, I jerk my car to the right and throw it into park.

RAT: Meeting with Silas.
R: Where are you, brother?
R: Something's not right.

Damn straight something's not right. In all of our years with Silas, we've never had a meet without both of us being present.

Shit. The texts came through about half an hour ago.

Wrenching my steering wheel all the way to the left, I execute a U-turn in the middle of the street. My foot hits the floorboard, and as Spencer's house flies by, a sudden sinking feeling lodges in my stomach.

The heaviness continues to churn until fifteen minutes later when I'm downtown, right around the corner of Silas's warehouse. Just as the stoplight in front of me turns green, I spot Juan's black

Mercedes AMG CLA45 turning onto the street with Rat in the back seat. I slow my speed, allowing a couple of cars to pass before falling in line behind them.

My eyes remain trained on the Mercedes as I continue to follow from a concealed distance. The gnawing feeling in my gut spreads, and I nervously tap my fingers on the steering wheel while my left leg begins to bounce uncontrollably. I crack my neck, my anxiety rising, and I find myself strangely comforted by the preparatory ritual, but the feeling doesn't last long. My calm is lost when I see the Mercedes hang a right onto a very familiar road—one that travels a path deep into the woods and is often used to conceal the bodies of anyone who dares cross Silas Kincaid. Bodies Rat and I have had to bury.

To get to Rat undetected, my best bet is to ditch the Camaro and cut through the woods on foot.

I switch off my lights and coast to a stop, then flip open the glove box and remove the Glock. After cocking it, I slide it securely in the back of my waistband and exit my car. As soon as my feet hit the ground, I begin to jog, making sure to stay on the clearing in front of me to muffle the sounds of my boots.

I know I'm getting close when lowered voices break the silence of the stagnant night air. I crouch down and creep behind a tree, mindful of my steps so as to not alert them to my presence.

I remain hidden, listening intently to Juan's voice in the distance. "Here."

Shuffling occurs before Rat responds. "What the fuck, man? I thought he was in jail."

Juan snickers. "Not anymore. He was released on a . . . *technicality*."

The quaking of Rat's voice is undeniable. "You want me to fucking shoot him?"

"Silas's orders. Him . . ." Footsteps precede the sound of a trunk opening. A whine, then more shuffling. "Or *her*."

"What the fuck did you do to my sister?" Rat's cry echoes through the barren woods.

With my heart pounding, I peek around the corner of the tree, curling my fingers around the handle of the gun. Rat's sister, Trinity, is on her knees, hands secured behind her back and head bent at the neck, lolling around as though she's been drugged. Eyes half-lidded, she tries to lift her head. After a couple unsuccessful attempts, she gives up, her chin falling to her chest. Rat bolts toward her, his face frantic, but the cock of a gun stops him cold. I watch as Juan places the muzzle of his own Glock 19 right against Trinity's temple.

"Your choice," Juan concludes, his eyes trained on Rat.

I draw my weapon carefully, sliding my finger over the trigger while tightening my grip. Rat's eyes dart to the man at his side. Beaten and badly bruised, his slumped frame mirrors that of Trinity, his knees barely able to support his weight. A man almost beaten beyond recognition, but I know exactly who he is.

Ed Jamieson.

At the sight of him, familiar fury is unleashed and my mouth dips in disgust.

My eyes slide to Rat, who hesitantly aims a gun in the direction of Jamieson's face. His hand trembles visibly as he cocks the hammer, prompting Jamieson to finally raise his head. His face crumbles at the sight of the gun.

"Please," Jamieson begs, shamelessly. "I'll pay everything I owe. I have it all in another account. This has just been a misunderstanding. Please!"

Rat's arm quakes as tears stream down his face. He looks back to Juan, who answers with a nudge to the side of Trinity's head with his gun. "Shoot him or she dies. Plain and simple, Rat. Your choice."

Rat looks between the two of them, manically shaking his head before turning the aim of his gun to Juan. "I never agreed to this," he states. "I never wanted to kill anyone. I just needed the money for my family."

I also train my 9mm on Juan, who simply smirks at Rat, then scoffs. "Did you really think being in the business you've been in for the better half of your life, seeing the things you've seen, that you would escape without any blood on your hands?"

Rat remains still as Juan's menacing laugh echoes around us. "You did, didn't you?" He tsks. "You delusional *child*."

Juan transfers his hardened gaze to Trinity. "Well, I see you've made your choice."

With an impassive shrug of his shoulders, he pulls the trigger.

Everything after that happens in slow motion. Trinity's body slumps to the ground, a red pool leaching into the dirt under her head. Rat releases a blood-curdling scream. Juan fires off a quick shot into Jamieson's skull before redirecting his aim at Rat. Rat holds his position, gun still pointed in Juan's direction, his expression warring between absolute anguish and uncontainable rage.

My own anger spreads like wildfire, and hearing nothing but blood as it roars through my ears, my decision is made.

With my finger pressed firmly against the trigger, I bolt out from behind the tree, running full-force in their direction with my gun directed at Juan.

I pull once.

But not before another shot is taken.

Rat's body folds in half and he falls to the ground, curling into himself as his agonizing cries echo all around me. I continue running forward, watching Juan grab his own shoulder, my bullet having missed its intended mark. He lifts his head and his blazing eyes meet mine.

Rat's screams pierce my ears, darkening my vision, and all humanity I foolishly thought myself capable of is lost in this moment. I want nothing more than to see Juan's head blown wide the fuck open by the gun in my hand.

I envision it.

I welcome it.

I will it.

My legs continue to carry me, and I duck as another bullet is fired in my direction. It whizzes by my head but I keep running, driven by pure fury. My throat releases a primal, rage-filled cry, and I allow it to build as I willingly approach the gun aimed right at my face. Completely enveloped in darkness and blind to any danger, I launch myself at the ape in front of me just as his gun goes off right by my head. Together, we hit the ground, the high-pitched ring in my ears all I'm able to hear. My fist strikes hard against his jaw, knocking him nearly unconscious. His eyes roll back into his head and my hands join, threading around the handle of my gun.

All rationality has long since disappeared into my blackness. Now, there is only rage. I straddle his body and line the muzzle right in the center of his forehead, point blank. Angry tears gather in my eyes and pour down my cheeks. "Fuck you, you piece of shit. And fuck Silas too." I press firmly against his head as I add, "Too bad you won't be alive to deliver the message."

His eyes fill with panic and I soak it in, bathing in his blood before it's even shed. Rat continues to whimper while his sister's lifeless body continues to bleed not even five feet from where we lie. I take in the scene, allowing the sight to fuel my fury as I begin to pull the trigger.

"Greer! NO!"

The words barely register before I'm tackled from the side, my body rebounding off another upon impact. Frantically, we grapple for possession of the gun in my hands, our arms tangling with each roll of our bodies.

We continue to wrestle until the dust settles and my eyes find focus on the brown stare of a person I never expected to see.

Lawson.

His expression is saddened as he wordlessly observes me. When I put up no fight, he gently pulls the gun from my stunned grip, his features softening. He jerks his head in the direction of Rat.

"Your friend needs you." He glances toward Juan, now hand-cuffed and being taken into custody. "We'll take care of him. Don't worry. Silas will never know you were here. I'll make sure of it."

Another cry hits my ears and I turn all my attention to Rat, not even bothering to dissect the meaning of Lawson's words. Nor do I bother to ask him what the hell he and his crew are doing here. All I can focus on is getting to Rat.

On my knees, I inch myself to where Rat lies, still curled into a ball. Moisture leaks uncontrollably from the corners of my eyes with the sight of his obvious pain. Only when I arrive does he find the strength to unfold his body, wincing as he twists to look at his sister. His tortured eyes are overflowing with tears and his chin trembles uncontrollably, but he holds his stare. Another sob is released as his eyes linger, the sound ripping a gaping hole in my chest that I know will never be healed.

He grimaces, breaking his stare to meet my eyes. Grabbing my hand, he gasps for air, then speaks. "Get. Out. *Now.*" He squeezes my hand with each syllable spoken, as though he's afraid of remaining unheard.

He coughs, blood forming a thick line as it begins to flow from the corner of his mouth. "You are better than this life. You have a choice. Use your *fucking* brain . . . Dante and shit . . ."

His laugh is strained, and he gasps for air. "If not for you, do it for Spencer. She's not"—the grip on my hand tightens as he looks to his sister before returning his unsteady gaze to my face—"*safe.*"

My jaw tightens with the mention of Spencer's name and the undeniable truth his statement holds. I clutch his hand just as tightly and respond in earnest, "I will, brother. I promise."

His face relaxes, as does his grip. "This is just purgatory, D. I look forward to seeing you in heaven. I'm gonna take my pass now."

Tears openly stream down my cheeks with the memory of the dreadful day I fucking coerced him to this death.

"Well, Silas. I have a friend named Rat who would also be good at running your errands. You bring him on board too, and you've got a deal."

As though reading my thoughts, Rat squeezes my hand one last time. "I would have been here with or without you, brother. Don't take that anger with you. I see it in your eyes. Just . . . revenge it."

"Avenge?" I ask, my throat constricting, the pain too much.

His chest heaves with laughter. "That's what I said."

I squeeze his hand with all the strength I possess, my words fierce. "I will fucking *kill* him."

He dips his head, and with one last gasp for air, his eyes glaze and fall out of focus. My hold on his hand remains as I lean over, placing my forehead against his.

And for the first time in more years than I can remember, I weep like a fucking child.

I weep for the death of my friend, a friend that has been by my side ever since I was six.

I weep for the loss of my youth, shredded from my existence with each beating received.

I weep for my blindness to the evil of Silas Kincaid as he fed on my weakness, hiding beneath the premise of protection.

I weep for the loss of the most beautiful feeling I've ever experienced, a love so freely given only to be left behind in order to guarantee its safety.

With my head pressed against Rat's, I continue to cry until my sorrow begins to transform, taking root as it burrows into concrete resolve.

It's then that my choice is made.

I will make this right.

I will avenge Rat's death. A life wasted to prove a fucking point.

I will take out Silas Kincaid and erase his parasitic existence.

And then God willing, I will recapture the love of my life.

Because I know now, without a doubt, I *have* to let Spencer go. I have to release her from the chains that bind me, until I'm fully freed.

That's the only way she will emerge unscathed.

And there's no way *my* angel will be forced to endure the depths of my hell. Not on my watch . . .

No matter how long it takes.

Part Two

Withdrawal

Chapter 20

Spencer

From: Mail Delivery Subsystem
To: Spencer Locke
Subject: Delivery Status Notification (Failure)
Date: Saturday, April 24, 2010 12:45 PM

Delivery to the following recipient failed permanently:

Dalton,

Where are you? I'm really worried. I tried texting and calling all morning, but nothing is going through. I'm hoping to get a hold of you this way. As soon as you get this, please call me. Please.

From: Mail Delivery Subsystem
To: Spencer Locke
Subject: Delivery Status Notification (Failure)
Date: Saturday, April 24, 2010 1:05 PM

Delivery to the following recipient failed permanently:

Dalton,

What's going on? I've never gotten a failed delivery back from this address before. Have you deactivated your account? And if so, why am I still writing you?

I guess I'm hoping this one will go through. If it does, PLEASE let me know you're all right. I need to know you're all right.

From: Mail Delivery Subsystem
To: Spencer Locke
Subject: Delivery Status Notification (Failure)
Date: Monday, April 26, 2010 1:01 AM

Delivery to the following recipient failed permanently:

Okay . . .

I don't know what's going on, why you're not answering my calls, or why your email seems to be rejecting my attempts to contact you. What I do know is that you would never hurt me intentionally. I know it with absolute certainty.
I told you I wouldn't give up on you and I won't. I will keep writing you so that when you do come back to me, I will have these letters to prove I meant what I said.
I love you, Dalton. I know you're still out there. I feel your heart as it still beats within my chest, alive and flourishing.
You told me to trust you, and I do. With everything that I am. And because of that, I have faith that you will come back.
Until then, I will continue to write these pointless letters. Both for you and for me because I miss you. I need you. And this is the only connection I have to you right now.
I love you. So much.

From: Mail Delivery Subsystem
To: Spencer Locke
Subject: Delivery Status Notification (Failure)
Date: Monday, April 26, 2010 7:18 PM

Delivery to the following recipient failed permanently:

Dalton,

Detective Lawson came by our house this evening. At first I thought he was coming to shed some light on your disappearance, maybe give some clue as to where you are, but sadly that wasn't the case.

With both my mother and I present, he began by telling us Penny's father had been found shot in the woods right outside town. While he didn't seem terribly upset about it, he did seem worried about what would happen to Penny and her mother, and asked Mom to please let them know he would help them in any way he could.

After she agreed, he explained that the death of Penny's father wasn't the only reason for his visit. He sat us both down on the couch and with his eyes full of regret, he informed us Rat had been shot during the same altercation that took Penny's father's life. One in connection with the infamous Silas Kincaid, your Silas Kincaid I assume, and that Rat was also . . . dead.

I began to cry as soon as the words left his mouth, and I haven't been able to stop since.

I'm so, so sorry Dalton. We were all close, but you two were like brothers. I know you're hurting, as am I. I want nothing more than to be there for you right now. To hold you and comfort you while you mourn the loss of your friend. To be your strength during this time. To erase the pain that his loss leaves behind. I would give anything to do that for you. Please know that.

I had to tell Cassie. She didn't take the news well at all. I consoled her, trying to remain strong for the both of us. But in my consolation, I felt nothing but the bitter pang of guilt because it was you I wanted to be holding in my arms. You I wanted to reassure with my words. But once again, I was harshly reminded that you're not here.

I know you have things you need to work out. I get that now, I'm sure this has all played a part in your absence. It all makes sense now.

Mourn, Dalton. I will be here when you get back.

I love you.

Always.

From: Mail Delivery Subsystem

To: Spencer Locke

Subject: Delivery Status Notification (Failure)

Date: Friday, April 30, 2010 2:26 PM

Delivery to the following recipient failed permanently:

Dalton,

Just a couple of hours ago, Rat and his sister were laid to rest side by side in Athens Cemetery. His family . . . God, Dalton, his poor mother. She was inconsolable, wailing and screaming that her babies had been stolen from her and how it should have been her to go first. It was one of the hardest things I've ever had to witness, watching her sob into the arms of her sister as she kept shouting that no one should ever have to bury their own children. My heart absolutely broke for her.

Detective Lawson also showed up and was very kind in his condolences to Mrs. Marchione. He made it known that he would do everything in his power to take down the man responsible for the death of her children. His eyes were warm and genuine as he held her hands in his while speaking. And as I watched, I found myself mesmerized by his gentleness in dealing with her. Mom also seemed fascinated by him, but for a completely different reason I think. I think she likes him. And surprisingly, I'm totally okay with that because I like him too.

He asked me if I had heard from you, and just when I thought my heart couldn't break anymore, it completely shattered with the mention of your name. I tried not to think about you today, to give Rat the respect of not tainting his death with more unfulfilled wishes that you would come back. But sadly, my efforts were futile. I kept expecting you to emerge from somewhere within the crowd, having convinced myself that you would be back in time to lay your friend to rest. To say one final good-bye before his body disappeared below the cold ground.

But you never showed, which pisses me off because Rat deserved better.

And as I type this letter to you, my anger continues to grow because I'm forced to recognize that a simple good-bye from Dalton Greer must be too much to ask for, even in death.

From: Mail Delivery Subsystem
To: Spencer Locke
Subject: Delivery Status Notification (Failure)
Date: Friday, May 14, 2010 5:13 PM

Delivery to the following recipient failed permanently:

It's been three weeks, Dalton. Three weeks. I'm trying so hard . . . so hard to be patient. To remain positive and optimistic. To not allow the simmering anger that festers, the fury that scorches every inch of my skin, to find its release.

But sadly, I feel I'm fighting a losing battle because with each day that passes, it urges me. It taunts me with this unfamiliar need to lose myself in rage. To punch a hole in the nearest wall in order to feel some sort of pain other than the one that cripples my ability to breathe. To cry and scream at the top of my lungs because I just don't understand.

I don't understand.

Why?

Three weeks, Dalton, and absolutely no word from you. No reassurance that you're okay or even alive. I know you are though because I feel you stirring in the depths of my soul . . . your presence. Your existence as you so willingly choose to disregard mine.

Am I not enough? Was I ever truly enough?

Was I not worth the battle that I so eagerly, yet so foolishly, waged for you?

I'm drowning, Dalton.

Falling victim to feelings I promised myself I would never feel again.

I believed in you. I still believe in you.

I just need something. Something from you to give me hope. Something to ease the pain.

Just something.

Anything.

Please.

From: Mail Delivery Subsystem
To: Spencer Locke
Subject: Delivery Status Notification (Failure)
Date: Saturday, May 22, 2010 10:05 PM

Delivery to the following recipient failed permanently:

Well, prom was tonight. I didn't go. Neither did Cassie.

However, while she chose to remain home and subject herself to a Project Runway marathon (or so she said), I did the unthinkable. Unfortunately, I seem to be a romantic at heart because tonight, instead of wallowing in my self-induced pity—which is exhausting by the way—I put on the dress Cassie bought me. The one I was wearing when you first kissed me on my porch, after you told me that you couldn't breathe without me.

Do you remember that? Because I sure do. It's a stubborn memory, that one.

Anyway . . .

I put on the dress, curled my hair, applied my makeup, and waited. I waited for you to show up on my doorstep and apologize for not calling. I waited for you to provide some outrageous explanation for your disappearance and we would laugh. Boy, would we laugh. Then you would lean into me and whisper another sincere apology in my ear, and the warm breaths from your mouth would send a shiver across my entire body, like they always do. You would kiss my temple, then my cheek, then the corner of my mouth before taking my hand in yours and asking me if you could still be my date to the prom.

Which worked out amazingly well because I happened to already be dressed.

Your apologetic blue eyes would plead for my forgiveness, and mine would willingly grant it.

Then you would flash one of your mischievous, lopsided grins, and my knees would go weak before we finally rode off into one of our sunsets in the limo you so thoughtfully procured beforehand.

I am literally blinded by tears as I write this. Blinded by tears of insane laughter at my own stupidity. Blinded by tears of surrender as I'm forced to acknowledge that there is a very distinct possibility you aren't coming back to me. Blinded by tears of frustration. Tears of anger. Tears of disbelief.

Tears that drown me because I am completely lost without you. So lost that I remain here, with absolutely no desire to leave this tortuous place as I continue to cry. I cling to every tear that falls because with each one shed, I find some sort of sick solace as I welcome the experience of the pain you left behind.

It's all I have to remind me that you ever existed.

I will leave eventually, but for now, I choose to remain.

Because foolishly, I still choose you.

Chapter 21

Dalton

August 24, 2010

It's been four months. Four. Fucking. Months.

I can't breathe, Spence. No matter how hard I try, I cannot seem to force the air into my lungs. My body rejects all attempts made to try to soothe the pain of not having you near me. I told myself I could leave you, that I would be able to walk away peacefully, secure in the knowledge that you're safe. But I can't fucking breathe.

The withdrawal of you from my system is complete agony. I want so badly to quit, to give up this fight and just run. Fucking run into your arms and allow your presence to blanket the constant ache, the burn that ignites my chest and sears my entire body.

I miss you so goddamn much. Your smile. Your touch. Your smell. Your taste.

And what kills me is you're so close.

So close.

Yet so far.

I made the trip once. Only once.

I saw you at Rat's funeral, talking to Lawson, and the sight broke me. Your eyes were dead, void of emotion even as tears rolled down your face. Your tiny frame was slimmer than ever, and your beautiful face was ashen, the bluish shadows under your eyes the only color present on your normally glowing skin. And it fucking killed me because I know I did this to you.

I almost ran to you right then and there, giving up on my promise to Rat just to hold you in my arms and tell you everything was going to be okay. That I'm okay. That we will be okay.

But as I heard the cries of Rat's mother as she buried not one but both of her children, I knew I couldn't. Rat lost his life because I made mistakes. Because I didn't shoot when I had the opportunity. Because I fucking handed him to Silas on a silver platter. Because I willingly sold both of us into his repugnant form of slavery.

Silas must pay.

He will pay.

So the step I fervently took in your direction was reluctantly withdrawn, and I forced myself to remain where I stood, masked safely in the background until everyone left. Only then did I approach the body of my friend that lay underground. I stayed there for hours, apologizing profusely before announcing my plan. A plan that will take years, but will work.

It will get me close enough to Silas, and then I will take him out.

I was indebted to him for so long, and mark my words, his payback is coming.

With a vengeance.

Trinity died because Rat loved her so much.

I know with everything that I am, the same would have happened to you had I stayed.

No one is safe until Silas Kincaid is in the grave.

YOU are not safe.

So now, during times of weakness such as this, I work to remind myself of the reason I must stay away.

I would die for you.

And as the loss of you swelters inside me and burns me alive, I feel as though I am doing just that.

December 4, 2010

I don't know why I feel compelled to keep writing. I know you will never see these letters, since I burn each one when I'm through. I guess it's because I feel as though I'm actually speaking to you when I write them. That I'm right there, directly in front of you, on my knees as I plead for your forgiveness. That you are actually able to witness the torture that I have experienced since walking away that night. That you understand how difficult this is for me, and that you will eventually forgive me because of that recognition.

And in all honesty, I guess I also find comfort in them as they keep you near, even if it's only in my mind.

I know the last couple of letters haven't been much. But this one, this one is important.

Today I completed the first part of my plan. I did something I never thought I would do, never thought I COULD do, but with the help of a very unlikely alliance, I took that step.

And what I did today was the first step of many to help me get back to you.

It's all coming together, Spence.

I have made the connections necessary to put myself in the position to move in when the time is right. I have made a new life for myself here, planting ideas and concepts as I continue to do what I do best. To be the chameleon that has gotten me through this life.

I can't help but laugh because if anyone would appreciate me utilizing the skills learned during the shitty situations in my life to bring about change, it would be you.

I wish you were here to truly experience it with me, my growth into the person you believed me to be. It's bittersweet. I can't truly be happy, excited, or overjoyed because I want you to be a part of it.

I find solace in the fact that you will be. Eventually.

Not a day goes by that I don't think of you. That I don't check up on you in order to make sure you're coping. All the while, you remain painfully unaware that my heart still resides with you. That I am yours.

And, unfortunately, these letters are the only way I can reassure you of that. For now.

Listen to your heart, Spence.

Because mine is beating wildly inside your chest.

I am with you. Always.

Chapter 22 ✳

Spencer

From: Mail Delivery Subsystem
To: Spencer Locke
Subject: Delivery Status Notification (Failure)
Date: Saturday, January 1, 2011 7:58 PM

Delivery to the following recipient failed permanently:

Mom took my computer away this summer. It seems she felt my incessant need to write you every day, blabbering about how angry I was with you for leaving, telling you about the pain of having my heart completely shredded into nothing because you weren't here, all while knowing my feelings would be . . . undeliverable . . . well, she thought it would be best to break me of the habit.

This is my first letter since getting my computer back in September. She kind of had to, considering I'm taking classes at Fuller Community College and need it for school.

I know it's a new year, but tonight I'm drowning in memories of what's transpired since you've been gone.

This past summer was not easy. I was fully immersed and lost in my anger. Memories of our night under the stars, the night I gave myself to you wholly and completely, when I gave you my most treasured gift . . . well, I hated every evening the summer presented. Every single fucking sunset reminded me of that night. Reminded me of you.

And yes, I said fucking.

I am not the same person anymore, Dalton. I'm bitter. Angry. Lost.

In fact, I am gray.

There are no colors present for me anymore. I have muted them all. Orange no longer reminds me of our many setting suns. White no longer reminds me of the twinkling lights that hung above us. Red no longer reminds me of the passion that burned so brightly between us. And blue? Well, there is no more blue. I loathe the color.

I am completely numb.

It's hard though. Sometimes a tiny shard of feeling manages to slip between the gaps of my resistance.

Like tonight, when I feel compelled to write you.

God, Dalton.

I still miss you so much. I just . . . can't.

I can't keep doing this to myself.

Because with each step I take through my newly muted life, I still somehow cling to the hope of you. The hope that my heart wasn't wrong. The hope that my belief in you was true.

And that hope that stubbornly insists upon transpiring? Well, it's false. Completely and utterly false.

The notification I will receive as soon as I press send will no doubt provide a much-needed slap in the face to bring me back to reality.

My sad fucking reality.

I can't do this anymore.

I tried.

I'm sorry.

Chapter 23

Dalton

April 23, 2011

I've been busy, not writing so much, as I am working a new angle. But Jesus, it's your birthday. One year since the night I was forced to walk away from you.

One year since Rat and his sister were shot right before my eyes.

One year since I almost made the biggest mistake of my life as I held a gun to Juan's head and almost blew his brains out.

One year since I knew we couldn't be. Not at that time.

One year since you began your protective need to hate me. The knowledge of that slays me, Spence.

I know you've moved on. I have connections, the ones that feed me information. You are constantly watched to ensure your safety, and it kills me that you have absolutely no idea. No idea that I am still protecting you. That you still consume my every thought. That you still drive me in this quest for revenge.

But everything is as it should be, as it has to be. I cannot exist for you anymore because your tie to me will only be to your detriment. So I'm forced to watch through others' eyes.

One year down and more to go.

I just hope by the end of all of this, you will forgive me.

I told you once and I will tell you again.

You are everything.

Getting back to you is the impetus that continues to drive me.

I just hope you're still there when I get back.

Hold onto me, Spence. I'm still there.

Chapter 24

Spencer

From: Mail Delivery Subsystem
To: Spencer Locke
Subject: Delivery Status Notification (Failure)
Date: Tuesday, April 23, 2011 11:42 PM

Delivery to the following recipient failed permanently:

Well . . . Happy birthday to me.

You want to know how I celebrated?

I boxed everything up. Every single thing that reminds me of one year ago today.

The magnetic puzzle heart with which you proclaimed how strongly we were bonded, the stupid champagne flute that I made room for in my purse by removing my very favorite perfume (!!!!), even the compass Mom gave to me from Jim. Everything is now safely stored away, never to be opened again.

The box is labeled FUDGE, just in case you're wondering.

Code for Fuck U Dalton Greer . . . Exponentially.

Sorry, I needed an "E."

Please excuse my lack of ingenuity, but I just can't try today.

I just can't.

From: Mail Delivery Subsystem
To: Spencer Locke
Subject: Delivery Status Notification (Failure)
Date: Saturday, May 21, 2011 12:12 AM

Delivery to the following recipient failed permanently:

I had a date tonight. Or last night I guess.
It was nice.
Brandon's nice.
Dinner was nice.
The entire evening was . . . nice.
So why am I sitting here, with only the light of my laptop illuminating my darkened room? Hiding the fact that I still write to you?
Because nice fucking sucks.
I want to feel what I had with you. Like a junkie, I crave the sensation. My entire body trembles for it.
I miss the surge of electricity that would resonate throughout my entire body when you were near.
I miss the fluttering of butterflies when I would see you and the goosebumps that would break across my skin at your slightest touch.
I miss the soothing warmth of your familiar scent as I would breathe it in.
And I hate you for it.
You are nowhere. Yet, you are everywhere.
Your presence haunts me. So much so, I don't even bother sleeping with the light on anymore. Mom thinks I'm miraculously healed, but that's not the case. Not really.
It's the simple fact that the hurt associated with my childhood memories is nothing compared to the agony I feel now. There's nothing a stupid night-light can do to protect me from the pain. So every night, I shut off my light, plug

in my headphones, and yield to it as I lie in bed, listening to A Fine Frenzy's "Almost Lover" on repeat. Because the nighttime is the only time I don't have to pretend it doesn't hurt. That I don't have to paint on a happy face and act as though everything is okay. That I'm no longer consumed by my addiction to you.

Darkness has become my light and I seek comfort in it.

And in that darkness I will remain for just a little while longer. Just a little while longer.

Chapter 25

Dalton

August 31, 2011

You looked beautiful today, Spence. Absolutely gorgeous.

I needed to see you as you begin this new chapter in your life. An entire chapter that will be lived without me in it as you enter Wilmington University as a full-time student.

But as much as it pains me, that's the way it has to be.

I saw Lawson was there, helping you move in. He and your mom look really happy together. She deserves that, someone like him. He will do right by her, and you. Keep you two safe as I continue to thread the intricacies of my plan.

Seeing both of you was a painful reminder of all I've lost.

It's funny how you really don't realize what you have until it's gone. I took my friendship with Rat for granted. I didn't understand what a huge part of my life he really was until he wasn't in it anymore. I would give anything to just tell him that. To tell him that the solidity of his friendship was the only thing I had to hold onto when we were younger. Before you, he was the only one who knew about my past. Who understood the pain of abuse, as he was often on the receiving end of his father's fists.

That will always be one of my biggest regrets. I was so lost in my rage for the life I was given, I didn't take the time to appreciate what I had. Now he's gone.

And you . . . I'm losing you too. I feel our connection weakening. Fissures are forming. Cracks are splintering. I just hope our foundation is solid enough to withstand the distance time is creating.

I'd like to believe it is because I think that when you truly give yourself to someone, you forever remain a part of that person. A part that unknowingly roots itself into the other, remaining dormant until it's sparked back to life when the time is right.

I have faith in that. In us.

I will come back.

I just pray that the part of me that rests safely inside your heart is resilient enough to be revived when I do.

Chapter 26

Spencer

From: Mail Delivery Subsystem
To: Spencer Locke
Subject: Delivery Status Notification (Failure)
Date: Monday, September 5, 2011 7:52 PM

Delivery to the following recipient failed permanently:

Well, I survived my first day at Wilmington University. It's a bit surreal, to be honest. To be in a new place, making new friends . . . no longer holding myself captive in my room as I relive our time together.

I feel as though I can breathe for the first time since you left.

I feel free.

Like I can do anything. Be anything.

It's a good feeling.

Brandon is here too, so that makes things a bit easier.

He's not so bad. It took him a while, but he finally managed to chip away at the angry block of ice encompassing me.

I mean, he's not you. No one will ever be you.

But he's Brandon. And Brandon makes me happy.

I still love you, Dalton.

I will always love you.

But I cannot continue to hold onto a ghost. To someone who just doesn't exist.

I need to move on with my life. To be happy and free, like I used to be.

I guess I'm hoping that college will be that time for me.

Wish me luck.

Chapter 27

Dalton

April 23, 2012

Happy birthday, my angel.

You are officially in your twenties. And growing more and more beautiful by the day, so I hear.

Newfound love suits you, I guess.

I keep telling myself that I should be okay with it because ultimately your happiness is what matters. I just . . . I want so badly to be selfish. You are so close, Spence. I want to drop everything I'm doing and drive the short distance to where you now hold him in your arms as you so gently once did with me. To where he is the one now gifted your laughter, your smile, your touch. The things that I once basked in, took comfort in, unknowing they would be ripped away from me so harshly.

But I can't. I'm in too fucking deep. If I left now, everything I've set in motion would have been for nothing. The time away from you completely wasted. I'm forced to remain here, all the while knowing you've moved on, into the arms of another.

There is nothing now.

No pain. No burning.

Just the numbing effect the need for revenge provides, washing over me as I turn my focus from you to the one person who is to blame for all of this. The person who tore my life completely apart with senseless actions.

And with each passing day, I am fueled by this need to stay on course and fucking finish this.

Because the farther you are driven from me, the more I want to make him pay for taking you away.

April 23, 2013

Happy birthday, Spence.

Another long year has passed.

I find myself stir-crazy as I begin to lose myself to this life. Lines are becoming blurred while I continue to blend. The only things keeping me sane are my memories of you and Rat. Of why I am here. Of why I must remain here.

So much ugliness surrounds me.

I forgot how this life grabs hold of you, digs its claws into your soul, and doesn't let go.

How it entraps you with its constant quest for power. Respect. Loyalty.

I try to focus on the memories, but I feel myself fading. The person I wanted to become as I so eagerly started this crusade is slowly drifting away, out of reach no matter how tightly I try to keep him within my grasp.

I need you so much right now. I know you are no longer mine to have, but damn, Spence, what I wouldn't give to have you here right now. To remind me of the good life has to offer. To remind me what the fuck I'm fighting for.

One more year. That's all I need.

I just hope I don't lose myself entirely by then.

April 23, 2014

Happy birthday.

I hear things are going great for you. Set to graduate early with a degree in sociology. I knew you could do it. I knew you *would* do it.

I'm so fucking proud of you, Spence.

I also have some exciting news.

One year to the day, and it's done. I have successfully integrated myself where I need to be, primed in the position to make my move when the time is right. I will begin the transition back to Fuller soon. I won't be there full-time, not yet, but I'm working to get myself where I need to be so I can remain there eventually.

I'm anxiously awaiting the day I see your face again. It's the one thing that has made these past four years worth the arduous journey, worth the internal struggles, and worth the pain that accompanied each and every one of them.

I hear that you are coming back to Fuller after graduation in December. About the same time I plan to be there full-time.

Funny how things work out sometimes. Almost as though it was meant to be.

Well, one can hope anyway.

I miss you, Spence.

I have done all of this so that maybe, if the fates are kind, I can finally be fully severed from this life and begin a new one with you by my side. One in which you are safe. And one in which I am the person you always dreamed I would be. The person I have indeed become.

All because of you.

And all for you.

You are my everything.

My angel.

My air.

Only time will tell if the damage that's been inflicted is reparable. If the distance between us can be diminished.

If you still love me.

Because I still love you.

With everything I am.

Chapter 28

Spencer

Dalton,

It's been years since I've written you, and I have no idea why I feel the need to write you and tell you this, but I do.
So here goes . . .
Brandon proposed earlier tonight. On my birthday, of course. The one day that seems to always bring heartache, no matter how hard I try to avoid it.
It seems par for the course again this year.
Because as he knelt before me, his green eyes shining with such hope and anticipation as he asked me to be his wife, I knew heartbreak was inevitable, for the both of us.
For him because I would regretfully be turning down his proposal.
And for me because I wanted it to be you.
I wanted to be looking into your beautiful blue eyes. I wanted your hands to be the ones trembling with nervous excitement. I wanted the question to come from your lips. And I wanted it to be your arms that would lift me off the ground in a

celebratory, laughter-filled embrace. Because to you, I would have said yes.

But now, as I sit in my apartment, I wonder why that is.

Why no one will ever compare to you.

Why I still, after all these years, stubbornly cling to the hope that you will come back to me.

Why I continue to hold onto you.

I am twenty-two years old today, no longer the eighteen-year-old girl you left behind.

Yet in moments like tonight, I still feel as though I am.

I'm still very much the smitten child who looked at you like you could save the world.

Who thought she could save you.

It's time for me to grow up.

And the only way to do that is to let you go.

I have to.

From: Mail Delivery Subsystem
To: Spencer Locke
Subject: Delivery Status Notification (Failure)
Date: Friday, December 19, 2014 4:48 PM

Delivery to the following recipient failed permanently:

Well, I will be graduating tomorrow and moving back to Fuller. I feel as though I need to write this one last letter in order to provide some sort of closure, some form of good-bye before I head back home, where memories of what we had used to completely devastate me.

The time has come when I'm finally able to do something I never thought possible. With my impending graduation, I feel it's time to close the door on our past. To make a fresh start with my head held high.

And this letter will be the first step to make that happen. After this, all emails will be deleted, and the proof of my weakness will no longer exist. Much like you.

I loved you once. A love I thought irrevocable. A love I mistakenly believed could transcend both time and circumstance. Under the influence of my dimwitted, naïve, traitorous heart, I became intoxicated with what I now know was simply a figment of my self-indulgent imagination. So drunk on the feeling, I couldn't see what was right in front of my face. So foolishly enamored, I blindly followed my heart into the depths of an emotion that would ravage me.

Years later, I know now what I wish I knew then. I am stronger. Smarter. Tougher. I will not allow myself to be broken again.

I loved you.

I raged for you.

I wept for you.

And now, I'm letting you go.

Good-bye, Dalton.

Part Three

Recovery

Chapter 29

Dalton

A bitter gust of February wind tugs fiercely on my cap. I pinch the bill tightly, pulling it low on my forehead before shoving my hands back in my leather jacket as I wait.

Hidden by the night sky, I'm right back where I was the night my life changed forever—in the godforsaken woods that witnessed the death of my friend. It wasn't easy to come back here, but since the woods are now the most secure meeting place in Fuller County, I wasn't given much choice.

My eyes try to adjust, but I can't see much other than the shadowy, harrowing branches that surround me.

Darkness. I'm so fucking tired of it.

Everything I do is concealed by it. Every move I make, every conversation I initiate, every deal I broker. I have practically lived the last five years in nothing but inescapable darkness—both emotionally and physically.

I arch my neck onto the back of the park bench, shutting my eyes while inhaling deeply in thought. If I make it through this, I'm fucking moving to Barbados. Warm sand, bright sun, clear blue skies, and God willing, Spencer by my side.

Stretching my legs and crossing my feet, I listen for the sound of footsteps but hear nothing other than the wind carrying the leaves. My eyes remain closed because I know from experience the stars above me will only beckon a distant memory that will addle my mind. And that's something I can't afford right now.

My closest thoughts, however, remain a slave to her.

Spencer.

Not one day has gone by since she's been back in Fuller that I don't see her. She doesn't see me, of course. I know that's the way it has to be for now, and I'm oddly content with the small amount of time I'm able to be near her. Just witnessing her laugh and smile the way she used to, feeling her strength as it radiates across the room and strikes my chest—those things give me the drive I need to keep going.

Still lost in my thoughts, a fallen branch cracks behind me and I grin, but remain in resting position. My voice is gruff as I inquire, "How in the world is it that you cannot walk quietly? Isn't that part of your job requirement?"

A familiar chuckle sounds from behind me as the rustling ceases. This is the fourth time we've met, and every time I can clock him from at least fifty yards away. As he passes in front of me, I open my eyes just in time to see a white piece of paper float mysteriously into my lap. Jerking my hands from my pockets, I snag it before the wind can take hold.

"That your handiwork?"

As soon as the question is asked, I break my gaze from the paper to eye the person standing in front of me. His dark trench coat stirs with the blowing breeze, its bottom slapping against the equally dark pants beneath it. I shake my head.

He's a fucking walking cliché.

"She needs to be able to protect herself," I assert.

"She wouldn't need protection if you would keep an acceptable distance, as we agreed on before beginning *any* of this." His tone is clipped and my lips tug upward. He's become almost as protective as I am.

"Spencer's been in danger since before I even left. My *proximity* has no bearing on her safety. Not anymore. Not now," I respond emphatically.

He stalls before answering, "You're getting too close. I don't like it."

"I have to stay close in case he decides to make a move."

His heavy sigh is carried on the wind. He knows I'm right.

I glance back down at the flyer in my hand. "She needs to be able to protect herself in case he chooses to come after her, plain and simple. I know him. And I also know we can't count on a fucking can of pepper spray to protect her if he figures out what's going on before this is all over."

He passes a frustrated hand through his hair, releasing another long breath before answering. "You're a smart man. I've always known that. But you're also cocky. You're walking a thin line here, and I won't have her or her mother going through what happened five years ago."

My jaw clenches, his words thrashing my insides. *As I'm sure he intended.*

He clears his throat. "Just make sure your heart doesn't start fucking with that brain of yours. If you lose focus, mistakes will be made. Mistakes that cannot be undone. Understood?"

"Understood," I relent, my voice controlled.

"Good. Now, any sign of him?"

I draw in a calming breath. "Not yet. He's shielded with constant protection and never shows his face. I've only dealt with his new second-in-command, Bates. After Juan was taken out in prison, things in the organization changed. He trusts no one, not anymore."

A hum fills the air. "He's hiding."

I nod. "He's paranoid."

"As he should be." He dips his hands into his pockets. "Vice has been running nonstop surveillance, as you well know. You've gotten us good intel so far. We have plenty to take him now, but we want to see how far we can extend our reach. We need you to find out who his supplier is. Talk to this Bates character, scan over any paperwork lying around, whatever you can do. The higher we can go, the bigger the impact we can make."

With his back still facing me, he adds, "We're gonna wire you. You've been cleared since they think you killed Garcia, yeah? They haven't been scanning you, not in the last year or so?"

"Not since Garcia, no."

"Good. Then I'll get something set up soon." I hear a light chuckle on the breeze. "She still has the pepper spray I gave her?"

I grin. "On her keychain. It goes everywhere she does."

His head bobs, then he clears his throat. "You will protect her?"

"With my life. But part of that protection is making sure she can handle herself."

"And you don't think Krav Maga is a bit extreme?"

I chuckle. Krav Maga is the shit. Street fighting mixed with martial arts? Sign me up. Spencer too.

"No, I don't. I think it's the best self-defense out there and there just so *happens* to be an instructor right here in Fuller, as you well know. Plus," I add as the leaflet rustles in the wind, "it was only a suggestion. *She's* the one who picked up the flyer."

"You put it on her goddamn windshield," his voice booms, echoing through the trees.

My laughter is silent as I rise from the bench, stretching languidly before stepping onto the grass. Just as I pass behind him, I offer barely above a whisper, "I've already got one made for a free visit to High Caliber Gun Range. FYI."

He whips around to protest, but I'm already long gone by the time he finishes the turn.

Sometimes being a lifelong chameleon has its advantages.

Chapter 30 ✦

Spencer

"Come on, Cass. We're going to be late."

In a hurry, I yank my yoga pants over my hips then shrug on my trusty Pink Floyd tank top. Toeing on my tennis shoes, I throw my hair up into a half-ass ponytail and fling my door open. As soon as I enter the hall, I come face to face with a clearly uninterested but thankfully already dressed Cassie, blowing a huge bubble as she leans against the wall.

She sucks the bubble back through her teeth. "What's your deal with this Kung Fu shit?"

I narrow my eyes. "It's Krav Maga. I told you that already. And it's awesome."

Her head moves back and forth, then she presses herself off the wall. "If only we could get you this excited about dating. Instead, for the last three weeks you've chosen to hang out in a smelly gym with sweaty guys who are most likely overcompensating for the small girth of their dicks. I don't get it."

I huff back. "I didn't ask you to. The only thing I've asked you to do is accompany me to this *one* class. It's 'bring a friend' night, and since you're like my only friend, you're officially obligated to attend. And you never know, you might actually learn something useful."

At the mention of friendship, thoughts of Dalton skirt the edges of my mind. I shove them forcefully into my mental FUDGE box, watching as another huge bubble is blown right in front of my face. I smack it with my hand, wiping the gummy residue from my fingers onto Cassie's retro *Star Wars* T-shirt. "Plus the instructor's hot. Like, *really* hot. Not my type, but maybe for you."

Her previously dulled expression lifts magically. "Well, then what the hell are we waiting for?"

I roll my eyes and turn down the hallway of our new apartment. She laughs as we both grab our water bottles, then head to my car. My baby. My fully restored, 1968, sonic-blue-with-black-interior Mustang coupe.

Just as I start it up, the engine roars loudly and Cassie throws me a horrified glare. She opens her mouth to shout her objection, and in return, I press forcefully on the gas pedal. And I continue to do it every time she attempts to speak. After a full minute of this incredibly immature, yet ridiculously funny scenario, she finally gives up, her dark ponytail whipping to the side when she turns her head away from me. Crossing her arms over her chest, she twists back quickly and sticks her tongue out at me, which earns her yet another growl from my engine. She narrows her eyes but the tiniest bit of laughter tugs at her lips.

I grin widely back at her.

She loves me.

Ten minutes later, we're walking into Crow's Gym, a small, ratty-looking warehouse filled with mats and mirrors. I don't know why, but I love it here. It feels like home, familiar. I can't really put my finger on it, but the feeling I get when entering the front door is akin to pure happiness.

Once inside, we set our water bottles on the edge of the main floor then find a place to stand on the mats. The class is larger than usual, which I expected since most people have a plus-one, but there's still adequate room for us to spread out. As we get settled, the instructor makes his way to the front of the room, and I swear I hear Cassie's panties hit the mat beside me. I start to check, then remind myself she's probably not wearing any, so I maintain my forward gaze.

The sapphire-blue eyes of the instructor roam the crowd and I note privately how those eyes linger a bit longer on Cassie before he clasps his hands in front of him.

"Welcome to Krav Maga. My name is Grady Bennett, and I will be instructing you this evening. For those of you joining us for the first time this evening, thank you for coming." With his head completely shaved except for a long strip of hair at the top secured by an elastic band, he's a walking contradiction: a wicked biker boy with angelic eyes.

"Krav Maga, which is translated as 'contact combat' in Hebrew, is a line of defense developed and initially only used by Israeli armed forces until the 1970s, when its instruction began worldwide. The most important thing to remember in the philosophy of Krav Maga—avoid confrontation when at all possible. Only when offered no other option do you utilize the techniques taught tonight. The art of Krav Maga is not about violence, but protection."

Protection.

The word most synonymous with the one person I'm constantly trying to forget. But as I glance down at the onyx-beaded bracelet I can't seem to take off my wrist, my mind wanders to a time when I felt safe and protected by *his* presence. *Why tonight? Why am I thinking this tonight?*

I shake my head and reassert the repeated notion that I don't need to rely on *him* for protection. I never did. I can protect myself. Protection from what, I don't know, but there's this unavoidable, foreboding feeling I can't seem to shake, no matter how hard I try. So as soon as the flyer for this class appeared under my windshield wiper, I took it as a much-needed sign and signed up the same day.

"We will go through various strikes and kicks, then pair off to visit particular situations that may be of use, which is the reason for this open class—take what is taught and utilize it as necessary." His eyes soften as he concludes, "Although I hope you will never be in a situation that requires the use of these defensive techniques."

With that, we break apart and perform elbow strikes, punches, and kicks monitored and corrected by Grady. It seems Cassie's taking his words to heart because she makes no complaints as we perform the exercises together.

Once the warm-up is over, Grady announces, "Ladies, please pair up with someone of the opposite sex. It's crucial for you to learn how using the energy naturally carried within your center can overpower someone larger than you. For you to understand where the vulnerabilities lie in someone who could be *perceived* as a stronger opponent."

At the inflection of his voice, I smile and soak in his words. But as he makes his way in my direction, I completely freeze. The cerulean coloring of his eyes reminds me of a time when I was weak, and that feeling has absolutely no place here. I shake my head and point toward Cassie.

His gaze is surprisingly apprehensive as it leaves mine. It grazes over my shoulder, almost as though seeking the permission of someone else. I turn my head, but there's no one to be found.

Glancing back, I see Grady turn and approach Cassie. He introduces himself and her smile is so bright, I grin right along with her. He begins his instruction, his corded, muscular forearms flexing to capacity while he grips her waist, teaching her how to properly twist her body. Her face is flushed, but I have a sneaking suspicion that her heated reaction has nothing to do with our workout.

Still grinning, I begin to seek out a partner of my own. My eyes land on a man standing alone, stretching his well-defined arm across his chest. A man I regularly see in class, but who mainly keeps to himself. And as I keenly observe him from afar, I find myself drawn to him for this particular exercise, mostly because his appearance is completely opposite of the person whose name shall remain unspoken.

His coffee-colored hair is secured into a man bun at the back of his head, which I find oddly attractive. It's the same shade of the full beard framing the bottom half of his face and a tad lighter than his dark eyes. From across the room, I watch those eyes intensely scan and scrutinize the crowd. As I continue to stare, something deep within me surges to life, sending the smallest of tremors through my body. My heart begins to blossom, opening into full bloom as it thrums lively within my chest.

His dark eyes find me through the crowd separating us. He holds my gaze briefly, then quickly looks away to focus on the red mat below him. I take a step in his direction, but an eager Cody Randall stops me. Cody, a classmate, unfortunately refuses to accept the notion that I come here to learn and not score a date.

"Hey, Spencer." He's winded as he speaks. Theatrically, he blots his face with the towel around his neck before blatantly eyeing my chest. I raise my brow and wait patiently for him to meet my eyes. Once he does, he smiles widely and inquires, "Want to partner up?"

I open my mouth to politely refuse, but my words are interrupted by a rough, gravelly voice. "She's with me."

My eyes fly upward to the bearded face towering above both Cody and me. The man's annoyed stare narrows on Cody, and I pinch my lips together to conceal my laughter at Cody's paling face.

The man says nothing else. He just continues to glare until it becomes so awkward, Cody is forced to relent with a defeated sigh. Clearly flustered, he nervously dips his head in my direction before slinking off to find another victim. Normally I would feel bad, but I'm reminded of his eye assault on my chest, so I don't.

The bearded man drops his gaze to me. I clear my face of any previous amusement because this guy doesn't look like he enjoys laughter . . . or humor . . . or much of anything, actually.

I extend my arm. "Spencer Locke."

He accepts my offer and shakes my hand. "Liam Kelley."

As soon as our skin makes contact, my chest flutters wildly. I gently extract my hand from his and wipe it on the side of my yoga pants, strangely dazed by the feeling. His gaze falls on my leg then lifts to meet mine. I just smile back as though my reaction is completely normal.

Liam's attention is broken when Grady hands him an orange rubber gun. We both watch in silence as he turns to face the class once all the guns have been distributed. "We're going to focus on what to do if your attacker is holding a gun to the side of your head from behind. Cassie, can you come up here for a demonstration?"

Cassie's ponytail whips from side to side as she happily bounces her way to where Grady stands. She turns, her eyes finding mine. Her mouth breaks into a broad smile, and she waggles her eyebrows as he moves to stand behind her. I try to suppress my giggle, but it escapes. For some reason, Liam exhales forcefully beside me. I don't dare look, keeping my eyes glued on Cassie, who's still smiling. Grady takes his stance behind her, then places the rubber gun to her temple. "There are four steps to take when dealing with a gun in use by an attacker. Redirect. Control. Counterattack. Disarm. For example . . ."

Grady reaches around the front of Cassie's body and moves her left wrist across her chest, securing her hand on the barrel of the gun.

Her fingers curl over the top as his hand envelops hers. "Redirect, control, and counterattack pretty much happen at the same time, so pay attention. The first thing you need to do is get a secure grip on the gun, as Cassie is doing correctly here. Then, you will lean forward and drop your base while redirecting the gun toward the attacker. Like this . . ."

He presses Cassie's body forward with his own and twists her wrist, removing the muzzle from her temple and pointing it backward. Her grin widens at their suggestive positioning, but she maintains her focus on the mat below them.

"At the same time you lean and redirect, you will also counterattack as you throw a straight arm back into this open area right here. Cassie, extend your free arm backward."

She does as instructed, swinging her arm back until it's lodged in his armpit.

"Good. Now, let's try it all in one motion."

Grady removes his hold on her and stands. When they both reset to their original positions, he places the gun back against her head, and surprisingly, she executes the technique perfectly. Grady's body falls off center, and once the gun is pointing in his direction, he continues.

"Excellent job, Cassie. Now, for the disarming. See this arm," he motions to the arm lodged under his, "you want to bring your forearm back toward your body and lock his arm with yours, like this." He bends Cassie's arm until it hooks around his as she pivots on her feet. With her grip still tight on the gun, she twists his wrist with her movement and takes the gun from his hand. He smiles widely at her before readdressing the class.

"What that does is effectively remove you from danger, but it also thwarts the attacker's hold, making it easier to acquire the gun, as Cassie has expertly demonstrated."

Thwart.

As soon as the word leaves his lips, memories of its use long ago flood my mind. The air whooshes violently from my lungs, which is unfortunate because I'm midswallow when it happens. As a result, I begin to choke and cough heinously. I cover my mouth and bend at the waist, my body apparently determined to expel my left lung.

Through my blurred vision, I see Cassie take a step toward me. I hold up my hand and shake my head, signaling that I'm all right.

"I'm okay," I force through sporadic coughs. As soon as I can breathe, I suck in a long breath and cough one more time before repeating, "I'm okay."

The whole class stares at me as I wipe the tears from my eyes, and my face heats with embarrassment. I crinkle my nose before smiling sheepishly back at the crowd, then turn back to my partner. I can't tell because of the blasted beard, but I think there is a hint of a smile.

His curious eyes scan my face before he asks in his rough voice, "You have an aversion to the word *thwart*?"

Yes, I do. A very strong one.

"No," I lie. "I just . . . choked."

Liam continues watching me and I feel my reddened face turn a shade darker.

Thankfully, Grady addresses the class, breaking the awkwardness of the moment. "Your turn. The larger of the two will be the attacker. The smaller will play the potential victim and execute the technique just demonstrated."

I clear my throat and turn to Liam with my brows raised. "I'm assuming I will be the victim in this scenario?"

He dips his head briskly and moves to stand behind me, rubber gun in hand. As he closes the distance, the heat from his body begins to seep through my tank top and I inhale deeply. His woodsy cologne fills my nostrils, and an electric current begins to hum through my body that I haven't felt in years. Not even with Brandon.

Every hair on my body stands on end and my pulse quickens. Liam sets his hand gently between my shoulder blades and places the gun against my head. His warm breaths hit my neck and I suppress a shudder. Yet, as I take in the situation in its entirety, I squash the temptation to burst out laughing because my response to his presence is just so odd. Odd because I have no idea why I'm reacting this way to someone I don't even know, and odd because there is a freaking gun pressed against my temple. Talk about inappropriate.

I force myself to refocus. "Ready?"

He chuckles. "You gonna ask the attacker if he's rea—"

I reach for the gun and twist its position, then lurch forward while locking his arm with mine and removing the gun from his grasp . . . all before he finishes his sentence. My face splits into a satisfied grin as I take in his stunned expression. Releasing the gun, I let it dangle from my index finger.

"Again?"

The whites of his teeth peek out from behind his beard, confirming that the man can actually smile. He shakes his head. "I think you've got that one down. Want to try something else?"

I nod eagerly, met with another grin from Liam. For the rest of class, we remain in our own little bubble as we go over other defensive situations. We cover various techniques such as breaking chokeholds, wrist manipulations, defensive punches, and kicks. Grady leaves us alone while he instructs the rest of the students, and by the time class is over, my tank is soaked and every part of my body aches.

Except one very important part . . .

Because with each punch thrown, my confidence grows.

With each kick landed, self-assurance brews within me.

And with each round of genuine laughter shared with my new fuzzy-faced partner, the gaping hole in my chest begins to close. For the first time in five years, my heart doesn't hurt. I feel . . .

Happy.

And as I walk out the doors of the gym, strong and assured, I find myself wanting to kiss the person who left that stupid flyer on my windshield.

Chapter 31 ✳

Spencer

Cool air hits my face as I lean forward, turning the air conditioning up full blast. Cassie giddily lands herself in the passenger seat next to me, face flushed, although this time I'm pretty sure it *is* due to the workout.

That is, until she states, "We've got a date set for tonight."

A rush of panic ricochets through my chest. "What?"

She nods, then pulls her phone out of her bag. An unknown number is forcefully shoved in my line of sight, so close I go cross-eyed while trying to read it. I press the phone away, refocus my blurry vision, then redirect my attention to her, still unsure what she means.

"Grady," she responds, lowering her cell and thumbing his name into her contacts, eyes filled to the brim with excitement. I, however, am stupefied.

"We're going on a date with Grady?" My tone is incredulous.

Brows pinched, she jerks her head back, clearly appalled. "No, hooker. *I'm* going with Grady Bennett—Krav Maga instructor extraordinaire and quite possibly the hottest guy on the entire planet. You will be accompanying his friend, Liam Kelley—the beautifully built, bearded wonder who made you smile for the first time since you've been back in Fuller."

I shake my head frantically. "Um, no."

A devilish smile is received in return. "Um, yes."

I begin to vehemently refuse, but I'm interrupted as Cassie launches forward and covers my mouth with her hand. "Spencer, you need to get out and go on a goddamn date. Since you've been back, you've done nothing but hole yourself up in your room and study for your master's. Other than going to work at the coffee shop and helping your mom at the center, of course. You chose to come back *here*, instead of staying at Wilmington, and so help me . . . if it has anything to do with Dal—"

At the mention of his name, a barely audible sound reverberates through my throat. My eyes widen and hers narrow into a determined glare. She firms her hold against my mouth, pressing her hand closer. "*Dalton*, I will throat-punch you. I know you say you're over him, but you're not. You weren't when you were dating Brandon and you're not now. I can see it in your eyes."

Her expression softens, a tinge of sadness flashing across her face with her whisper. "He's gone, Spence. He's not coming back."

Our gazes remain unbroken as I allow her words to penetrate the fortitude of my self-delusion. She's right. I know she's right.

And I hate myself for it.

I exhale through my nose and give her a defeated dip of my head. Then I lick her palm because I can't breathe.

"Ewwwww! Spencer!"

Laughing, she whisks her hand away only to press it against my cheek and drag it down my face. Giggling, I swat her arm away before rubbing my face against my shoulder. "Fine. I'll go. But for your information, I came back here because it's less expensive and Jim's college fund was almost depleted."

Cassie winks, relaxing back into her seat. "Right."

I roll my eyes before starting up the engine. Now that his name has been spoken, I can no longer avoid the memories associated with it. Thoughts of Dalton flood me: shaggy blond hair, crooked smiles, sweet scent, soft lips, laughter, sunsets, stars, crystalline-blue eyes holding the promise of tomorrow.

I swallow deeply, trying to control their progression, then turn to Cassie for a much-needed distraction. "You know, the last double date we went on didn't turn out so well."

She laughs. "Yeah, but at least this time if you throw a punch it will be with correct form." Her smile softens with her squeeze of my hand. "Give him a try, Spence. You never know."

I place my other hand over hers and offer with sincerity, "I promise to give Grizzly Adams a fair try." A goofy grin crosses her face and I ask, "What's the plan?"

As though jolted back to reality, she stiffens and grabs her phone. Her home screen flashes the time as she exclaims, "Shit. Showers. That's the plan. We're meeting them in an hour and a half at Bambino's."

I throw the car in reverse. "Seriously? You couldn't give us more time?"

"I didn't want to give you time to think about it."

"Well, shit . . ." I shift into drive, then practically peel out of the parking lot. "Mission accomplished."

An hour and a half later, we pull into Bambino's. We're right on time and surprisingly put together for the amount of time allotted.

Cassie's dark hair is pulled into a tight bun at the base of her neck, the smooth effect matching the sleekness of the black, one-shoulder mini dress practically painted on her body. Her dark eyes are framed top and bottom with smoky gray, and her lips are coated in a light-colored gloss, bringing out the dramatic effect of the eyeshadow. And, of course, her feet are donning six-inch heels with thin black straps crossing over both her toes and ankles. She looks incredible.

Not nearly as overtly sexual, I glance down at my off-the-shoulder, rust-colored peasant top that rests above a pair of dark skinny jeans. My hair is down as usual, with tiny braids crowning my head. The only thing remotely out of the ordinary for me is the pair of heels on my feet. The style is similar to Cassie's with the exceptions of color (mine are beige) and the fact that they're not stilts (only four inches).

After pulling into an open spot, the growl of my engine dies and we both look at each other, our nervous excitement charging the air. We smile in unison, then both release a calming breath, nodding when we're ready to exit the car. As we approach the restaurant, two *rather* handsome gentlemen standing by the front door meet us.

Grady looks delectable dressed in a navy-blue button-down folded over his muscular forearms and tucked into a pair of dark-charcoal dress pants. The color of his shirt highlights his bright-blue eyes, and I shake my head to rid the involuntary comparison my mind brings forth. His light-brown hair is still secured at the back of his head, showcasing his chiseled jaw, and the wide grin on his face tells me he's very pleased with the appearance of his date. As he should be.

Cassie releases a light sigh and steps ahead of me, taking his offered hand as he guides her toward the door. I grin as I watch them, then turn my attention to the man now heading in my direction.

My grin broadens when I see the smile through the full beard of Liam Kelley with his approach. Like Grady, he's donned a button-down shirt that hugs the muscles of his chest and is also clad in a pair of dark dress pants. Unlike Grady, the shirt is medium gray, and instead of being tied, his coffee-colored hair flows freely, grazing the tops of his shoulders.

A nervous flutter stretches the expanse of my stomach. "Hi," I offer meekly.

"Hello, Spencer." The low register and rasp of his voice hits my ears and the flutter spreads to my chest in response. He glances down at my wrist. "Nice bracelet."

My hand involuntarily crosses my body to cover it, almost as though I've been caught wearing something I shouldn't. "Yeah, I've had it for years. I can't seem to take it off. They're"—I lightly trace the tips of my fingers over the beads—"onyx."

He hums. "The stone of protection."

I give him a small smile, and the sides of his eyes crease as he gestures toward the door. "Shall we?"

I nod, falling into step with him. He places his hand at the small of my back as we walk. Leaning in, he states, "I'm sorry. This kind of came out of nowhere. Once Grady gets an idea in his head, there's no stopping him."

I laugh. "Yeah, Cassie too. I have a feeling they're very much alike."

Liam chuckles. "You have no idea."

My eyebrows quirk upward with his response because truly, he shouldn't either. It's not like he knows her. I let the oddity go without comment and smile as we enter the restaurant. Once we're seated, I order a glass of Pinot Grigio while Grady and Cassie both order Cabernet. Liam asks for a glass of water, and I find myself praying he's not one of those health food gurus. The thought, however, is quickly dismissed when he orders chicken parmesan instead of a salad. I breathe a small sigh of relief, then order my own chicken parm.

After a small session of obligatory small talk, Grady and Cassie quickly abandon us, falling into their own discussion and an awkward silence begins to filter between Liam and me.

I trace the condensation on my wineglass, haphazardly glancing over at Liam, his face completely relaxed for the first time since I met him earlier today.

And what I see drives a molten-hot spear right through my ribcage straight into my heart.

Because with the orange glow of the candle on the table highlighting his features, it's freakishly uncanny how much he resembles the person once seated by my side during many a sunset. I didn't see it before, but with the lighting . . .

My eyes widen and a current of surprise jolts my entire system. Reflexively, my hand shoots forward, sending my glass of Pinot Grigio flying across the table.

And onto Cassie's dress.

As soon as she's splattered with the cold liquid, she gasps out loud and swipes madly at the black fabric. I grab my purse, lean over the table, and down the rest of her Cabernet before announcing, "Cassie, we need to go to the bathroom. *Now*."

Grady and Liam stand. Cassie bolts to her feet, giving me a deadpan expression. "Ya think?"

I wrap my fingers around her forearm and tug her in my direction, offering a quick apology to our dates before marching us both to the bathroom. She stumbles behind me, but my feet are undeterred and on a mission. As soon as the door closes behind us, I whirl around.

"What is *wrong* with you?" Cassie seethes.

I'm seconds away from a panic attack. My heart is racing uncontrollably and I bring my hand to my chest.

"I'm losing it, Cass. Losing. It."

I begin drawing in long breaths through my nose and exhaling them slowly. She tightens her stare. "I'm about to lose it if you don't tell me what the hell is going on."

As though my body is rejecting the idea, my head moves back and forth on its own. Only when Cassie takes a menacing step in my direction does it cease.

After forcing a swallow, I respond. "I just saw Dalton. Well, what looked like Dalton, only not really, but kinda."

It's Cassie's turn to shake her head. "What? I'm not following. What are you talking about?"

"Cass"—I hold my hands up, palms out—"please don't freak out, but Liam . . . he looks like Dalton, kinda. In the right light, I mean, I know that's completely crazy but . . ." I bounce on the balls of my feet. "Oh!" I add breathlessly. "And he said something outside that made it sound like he knew you. I thought it was odd, but now . . ." I take in another breath, replaying the crazy words that just left my mouth. "Okay, I am *definitely* losing it, Cass."

She cocks her head disbelievingly and plants her hands on her hips, giving me a stern look. Knowing there's only one thing I can say that could possibly sway her belief, I void my face and drop my left hand, leaving the right on display.

"I swear on your Kindle, Cass."

Her eyes widen and she gasps. "Noooo . . ."

I nod slowly.

"Noooo . . ." she repeats.

I continue nodding.

She opens her mouth again and I clamp my hand over it as I whisper, "Yesss . . ."

We hold our stares until she quickly pivots, darting out of the bathroom with me on her heels. We find the cover of a six-foot plastic plant and root ourselves there, Cassie in front of me as we peek around it. Disregarding the stares of several gawking patrons, we watch Grady and Liam, who seem to be in deep discussion. Liam's expression is drawn taut as Grady speaks.

Cassie squints. "I don't know, Spence. I mean"—she angles her head to the left—"maybe?"

"*Maybe* I'm just losing it. I saw it, but from far away, now I'm not so sure," I whisper in her ear.

"No, I can see it. Kind of," she affirms. "Now that you've pointed it out, I mean, I see the resemblance."

"What the hell are we going to do?" My voice is trembling as my fingers clench the tops of her arms.

A waitress passes us, then pauses briefly. "Are you ladies okay?"

We both turn in her direction. "We're fine," we state in unison.

Her brows furrow before she turns away, heading in the direction of the kitchen.

Cassie turns back to me. "What do you want to do?"

I shrug. We look back at the table, then again at each other. "I guess just have dinner without looking at him? Maybe my mind is just superimposing Dalton's face on Liam's as payback for the last five years of useless pining?"

Cassie scrunches her face. "Highly unlikely."

Together, we turn our gazes back to the table.

After a few more seconds, I gather my wits and press myself off Cassie's back, smoothing my dress. "Well, I guess we just go over there and act like normal. Like nothing happened."

Cassie huffs skeptically. "Right."

I bite my lip, holding her stare. Once my heart rate has finally slowed to normal, I breathe in deeply. After a resolved nod between the two of us, we step out from behind the plant and head in the direction of our dates.

Time to get this show on the road.

Whatever the hell this show may be.

Chapter 32

Dalton

"She knows." Grady's voice is faint, almost inaudible as he lifts the glass of wine to cover his mouth. "Lawson's gonna shit."

I fight a smug grin and shrug. "He told me I couldn't tell her. He said nothing about her figuring it out for herself."

Grady sets the glass on the table and glares at me disapprovingly. "You're jeopardizing the entire investigation. Five years of work down the drain if your cover is blown. You're willing to sacrifice that?"

I lean forward, my expression serious. "There's nothing I *wouldn't* sacrifice for her. She's unsafe otherwise, regardless of what Lawson believes. I feel it in my gut, and it's time for her to know."

Grady inhales deeply, glancing to the side before leaning over the table. "You're lucky I trust you. Anyone else would have you extracted, *immediately*. But you know Silas's operation better than any of us, and because of that, I will grant you this."

I laugh. "And I'm sure your granting me this date had absolutely nothing to do with her very attractive friend. The same friend I knew would be invited to the open class I convinced you to have for that *exact* purpose." I tighten my stare for emphasis. "Just another *gut* feeling."

He says nothing, but eases back in his seat.

"You're welcome," I add, just as the girls make their reappearance.

They're blatantly staring at me, shock paling both of their faces. I rise with their approach and offer my hand to Spencer. "Wanna take a ride?"

My voice is still gravelly, as it's been trained to be for the last three years. I clear my throat and she remains where she stands, the caution in her eyes fucking slaughtering me because I'm the one who put it there.

Not taking my hand, she glances hesitantly at Cassie, who's still watching me with uncertainty. Spencer looks back at me before stating, "We can take my car?" I lower my chin in affirmation, watching as she turns her attention to Grady. "I'm going to get your license plate number, just in case." Spencer jabs her index finger in his direction. "Cassie better make it home safely because I *know* people."

Grady's entire face tightens to suppress his laughter, then he concedes with a dip of his head. "She'll be home by eleven. Scout's honor."

Completely straight-faced, he demonstrates the universal sign by displaying his first three fingers for Spencer to see. Cassie notes her objection with a considerable huff, taking her seat next to him. Spencer turns to me and I watch over her shoulder as Grady winks at Cassie, their faces breaking into equally rebellious grins.

I extend my arm. "Keys?"

"To *my* car? No, I'll drive."

My palm remains open, silently requesting the keys. She doesn't budge. Our eyes remain locked until Grady's deep voice states from behind her, "Looks like you're going to have a fun evening."

Spencer twists around and glares while Cassie covers her mouth to hide her laughter. Reaching in my pocket, I grab my wallet and toss a couple of hundreds on the table. "Dinner's on me."

Grady glances at the money before turning in his chair to signal the waitress. Once she's on her way, he faces me, shit-eating grin on his face. "Well then, I'm changing my order."

Cassie giggles as I respond with lifted brows of warning. "Then cancel ours."

Still smiling, Grady lowers his chin. "You got it."

I curl my fingers around Spencer's forearm and surprisingly, she steps willingly without me having to haul her ass over my shoulder. Side by side, we exit the restaurant in complete silence.

She takes the lead once we're outside, digging in her purse in search of her keys. My eyes slowly graze up her body from behind, starting from the sexy heels on her feet, then moving up her long legs to her beautifully rounded ass, finally landing on her long blonde hair as it dances in the wind. My chest ignites as the smell of Love and Happiness fills my nostrils with the breeze. The bitter-sweet fragrance reminds me of the times of our youth, as well as the many nights over the past five years spent with that fucking perfume bottle glued to my nose.

Spencer wheels around to face me, and I avert my eyes to the ground.

"Which one is Grady's car?"

I point to the gray Nissan Maxima parked a couple spaces away, chuckling when she whips back around. She walks directly up to the trunk, then digs around some more in the purse, and removes a pen and small notepad.

My grin breaks free as she jots down his license plate number. As though memorizing the car's appearance, she gives the car a long look then pivots on her heel, putting everything back in her purse while heading back in my direction. She bypasses me without meeting my eyes, giving me no choice but to step in line behind her.

After cutting through a couple of rows, her steps begin to slow as she approaches a blue vintage Mustang coupe. The corners of my lips lift in appreciation. "This yours?"

She twists back in my direction and nods, proud smile on her face. My fingers linger on the rear of the car.

"'67?"

Spencer shakes her head and points toward the rear lights. "'68. You can tell by the side marker lights. The '67 didn't have them. They were installed the next year due to federal safety regulations."

Nothing sexier has ever come out of her mouth, and my cock stirs with thoughts of taking her on the hood of this '68 Mustang. I shift in my pants. "You seem to know a lot about cars."

She sighs as her eyes remain on the rear lights. "Yeah, well, I had a friend who had his own restored muscle car back in the day. I couldn't help it. I fell in love."

Her stare slices to me, and the absolute resentment in her expression pierces my fucking soul. Words fail me, and as though sensing it, she clears her throat. "Look, I know I said we could take my car, but that would leave you stranded in case you need to *leave*."

Another gut punch landed.

She continues. "So maybe you should just follow me."

I debate telling her I didn't bring a car, but I get the feeling she needs some time to process everything. I can't say I blame her. Plus, my Rubicon is parked three spots over.

I nod, then grab my keys from my pocket and head toward my Jeep. The glorious growl of her engine fills the air and I grin while sliding into my driver's seat. After turning the key, I pull directly behind her as she turns out of the lot.

We make the ten-minute drive to the apartment she's shared with Cassie since moving back to Fuller in December. Two and a half months of regular surveillance at this very location. I know it well.

Once parked, I exit my car and follow her to the front door. She unlocks it and steps inside, leaving the door open for me to enter behind her. Saying nothing, she just tosses her purse on the couch and heads straight for the kitchen.

"You should set the alarm," I remark, eyeing the unused security pad while locking the door.

Spencer sets a freshly poured glass of wine on the counter, then bends, hooking her finger in the strap of her shoe and tossing it aside. Stepping her bare foot on the wood floor, she switches to the other. "We were in a hurry."

I forgo the safety lecture and remain silent, watching as she rises. Once standing, she sighs, looking to the glass in front of her before finally bringing her tired eyes to mine. "I'm going to change, and then we can talk."

Silently, my eyes follow her as she enters the hallway. After her door shuts, I head over to the living room window and move the beige curtain aside. Noting the unmarked vehicle is stationed where it should be, I pray they haven't called Lawson with news of my appearance here.

A slight shuffling sound alerts me to Spencer's presence, and I lower the curtain before turning to face her. Wearing a simple Led Zeppelin tank top and baggy gray sweatpants, she still manages to steal my breath. It doesn't matter how many times I've seen her through the years. Watching from a distance, I've witnessed her growth from a beautiful young girl into the striking woman who stands before me.

But that isn't why I struggle to breathe.

For the first time since I was forced to leave, she finally *sees* me. She's fully aware that I'm here, right in front of her, and the knowledge of that renders me completely breathless.

She warily watches me, her eyes never breaking from mine until she turns to enter the kitchen. After grabbing her glass of wine, she downs half the glass in one large gulp before focusing her narrowed stare on me.

"Am I seeing things? Because you sure as hell resemble someone I used to know. Someone I haven't seen in a very long time."

Ripples form in the wine, her hand trembling almost as much as her voice. As much as I want to comfort her, I remain where I stand. I clear my throat and attempt to regain the use of my normal voice.

The sound is foreign to my ears with my reply. "You're not seeing things. It's me, Spence."

The glass begins to quake. She inhales deeply, closing her eyes and tilting her head backward. When she regains her composure, she looks back at me, eyes filled with tears. "Why? Why now? After all this time?"

I lean my hip the window and cross my arms. "Truth?"

"You owe me that, yes. I think I deserve an explanation." She sets the glass down on the counter, her tone as sharp and cold as ice. And her stare rivals it.

Drawing in a long breath, I begin. "I was there the night Rat was killed. The night he and his sister were murdered." My throat constricts as the agony of the memory resurfaces. I clench my fists and swallow as the pain runs its course. "It was the night of your birthday, as you remember, I'm sure."

Spencer's lips pinch tightly, but she remains quiet, allowing me to continue. "I had just pulled out of your driveway when several of Rat's texts came through on my phone. Something had gone wrong with a meeting he had with Silas, so I went straight to the warehouse. As I was pulling up, I saw Rat in the back seat of one of Silas's cars, so I followed them. We all ended up in the middle of the woods, where Rat's sister was shot and subsequently, Rat. I tried . . ."

My throat clamps shut. No matter how many times I've covered this night in therapy, the pain of not being able to save him is still so fresh in my mind.

"I tried to save him, but I couldn't. I . . ." I shake my head. "I wasn't fast enough. So I jumped the person who shot him, held a gun to his head, and started to pull the trigger."

Spencer's sharp gasp cuts through the air, ripping off the scab of a wound that's never really healed. I can't bring myself to meet her eyes because I know what I'll see. Pained horror will be staring back at me with the knowledge of my true nature, of the monster I once was.

And I can't handle that right now.

"That night, Lawson saved me from making the worst mistake of my life. I didn't kill anyone. I wanted to, but I didn't. Lawson's people apprehended the man, and Lawson stashed me somewhere safe until we could figure out what to do next. Because I made Rat a promise that night as he lay dying on the ground in front of me that I would make it right. That Silas would pay. So that's what I set out to do. What *we* set out to do."

I find the courage to lift my gaze, leveling it on her as she agitatedly drums her fingers on the counter.

"Lawson? As in *Kirk* Lawson? The man who's been dating my mother for the past five years? Who's become like a father to me? The same man who's made absolutely no mention of any of this to either of us during that time?"

As the conversation starts to veer, I reassure her in a steady voice. "He couldn't. Telling you could possibly jeopardize everything we've worked so hard to put in place."

Spencer shakes her head impatiently, silencing me with the slam of her palm on the counter. "And what would that be? Because I still haven't received any definitive answers to my original question. As harsh as this sounds, I don't want to know what happened that night. I need to know *why*." Her voice trembles with her questions, brewing anger barely contained. "Why did you choose to leave? Why did you cut me completely out of your life? And why, after all this time, have you decided to come back?"

I pin her with the sincerity of my stare. "First of all, I was forced to leave, Spencer. It wasn't my choice to make."

The knot in my throat swells, so much I have to clear it before continuing. "I had to go into hiding because it was the only way I could get out from underneath Silas safely. I had to go missing. I had to break ties. I had to cease communication. I had to *completely* disappear, leaving absolutely no trace. And I had to do it for years, in order to give us ample time to create a way for me to infiltrate his organization. I'm the only person who knows the intricacies. And I'm the only one who knows Silas well enough to predict what move he will make next."

"So, the hair, the beard, the eyes . . . You're undercover?" she concludes out loud. "The voice?"

"Lengthy vocal cord training," I respond. "With Lawson's recommendation, I attended and completed Langston Police Academy in 2011 and was able to go straight into undercover work, setting up the connections necessary."

Her blue eyes widen in shock, no doubt because of the close proximity. Langston is only four hours away.

"It was far enough to keep me out of Fuller, but still close enough to use my knowledge of Silas's customers to begin infiltration on the outside to work my way in. I acted as a small-time distributor until Silas's people recruited me to come back to Fuller, where we knew I eventually would be. We made sure my points of sale were widely dispersed, giving me an extensive range of distribution, one he would want to claim for himself."

Spencer takes in the information provided, then asks, "And Lawson is leading the investigation into Silas?" I dip my head, allowing her to continue putting the pieces together.

Minutes pass before she asks, "Grady?"

I fight a smile. She misses nothing. "He's part of Lawson's unit. An officer for the Fuller Police Department. Also a part-time Krav Maga instructor. We've become . . . friends."

Years later, I still stall on the word, as though they're a betrayal to Rat.

Her expression remains blank. After another long pause, her keen eyes find mine. "Krav Maga. So I assume *you* are the one who put the flyer on my windshield?"

I say nothing, but my lips barely lift in answer. She narrows her stare. "How long have you been back here? And have you been watching me? In class, I mean. I've seen you in there."

I shrug. "I've been back for about the same time you have. Since December. And yes, I've been watching you from a distance. To make sure you're okay."

She swallows deeply, then asks, "Then why tonight? As you said, you could watch me from a distance. Why put yourself so close that there was absolutely no way I wouldn't figure out who you were?"

"Well"—I take a breath before answering, completely aware of the ramifications of what I'm about to impart—"because it's time you knew. Lawson made it clear he would have my balls if I said anything, so I couldn't exactly tell you. However, if you figured it out for yourself, well . . . there's nothing he can do about that. Plus, we both know I've never really been one to follow the rules."

Her drawn expression remains uncompromising, so I abandon my attempt to lessen the tension and continue. "Lawson is convinced you'll be in more danger if you know. I, however, don't share his opinion. I think since you are directly involved, you need to be prepared. It's just a *feeling* I have. Things are about to go down and I want to make sure you're protected."

Her mouth tips downward. "I don't understand why my protection is necessary."

"Silas had already discovered our connection before I left. As soon as we figured out that he knew who you were, Lawson and I made sure you were constantly watched, just in case he decided to make a move. You were always protected from any possible retaliation from Silas as you went about your life, completely unaware of the danger you were in."

Her head jerks, clearly surprised by that information, then she voids the shock from her expression. "And now you're back. You don't think Silas recognizes you? That he hasn't caught on?"

I shrug. "I haven't seen him. He's barricaded himself behind layer upon layer of security. But this is my honest-to-God opinion. On his own, Silas has probably put together that I was there that night due to the timing of my disappearance. He wants revenge because of my betrayal to his organization. And if I'm back in Fuller, I feel a hell of a lot safer being close to you instead of watching from a distance. Regardless of what Lawson believes."

Instead of fear, the burn of anger mixed with the chill of detachment stems from her body.

She has to understand.

I *need* her to understand.

Desperation takes over and my voice shakes with intensity as I try desperately to make my point. "Don't you see? My leaving. My staying away for as long as I have. And now my coming back. It has *always* been about you. Every decision I have made over the past five years was made with *you* in mind. *Your* safety. *Your* protection. And how to end one life so I may be able to begin a new one with *you* by my side."

I clench my teeth. "I also made *you* a promise that night, a vow, that I would sever those ties to Silas and his organization. Mark my words, I'm not only going to sever them, I'm going to completely annihilate them. I will avenge everything that happened that night. Losing Rat. Losing you. Losing five fucking years. He will pay for every single thing he took from me and for every second not spent with you."

My heart is pumping with such force, my entire body pulsates as I watch her reaction. But she gives me nothing. Silence coats the air between us, the weight suffocating. Because as her eyes break from mine, I feel it. The part of me that resides inside her heart begins to extinguish.

I inhale deeply, supplying myself with the oxygen needed to fan our flame. To keep our connection alive.

I will *not* lose her.

Not when I just got her back.

Chapter 33

Spencer

I focus on the floor, observing the grooves in the wood in effort to conceal my burning eyes.

I want so badly to believe him. To hope that the loss of him over the past five years hasn't destroyed me. To embrace the belief that we can pick up right where we left off, past transgressions forgiven.

Yet as that hope rises, I pummel it until it no longer exists. It only serves as a reminder of my weakness. Of endless tears, sleepless nights, and the anger and rage that once ruled me. All the things I worked so hard to overcome surround me as he watches me from a mere ten feet away.

I can't be that foolish girl anymore. I refuse to subject myself to the heartbreak brought by yet another false notion. I'm a grown woman now, and Dalton needs to understand that I'm no longer the same infatuated child he left pining for him five years ago.

Inhaling deeply, I fortify my resolve, then lift my gaze to meet his.

"I can't, Dalton. I cannot jump blindly into this life you expect from me. A life lived in constant fear that one day I might wake up to find you're not there, knowing you're never coming back. A life plagued with the constant worry about where you are, mind-numbing fear of what has happened to you, and agonizing uncertainty of not knowing whether you're dead or alive." I slam my hand down on the counter.

My jaw clenches, fury threatening to supersede my fabricated composure. "You just waltz in here and expect me to accept your explanation, ready to move on as though nothing happened. To conveniently dismiss the fact that it was *my* heart left completely demolished, and that *I* was the one who had to pick up the shattered pieces your disappearance left behind." More tears start to fill my eyes, but I swallow them forcefully, refusing to display any sign of weakness.

I attempt to gather myself before speaking. "I appreciate what you've done, the protection you've coordinated for my benefit over the past five years. I will discuss my safety concerns with Kirk moving forward. But for the time being, I need you to leave. I need . . . space."

Dalton's face is expressionless as he remains still. I gesture toward the door, but still, he makes no movement. His feet remain bolted to the floor, until finally, he heaves a breath and takes a step.

In the wrong direction.

The rhythmic echo of his heavy steps sound as he crosses the room and enters . . . *the bathroom?*

Dumbfounded, my jaw drops and my eyes bulge when the door shuts behind him. Seconds later he reappears, and much to my detriment, stands right in front of my face. Because instead of the previous brown coloring, steely blue-gray eyes—eyes that have haunted me for years—peer down at me. I begin to take a step back, but stop. I pin him with an angry stare, square my shoulders, then close the distance between us.

If he thinks he can intimidate me, he's got another thing coming.

His jaw ticks with our continued standoff, and he narrows his furious eyes on mine. "If you're going to keep coming up with bullshit excuses, you're going to do it while looking at me, into *my* eyes. Not *his.*"

With his harsh tone, fury flares within me, and I no longer bother to restrain the bitterness that's been simmering throughout this entire conversation. "They're not excuses, Dalton. They're fucking *facts*. While you were off planning the demise of Silas Kincaid's organization, I was the one left behind. Alone. Scared. Angry. Because I *knew* you were alive, Dalton. I knew it. And because of that, I cried myself to sleep at night and pined my life away wishing you would come back to me. Convincing myself that I wasn't good enough for you. That you didn't want me after you'd had me." My lip curls, my face pinching in utter disgust. "You might as well have locked me up in a fucking pantry like my parents."

Dalton visibly flinches, then his eyes turn cold. "Yeah, I know exactly how much you were pining for me. While I was away fighting tooth and nail, doing things I swore I would never do again—all to get back to *you*—imagine my surprise when I found out you had already moved on. Brandon, was it?"

My entire body jars as the name passes through his lips. His eyes are pure ice as they stare back at me. "I haven't just been watching you since I've been back in Fuller. I've watched you through the years. I checked up on you through Lawson. I was at Rat's funeral. Jesus, I even went to watch you move into Wilmington. All because I fucking needed to remember what the hell I was fighting for, *who* I was fighting for."

His features tighten in frustration. "Regardless of what you think, what you've convinced yourself of, the truth is I never forgot you, Spence. Not one day went by that I didn't think of you. That I didn't crave your presence. That I didn't pray I was making the right decisions while forced to watch you start a life without me. You think I didn't hurt too?"

He shakes his head. "You will *never* fully understand what I went through knowing I had to leave you. And you will *never* be able to comprehend the agony of knowing you were with someone else when everything I did, every move I made, was for you."

Heavy breaths escape the both of us, our gazes locked as he steps forward. I retreat, and we continue our movement until my back is flush against the counter. Now only inches apart, my traitorous body responds to his overpowering presence. My heart fires to life, thrashing wildly beneath my ribs, and my body heats to the same warmth I've always felt around him. Ever since we were kids.

As the sensation spreads, Dalton glances at my rapidly rising chest, then back at my heated face. His hardened features relax and he slowly shuts his eyes, inhaling deeply, as though blanketed by the same feeling. When his eyes open again, gone is his anger, and I find myself staring into the soulful orbs of *my* Dalton.

When he finally speaks, his voice is steady and calm. "I would do it again, though. I need you to *know* that, if nothing else. I would take the risk of losing you a thousand times over just to be guaranteed your safety. To know you're alive and breathing. Because if that's the case, my loss is the rest of the world's gain. Your existence, your happiness, your very life . . . those things are all that matter to me."

Hesitantly, he lifts his arm to place his palm above my racing heart. Then just as slowly, he captures my wrist with his free hand, and I swallow back more tears when my palm is secured against his chest. His heart thrums beneath my fingers as he whispers, "You can avoid me, ignore me, be pissed at me . . . hell, even hate me. But as sure as I still feel your heartbeat alive in my chest, you will never, ever lose me."

He searches my eyes, and his face swims in my vision as he continues to whisper what I already know. "Your heart is telling you the same thing, Spence. Just allow yourself to hear what it's saying."

Overcome with every single emotion that could possibly invade my soul, I look toward the ceiling and close my eyes. Warm tears finally break free, overflowing and trailing into my hair. A war wages in my mind. I long to believe his words but battle the fear that refuses to surrender.

He makes no effort to stop my crying. He remains silent, pressing my hand firmly against his pounding chest. Minutes pass until I lower my stare, finally able to speak.

"I need time, Dalton. Just to get my bearings. To process all of this."

His eyes roam my face. "You're scared," he states softly.

I nod my answer.

He steps closer, then places his palm on my cheek. "Take all the time you need, Spence." His thumb grazes lightly over my skin. "I know it's hard for you to believe, with everything that's happened. I don't expect you to trust me overnight. I would never ask that of you. All I can ask is that you give me a chance to prove that I never really left."

Dalton releases his hold on my hand to frame my face, then lowers his stare into my line of sight. His pleading eyes search mine, and he's so close, my entire body hums with electricity. Instinctively, I lick my lips, and his gaze darkens before it lowers to my mouth. When I don't refuse him, he dips his head closer, his sweet, warm breaths fanning my face with his slow approach. Suddenly, his forward movement stalls, leaving our lips millimeters apart.

"Please. Give me a chance, Spence."

We stare at each other. Panting. He remains motionless, awaiting my permission, and I'm completely helpless to do anything other than give it to him. My head dips in consent, and only then does he finally close the distance.

My lids slowly lower as soft lips brush gently, apologetically, against mine. The soft hairs of his beard tickle my skin, which is a foreign feeling, but his lips are so undeniably familiar. The same sweet taste fills my mouth as his tongue darts lightly between its seam, probing for more. When I willingly comply, he presses his body against mine, the sensation so soothing, so comforting, a relieved moan rises in my throat.

I lose myself in the gentleness of the kiss, finding solace in the warmth of his lips as they silence the war in my mind. He continues to calm me with feather-light touches of his tongue against mine. After a few more tender caresses, he breaks the kiss, then runs his nose down the length of mine.

I inhale contently, the same woodsy cologne I smelled earlier today invading my nostrils. I crinkle my nose.

Dalton gives me a crooked smile, then places his hands against the counter beside me. He presses away, but I remain pinned between his forearms as he asks, "What is it? Is it the beard?"

"No, it's not the beard," I answer a little too quickly. My cheeks begin to burn with embarrassment.

His eyes take in my reddening face and he grins. "Then what is it?"

My head falls into my hands and I mutter under my breath, "So embarrassing."

His familiar chuckle spurs my own grin, one I try to keep hidden, but my hands are soon peeled away from my face. I hesitantly glance upward, and his expression is filled with obvious humor as he stares down at me. I know from experience there's no way he'll let this go.

"It's just . . . you don't smell the same."

Dalton widens his eyes, then dips his head toward his chest. After a couple of sniffs, he lifts his face, laughing under his breath. "So you're saying I smell?"

My eyes close in complete mortification before focusing on the shiny buttons on his shirt. "Well, yeah." I shrug. "When we were younger, you used to smell sweet, like almonds or something, but now you smell like cologne. It's just . . . *different*."

I groan, covering my face again as his shoulders shake with laughter. Once through, he wraps his arms around me and hauls me into his chest, enveloping me in a tight embrace. My cheek settles against the soft cotton of his shirt, and I listen as he inhales deeply, then his voice reverberates in his chest. "You still smell the same."

Then, the warmth that is Dalton encompasses me. I grin into his shirt and circle my arms around his waist. He tightens his hold, firmly pressing his lips to the top of my head. "I've been waiting for this night for *five* long years."

His hand finds my hair and strokes it gently. "You're my home, Spence. I've never really had one, so I haven't been able to experience the feeling, but as I'm finally able to hold you after all this time, I get it. I now understand what it feels like to come *home*. I know you may not believe me, but I'm yours, completely. I have been for years now because when I gave myself to you, I gave all of me. You completely possess me, and if it takes time for you to trust that, to trust *me*, then that time is yours without question. Take all you need because I'm sure as hell not going anywhere."

I remain close, stubborn tears soaking into his shirt. His arm falls, closing me in as his heart pounds in my ear. I continue to listen, my own heart finding and matching his rhythm, growing stronger with each of its pulses.

I feel it.

I feel *him*.

Just as I always have.

And the sensation is so comforting, so soothing as it encompasses me, that I forget all the protective rules I conjured years ago and allow myself to bask in the comfort of his presence.

Everything Dalton did over the past *five* years, he did for me. To protect me. So he could be . . . *with me*.

And now he's back.

He's alive.

He's here.

And with his arms wrapped tightly around my body and as my heart continues to swell, I also know another thing for certain about Dalton Greer.

He's forgiven.

Chapter 34

Dalton

It's been four weeks since I kissed Spencer that night in her kitchen. The night I held her beautiful face in my hands, searching for any sign of my existence in her eyes. The night I tasted the salt of her tears and felt her tremble against my body.

The night I have constantly been reliving in my mind, patiently waiting for more.

Because it's also been four long weeks since I've felt her warm, full lips. Experienced her taste and the softness of her tongue as it connected with mine. I was weak that night. Selfish greed overruled my original intentions. My plan was to simply inform her of the details of the investigation, to warn her of her involvement, then get the hell out of there. But goddamn, the hurt in her eyes, the trepidation in her voice . . . All I could focus on was the fact that I fucking did that to her. *I'd* caused her unnecessary anguish. And there was nothing more I wanted in that moment than to take it all away. Over the years, she's convinced herself that I abandoned her. But I was never really gone. Because of that, my plan changed. She needed to see *me*. To hear *me*.

And as I spoke, I could feel my words chipping away at her strategically placed walls. With each new revelation, her anger lessened and her insecurity diminished. By the end, we were just Spencer and Dalton, standing alone in her kitchen while silently allowing the presence of the other to heal past wounds. I held her for hours after that, and she clung to me just as tightly, both of us refusing to let go for fear the other would disappear. I know without a doubt, she forgave me in those moments.

But forgetting . . .

I see it in her eyes, her fear I will abandon her.

I feel it in her heart, her refusal to believe me. To trust me again.

It will take more than a few hours for the honesty of my words and the truth of my intentions to sink into her stubborn head. For her to realize I would never, ever leave her. Not fully.

I can't force that trust, nor can I force her to feel secure with my presence.

That will take time.

And because I promised her that, I will not kiss her again, not until she finally believes in me. In us. That will be her move to make when she's ready.

Four. Long. Weeks.

It's 2:30 a.m., and once again, I'm sitting in her parking lot, my Rubicon pointed right at her bedroom window.

Guarding her.

Protecting her as I always have. As I will always do, whether she realizes it or not.

I know Lawson's men are casing the building, but I don't fucking care. I'm bound by an intrinsic need that refuses to be satisfied unless I'm the one providing her security.

After a short meeting with Bates to update him on my progress with the expansion of Silas's territory, and after another unsuccessful attempt to acquire information about Silas's supplier, I crawled into my Jeep, put it in drive, and just drove. Unsurprisingly, Spencer was at the forefront of my mind the entire time.

I don't see her as much as I would like. I get an hour in at Krav Maga and maybe thirty minutes afterward while we spar. During class, knowing glances are traded, unnecessary touches are given, and my lingering stare often finds itself locked onto her gorgeous fucking mouth. That, it seems, cannot be helped.

But other than that, nothing about my routine as an outside observer has changed, with the exception of my nightly stakeouts outside Spencer's apartment. Visits in which I know I'm not being followed because I drive for hours before ending up right here. Although tonight, I'm closer than usual, since some fucker parked his Corolla in my favorite surveillance spot.

I'm leaning my seat back, getting comfortable, when her bedroom light turns on. I find comfort in the fact that she no longer needs it to sleep through the night.

Her slim figure passes the window, the outline of her body curling my fingers with the need to touch her. I scrub the palms of my hands against my thighs and continue to eye her bedroom.

After a couple seconds, a row of the blinds dips at the center. I scoot lower into my seat, then pull the bill of my cap down while lowering my chin. A couple seconds pass, and when I look back up at her room, the light is off.

A relieved breath passes through my lips. Everything around me is silent as I remain hidden in darkness. Only my breaths are heard . . .

Until someone pounds on the window next to my head.

"FUCK!"

My heart hammers, sending a massive rush of adrenaline coursing through my veins. I feel like Mia Wallace in *Pulp Fiction*, post intracardiac injection, when her body is catapulted off the floor.

I also feel like I'm about to pass out.

Wide-eyed, I turn to the side, greeted by the tear-filled laughter of Spencer Locke. Right outside my window, she's bent over, holding her waist and gasping for air through her obvious amusement. I scan her entire body, from the messy mound of blonde hair topping her head, to the tight pink tank top molded to her breasts, down to the tiniest shorts I've ever seen in my life. I quickly survey the parking lot to confirm no one has been alerted to our presence. Once that's done, we make eye contact and I press my finger to my lips, signaling her to be quiet. This just makes her laugh harder and much louder, so I'm forced to take things into my own hands.

I lower my cap as far as I can, then swiftly press my door open. Her body stills with the sound and her eyes widen when my booted feet hit the cement. She turns away and cocks her leg to run, but she's not fast enough. Before her bare foot hits the ground, I place my hands on her shoulders, twist her to face me, then scoop her onto my shoulder into a fireman's hold. She giggles as I carry her across the parking lot, and damn if a smile doesn't break across my face at her laughter. The sound transports me to a time when her beaming smile and contagious laughter were the only things I had to look forward to.

Honestly, they still are.

Once we're at the front door, I lean to open it, then deposit her safely onto her living room floor before closing the door behind me.

As I turn around, my attempt at a threatening glare is completely offset by the grin on my face. "I cannot believe you did that."

Her smile is just as wide, her eyes luminous. "I cannot believe you didn't see me coming. What kinda cop allows someone sneak clear up to their car window?"

I belt out a laugh. "I was busy not looking."

She smiles wider and shakes her head. "You are so busted. Don't you get tired of sitting out there every night?"

My fingers itch to touch her, so I force them into my pockets. "You knew? Why didn't you say anything?"

She shrugs. "I don't know. I kind of like having you out there. I sleep better knowing you're watching over me." Her voice is small with her admission.

I smile, pride fills my chest, and then I redirect my attention to her living room. "Where's Cassie?"

Spencer huffs. "Where do you think? She's with Grady again. I should punch your face for introducing them because I pretty much don't have a roommate anymore."

All humor is lost and my face draws tight. "What? No one has been here at night?"

She shakes her head.

"Please tell me you're using the alarm?"

Her laughter echoes through the air as she walks past me, heading directly to the white keypad and entering the code. "Of course."

I begin to release a breath, only for it to become lodged in my throat when she takes my hand. Our fingers intertwine naturally, as though my hand is merely an extension of hers. She says nothing, but tugs me behind her, leading us down the hall to her bedroom. Once inside, she releases her hold to flip on the light and close the door, then gestures to her desk chair. "Might as well come inside. I mean, I can't be much safer than that, right?"

She cocks her brow and I give in, finally allowing my eyes full perusal of her body. Her legs look fucking phenomenal, their length accentuated by the shorts—*or lack thereof*—and her arms are tanned and toned, most likely from repeated punches thrown in class. I scan her quickly as to not be noticed, but when my eyes land on hers, her bottom lip is drawn between her teeth and a hint of a smile curves her lips.

"Busted. Again."

I shrug innocently and she laughs while I take my designated seat. Far away from the bed. She plops down on the edge, drawing her legs to her chest. When she perches her chin on her knees and smiles back at me, the distance suddenly isn't near enough. A primal urge to push her back and settle my body into hers rushes my mind. Memories of the only night I was granted with her, of her hair fanned out underneath her bare shoulders, of the innocence in her big beautiful eyes as she stared back at me, of the extraordinary gift she so willingly offered . . .

I clear my thoughts and recline back in the chair, stretching my legs and crossing them at the ankle. Spencer curls her fingers over her toes, focusing on her hands.

"I've missed you. I just wanted to tell you that." Her eyes slowly slide upward, meeting mine. "I miss us."

My mouth curves downward in a saddened smile. "I know, Spence. Me too."

"Do you think that, maybe, you could sleep with me tonight?" The bridge of her nose creases as a pink blush stains the tops of her cheeks. She looks fucking adorable. "I mean, *by* me. Not like *with* me, with me."

Laughter bubbles through my nose, and I couldn't hide my smile even if I tried. Lifting my arm, I snag my cap and toss it to the side. A bright smile graces her face, and then she turns to crawl toward the head of her bed.

I grind down on my molars, fighting the urge to moan out loud when I spot the cheeks of her ass peeking out from underneath the shorts. Dragging a tense hand through my hair, I breathe in deeply, but continue to watch because, as usual, I can't tear my eyes away from her. I shake my head, then bend, untying my boots and removing them.

I rise and gesture to the lights. "You don't sleep with the light on anymore."

She nods, nestling into her sheets. "Yeah. Years ago, I used to lie in bed, thinking of you in the dark. I guess I just got used to it." The sadness in her eyes sears my heart like a branding iron. She smiles in spite of it as she pats the open space next to her. "So consider me cured of that unfortunate habit."

After shutting off the light, I make my way to the side of her bed, fully clothed as I kneel on the mattress. She scoots her body back until she's flush against the wall, then lifts the bedding, allowing me to slide in next to her. As soon as my back hits the sheets, my arm extends to the side and her head finds my chest. Love and Happiness wafts around me as I curl her snug into my body, not willing to put even an inch of distance between us. Her arm drapes across my chest and we both release a contented sigh.

Our chuckles echo in the still of the darkness, the only light in the room being that of the moon, its rays dim as they're cast through her blinds. Slowly, my eyes adjust, and I watch as she sets her chin on my chest, grinning back up at me.

"This is nice."

I reach forward and graze her cheek with the pad of my thumb. "It is."

"Your hair is so long. Do you hate it?"

I shake my head. "Nah, I'm used to it. The color and length and everything. The beard though, that will be the first thing to go."

"It's not so bad." Spencer lifts her hand to tug it gently. "I vote the contacts should be the first to go. I'm glad you don't have them in tonight."

"They're annoying. I hate wearing them."

Her eyes roam my face. "Yet you wear them anyway. For me."

I run my index finger down her nose. "There's nothing I *wouldn't* do for you."

Spencer gifts me another small smile, then releases her hold on my beard to thread her fingers through the length of my hair, brushing it tenderly. Once done, she rests her palm against the side of my face, her eyes glistening in the moonlight. "I'm sorry, Dalton. I was so angry at you, so furious for years, that I actually grew comforted by the feeling. I felt strengthened in it, and just when I finally thought I'd let you go, you magically reappeared out of nowhere, throwing my life completely off-kilter. I was terrified to believe what you were telling me, knowing that if I did and if I lost you again . . . God, Dalton—it would destroy me. There would be no coming back from that."

Her head moves back and forth, still resting on my chest. "I've never said thank you. For all you've done over the past five years. For setting your life aside to make sure that *I'm* safe. For putting it on hold while I went on with my own—or tried to anyway." She shrugs lightly. "I just, well . . . I should have said that a long time ago."

I mirror her gesture, sweeping my hand through her hair. "Spencer, I would have been angry too. I've never faulted you for that." The corner of my mouth lifts. "And you're welcome. But I didn't put my life on hold for you. You *are* my life. I've never known anything more certain, more sound than that. And it was that very certainty that kept me sane over these past five years."

I snag a tear falling from her eye, then run my knuckles down the soft skin of her cheek. Our gazes remain locked for seconds, maybe even minutes, before she presses up to place a tender kiss on my mouth. Her hair falls forward and she tucks a section behind her ear, another rogue tear disappearing in my beard. I make no attempt to deepen the kiss. As much as I want to lace my fingers into her hair and crush my mouth to hers, this is *her* time. Her acceptance of my words. The sealing of her faith in me by way of her lips.

Hours later, she finally finds the courage to say it.

After having a near panic attack when I wake, I find her standing on the front porch of her apartment. The sight of the rising sun reflecting on her face is one of such serenity, I forgo my lecture and silently step behind her. Placing my forearms on the rail beside her body, I cover her hands with mine, thumbing lightly over the onyx bracelet that still lines her wrist. Her scent fills the air, and I nestle my nose in the crook of her neck, inhale deeply, then raise my eyes to take in the sight in front of us.

Corals and bright pinks painting the skyline, we watch in silence. After the sun hovers in its entirety over the horizon, I whisper, "I thought sunsets were our thing."

She maintains her forward stare, but replies softly, "They are. But *this* sunrise right here, I needed to see."

Her nose skims my cheek as she turns to face me. I lean away, my eyes roaming her face, still mesmerized by her beauty in the early morning light.

"This sunrise is special. It's the dawn of *our* new day."

She leans in, places her lips sweetly on the corner of my mouth, then faces forward. Wrapping my arms around her shoulders, I pull her close, knowing I'll never again let her go.

Four. Long. Weeks.

Worth every fucking second.

Chapter 35 ✦

Spencer

"Cass. I'm going to Mom's. Want to go with me?" I shout, slipping on my black Chucks. When I stand, the hems of my jeans drag the floor and I grin goofily. They remind me of my youth, of being eighteen years old, and of the whirlwind experience of falling in love for the first time. Feeling much like I do now, years later, as I fall in love for a second time. With the same person.

We're not the same kids we once were. We've changed.

He's grown.

I've grown.

But I think that as we begin this journey together, finally on the *same* path, we'll adjust to the changes as we remold, evolving into a stronger version of what once was.

And because of that, I have made the decision to officially retire the FUDGE box today. I no longer need to keep that part of my life hidden, nor am I afraid of the pain the contents inside once represented.

Not anymore.

Cassie magically appears in my doorway, holding a spoonful of peanut butter. She points it in my direction, then inquires, "Across the street from *my* parents' house?" When I nod, both of her dark brows press together. "Oh hell, no. Mom found my diary from eighth grade when she was cleaning out my bedroom. I won't be going back over there . . . *ever.*"

She licks the spoon, then settles her hip against my door frame. "Do you think you can sneak in my window and grab it? There were some really inventive positions practiced with Pete Johnson noted in there." She waggles her eyebrows. I roll my eyes, but smile nonetheless.

"Your parents put an alarm on that window the summer of our senior year, remember?"

Her face dips downward, sadness claiming her features. While I locked myself in my room, mourning the loss of Dalton, Cassie went batshit crazy the summer after Rat died. I guess the realization that we weren't immortal hit her pretty hard. Her parents' last-ditch attempt to control her behavior was to put a security system in their house, including her infamous window, and set the code without telling Cassie. It didn't go over well, needless to say, which led to Cassie pretty much never coming home that summer. Looking back, I feel bad that I wasn't there for her more during that time. But honestly, I was so far gone, there was no way I could have led her out of her darkness when I was lost in my own.

But eventually, we both found our way. *I think.*

Sometimes I wonder if there's something she isn't telling me. I felt it then, when we were younger, the unspoken anger accompanying her need to rebel and lash out. To escape. *Literally.* Like, through her window.

But no matter the angle of conversation, to this day, I've never been able to uncover the reasoning behind it. I just pray that one day, when and if she's ready, she'll come to me, need me. I know better than anyone, you can't force someone to face demons until *they're* ready.

Snapping back to the present, her far-off stare finds focus on me. "Yeah, I forgot. Man," she whines, "that sucks. I was gearing up for the big night with Grady."

She smiles at the mention of his name, and I try to banish the image of them having sex from of my mind.

Yet still, I ask. "You haven't had sex with Grady yet?"

She shakes her head. "No, just good ol' fooling around and spooning. Nothing else . . . *yet.*"

"Good." I grin.

Cassie winks then asks, "You?"

"With Grady? Ew." I mock vomit.

Cassie narrows her eyes. "No, hooker. With Dalton."

I smile, still somewhat stupefied when I hear his name come out of her mouth. According to Dalton, the night we figured out his identity, Cassie asked Grady about it. He explained that he was a cop and Dalton was helping him with a case, but that's all he told her. It seems to have satisfied her curiosity because she hasn't asked me anything since that night. I didn't really expect her to though. She's a just-roll-with-it kind of girl.

"No, not yet," I reply.

She licks the spoon free of peanut butter before announcing, "He owes you another birthday night. Like, complete redo."

I laugh at her protective tone, but the idea plants itself in my mind, taking a firm root. Grabbing my purse off my desk, I inquire, "Are you going to be at Grady's tonight?"

An impish smile crosses Cassie's face. "Why yes, yes, I am. Looks like we're both doing the dirty."

Laughter escapes me and I shake my head, passing her to enter the hall. Just as I hit the living room, she shouts in a motherly manner, "Make sure he wraps it before he taps it. Safety first."

I shut the front door behind me, full grin on my face.

Twenty minutes later, I arrive at Mom's house, pulling in behind a familiar black Chevy Impala. I stall, nibbling my lip while debating if I should go inside. For a couple reasons. One, with all this sex talk, I'm freakishly paranoid I'll walk in on something that can never be unseen, therefore scarring me for life. And two, I've been avoiding Kirk due to the fact that I know details about his investigation that he specifically does *not* want me to know. I'm not upset with him for keeping it from me. I understand he did it with the best of intentions, but I fear one look at my face and he'll *know*.

I mean, come on. He's a detective. Reading people is what he does.

While I debate internally, the decision is soon made for me when Mom opens the front door and waves at me from the porch. I grin, memories of time spent on that porch with Dalton crossing my mind. I allow them to run their course, then go to meet my mother.

Still wearing the same pink terry cloth robe, she's fresh from the shower, her brown hair secured in a towel wrapped around her head. As I approach the door, the smell of garlic and basil saturates the air and I inhale it, still smiling.

Mom glances over her shoulder. "Kirk's cooking an early dinner if you would like to join us."

I still can't get over the transition of my mother over the past few years. She looks happy. I know she still loves Jim, but I'm also certain she's in love with Kirk Lawson. A love that shines from the depths of her soul.

I reach out and wrap her in my arms.

Taken aback, she laughs. "What's all this?"

"Nothing. It's just good to see you happy. And no, I can't stay. I have some things to do today. I just stopped by to grab something from my room, if you don't mind?"

Releasing me, she shakes her head. "Of course not. Go ahead."

I nod, then enter the house. Kirk stands in the kitchen. Low-waisted jeans and a gray V-neck T-shirt covering his muscular chest, I watch him stir whatever he's cooking in the skillet below him. His brown hair has grown longer of late and is messy as it sticks out every which way from the top of his head.

He looks like a teenager. It makes me smile.

His kind brown eyes break from the stove to meet mine, and the familiar creases at the sides deepen as he grins back. "Hey, kiddo. Are you eating with us? There's plenty to go around."

I shake my head and throw a thumb over my shoulder. "I'm just here to grab something. I won't be long."

"I'll pack some up for you and Cassie then. Lord only knows what you two have been surviving on since you moved in together."

I grin. "Peanut butter, of course." His eyes widen and I let out a laugh. "Kidding, Kirk."

Shaking his head, he returns his attention to the skillet. I join my mom in the hallway and together, we walk to my old bedroom. Once inside, she plops on my bed while I head to my closet.

"How's school?" she asks, smoothing her hand over my old purple comforter.

"It's good. Mainly more coursework this year. Next year is the dreaded dissertation."

She remains quiet and I twist to face her. "What is it?"

"I wish you could have stayed at Wilmington. I know the cost is more affordable here, but I also know what a hard time you had in Fuller before you left. I just wish I could—"

I interrupt her with a flash of my hand. "Mom, no. I needed to do this for myself. I'm twenty-two, almost twenty-three years old. I needed to come back here." I smile. "I'm *glad* I came back here. It was time."

And boy, was it. To know I landed back in Fuller the same time as Dalton gives me the feeling that maybe, just maybe, this is the way things were supposed to happen all along. And I find comfort in that. Our time wasn't wasted but utilized until we could grasp things we couldn't understand at eighteen.

Relief relaxes her expression as she smiles back. "My little girl, all grown up. I'm so proud of you, Spencer."

"Aw, thanks, Mom." I grin, then turn my focus back to the closet. Once my eyes land on the box, I face her in preparation. "Okay, I need you to remember how grown up I am in about two seconds. Can you do that for me?"

You could hear a pin drop in the silence I'm given in response. With both hands, I heave the FUDGE box out of my closet. Mom's features tighten as I hold it close to my body, then she eyes it like a diseased rodent when I set it beside her.

"I need to retire the box, that's all. And there are some things I would actually like to keep in here."

Her face softens, and once I feel she's not going to call Kirk in here to have me arrested for my own safety, I curl my fingers over the top and lift.

At that exact moment, Kirk pokes his head in my doorway. I tear my eyes away from the box, met with his saddened stare as he speaks. "Spencer, Dalton loved you very much. You know that, right?"

The genuineness of his tone warms my heart. His gaze falls to my hands and I curb my smile, knowing he's trying to reassure me. Trying to convey what he *can't* say. Trying to keep me holding onto a love I believe dead, because he *knows* it's alive and that Dalton is coming for me.

And for that, I love him. I really do.

I drop the lid onto the bed, then peek inside, slowly reaching forward to press the release button on the compass.

And as it flies open, what I see sends a spasm throughout my chest. My eyes widen, taking in the contents of the box, and I swallow deeply.

Love is a stubborn thing it seems, both in life and in death.

Because now, *right now*, I finally get it.

What Jim has been trying to tell me all this time.

But just like the compass, my heart has been closed. I was unable to see, blinded by my fury.

Until this very moment.

Now, with both my heart and eyes wide open, it all seems so clear as I look at the compass . . .

The needle is pointing in the direction of Dalton.

Chapter 36

Dalton

"It's all there." My voice is low as I set the aluminum briefcase on the cement floor of the familiar warehouse.

Bates bends to retrieve it, his shoulder-length blond hair falling over his shoulder. I privately note how the fabric of his blazer pulls against the buttons with the movement. What is it with Silas and these fucking meatheads?

His lifeless eyes meet mine when he rises. "I trust you."

I smile inwardly. Trust. The word has no place in this business.

The money in his grip was supplied by Fuller PD, and the drugs I "sold" now reside safely in their evidence locker for purposes of tracking the supplier.

I survey the room around me, my chest heavy. Rat is everywhere, his presence at the forefront of every memory looping my mind. Our first time in this very warehouse, blown away by the piles of uncut heroin and coke stashed in cargo containers. Our reactions after our first "errand," when we broke into William O'Malley's office and stole the twenty large owed to Silas. We were heftily rewarded with wads of cash, giddy with the realization of being able to afford things we'd only dreamed of buying. Which, at that age, were stupid-ass PlayStations.

My stomach rolls.

We were just kids, trying to make it in a world that didn't give two shits whether we lived or died. And we were preyed upon for that very reason.

I force myself to focus on the task at hand instead of taking a fucking Uzi to this entire room. I crack my neck, then state, "Let me know when you get another shipment. Langston and Rockdale are running low."

A smile spreads across Bates's face. "I knew I was doing the right thing bringing you on board. That's another 500K each, easy."

"Any idea how long that's going to take? They're getting antsy."

"We've got one hundred kilos set to come in from—"

"Well, well, well . . ." a voice bellows from across the room. A very familiar voice. "If it isn't the infamous Liam Kelley."

Adrenaline spikes, pricking my entire body. I school my features, praying the jolt of shock ricocheting around my chest isn't on clear display, then wheel myself toward his emerging presence.

Silas enters the warehouse in all his self-deluded magnificence, his Gucci loafers echoing as his strides hit the floor. Eyes narrowed, he trains them on Bates in clear warning. A look I know all too well.

Silas slices his stare to me. The olive-green button-down highlights the prominence of anger brewing in his green eyes, but the ease of his smile contradicts it.

He extends his arm in greeting. "Silas Kincaid. I apologize I haven't been able to properly introduce myself since you migrated over from . . ."

"Langston."

"Ah, yes. Langston. A blossoming community it seems. Your sales are increasing exponentially."

I dip my head but maintain my stare, placating his tendency to size up a person by their displays of weakness. His smile widens with my refusal to break eye contact. Several seconds pass before he finally breaks the silence.

"Well, Liam. It's nice to finally meet you. We're glad to have you on board. If you need anything, please don't hesitate to give Bates here a call. He relays all information to me." His hold on my hand tightens and I firmly clench my grip in return.

He smiles grandly before finally releasing me, then addresses Bates with a stern nod. "Office."

"Yes, sir." Bates dips his head in my direction before following Silas.

As soon as I'm in my Jeep, I grab my cell from the center console, shifting into drive.

"Greer." Lawson's voice is muffled. I look down at the clock and cringe. 12:45 a.m.

"Just met with Silas." I veer right without having to think. I drive the same route every night before ending up at Spencer's.

More shuffling. "What? What did he say?"

"Nothing. Don't get your hopes up. His number two almost spilled some very valuable intel, but Silas cut him off, obviously having listened to our entire exchange before entering the conversation."

Lawson sighs. "Well, that's promising. Maybe he's starting to let his guard down."

Maybe. Or maybe he had a particular reason for showing up when he did. As much as I would prefer the former, my gut tells me it was very much the latter.

"Maybe," I offer.

He releases another long breath. "Good. You did good, Greer. I'm proud of you, kid."

As soon as the words leave his mouth, my throat clogs with foreign emotion. Pride, maybe?

I have no idea.

All I know is, once spoken, his words open an emotional floodgate of feelings I can't deal with right now. So instead of dealing, I drive.

Hours later, I find myself parked at Spencer's, staring up at her dimly lit window.

Weeks ago, I announced to Lawson's patrol unit that I would be making regular visits and that Lawson was aware of this contact, thereby nullifying their need to mention my comings and goings to him. Their response? They grinned like buffoons, while muttering jabs about "young love." I'm pretty sure they know Lawson doesn't know a goddamn thing about my visits to Spencer, and I really don't care, as long as they continue watching her apartment like hawks and keep my visits to themselves.

After removing my contacts, I secure my hair at the nape of my neck, then step out of the car. My feet shuffle, impatient as they carry me to her front door. Relieved to find it locked, I knock gently, and another wave of relief passes with the beeping of the security keypad next to the door. The locks sound, the handle turns, then the door flies open, along with my mouth.

Spencer's silhouette is traced with candlelight, the sight alone seizing my lungs. She's wearing a white nightie, the top lined in pearl beading that covers her breasts, the two sections held together with a simple bow that my fingers ache to tug and release. Her blonde hair is loose, sexy as it curls over the white straps on her shoulders. And as my gaze drifts downward, I find the rest of the gown is completely sheer, falling loosely to her midthighs, with a matching set of white lace panties displayed through the fabric.

I stand there, completely amazed at the celestial being standing in front of me.

An angel.

My angel.

"Hi." Spencer's voice is shy, wavering slightly when she speaks. She shifts her weight, then gestures for me to enter the apartment.

"What is this?" I ask, drawn in by the incandescent light.

The door shuts behind me, but my eyes remain captivated by the dancing flames that cover every inch of the room. I take them all in before I notice the picnic basket in the center of the room atop a blanket. I chuckle, the sides of my mouth tipping toward the ceiling as the pieces begin to fall together.

A small hand takes hold of mine. I look down at Spencer, struck by her bright smile when she looks toward the center of the room. She shrugs, then meets my stare.

"I need a birthday redo."

"It's not your birthday. That's like two weeks away."

Spencer laughs lightly, her eyes filling with humor. "It's meta-phorical, Dalton."

She tugs my hand and directs me to the blanket, but my eyes remain glued to the line of her body in front of me as she walks. The soft angles of her shoulders, her hair blowing gently with the breeze generated by her movement, the *V* of those white lace panties peeking at me, her long legs carrying her across the room, her bare feet padding the floor . . .

Everything about her, her very essence, robs me of my breath.

And as I begin to come out of my stupor, it sure as hell stirs my cock, its hardening painful with my need to touch her. To *feel* her.

She perches herself on bent knees, then pats the area beside her. I willingly comply, lowering myself to the floor and leaning back against the couch, my eyes never leaving hers. Leaning forward, she removes my boots then sits back on her ankles, nervously tucking a section of loose curls behind her ear.

"I, uh . . . yeah. So, I think it's time for a redo." She pins me with her stare. "For the longest time, that night haunted me. A night full of beauty, then tarnished by the loss of you hours later. I just . . . if we're going to do this, if this is a new beginning for us, I wanted . . . I wanted the slate wiped clean. I want a new memory, with you."

As she sits on her knees, her eyes break from mine when she leans toward the picnic basket and begins to draw out the same contents as before. Daisies in a glass vase, plastic champagne flutes and cheap champagne, napkins and plasticware, paper plates, a huge tub of . . . *mac and cheese.*

I grin as she eyes the container. "Sorry, I didn't have a Crock-Pot. And this is Kraft, not homemade." She crinkles her nose and my heart nearly implodes.

I shake my head, overwhelmed. "Spence, you didn't have to do all of this. Not for me."

Her eyes cut to mine, then she repeats my familiar words. "There's nothing I *wouldn't* do for you." She reaches to take my hand. "I want to give you this. Give you me, again. To share this experience with you knowing that the last five years, no matter how difficult, led us right back to this moment because we were meant to be. Forever and as one. Always."

I'm forced to swallow because she's all I've ever wanted in this world, and to know I had her just barely within my grasp before she was ripped away . . .

There's nothing I want to do more than to reclaim her.

She's mine.

Interlacing our fingers, I pull her gently onto my lap. Her long legs straddle my hips, and her blonde tresses cascade over her shoulders as she leans to tug the elastic band from my hair.

It falls loosely, and she threads her fingers into the sides, pressing the strands away before gently touching her lips to my forehead. Then my temple. The top of my cheek. The tip of my nose. And after sweeping her mouth lightly across mine, she performs the same ritual on the other side of my face.

My hands disappear under the fabric of her gown, my palms flat against the warm, smooth skin of her thighs. I skim the sensitive skin with my thumbs, trailing upward, stopping only when I reach the tops of her legs. As soon as I hit lace, I leisurely trace the lines of her panties with the tips of my fingers. Her breathing quickens, heated as it fans my face. She lowers her head, and with feather-like movements, gently brushes her lips across mine.

My fingers continue their plight, trekking upward along her stomach, and she smiles against my mouth when her muscles quiver under my touch. I grin back, then use her already parted mouth to my advantage as I plunder it. She moans, tilting her hips and pressing her core into my throbbing erection.

I hiss with the movement. "God, Spencer. You feel so"—she slides her hips downward and I finish on a groan—"good."

After a deep sweep of her tongue, she leans away just as my fingers find the lining under her breasts. My eyes rake over her entire body, completely vulnerable and waiting for my touch. Slowly, I remove my hands from under the sheer fabric, allowing my fingers to linger on her soft skin before pressing her hair over her shoulder. With my view no longer obscured, all I can do is stare at her breathtaking beauty while she strokes me with her movements.

Her hips continue to rock back and forth, eyes half-lidded and lips parted. "I need to feel you, Dalton. Please, I need this. I need you."

Inhaling deeply, I reach forward to touch the top of her throat. Her head falls back and I drag my fingers down the skin of her neck, then splay them across her collarbone, reveling in the feel of her body as my hand continues downward. Finding the bow between her breasts, I pinch the ribbon, then tug it slowly, deliberately. The two halves fall open, the center line of her body completely bared to me as the material clings to the tops of her breasts. I gently trace along the curve of her inner breast then move down her stomach until my fingers find the hemline of her panties. Tenderly, I stroke the skin just above, watching her breasts bounce with her movements. Filled with need, I lift my hands to cup those breasts, skimming along the hardened peaks with the pad of my thumb.

"Spence . . ." I need to get this out before we go any further. After five years without sex, I'm not accustomed to carrying around protection.

Knowingly, she silences me with a shake of her head. A tinge of sadness streaks her eyes before she reaches forward and presses her palm against my cheek. Her tone is reassuring. "There was only Brandon, and we always used a condom. We didn't need to . . . I mean, I'm still on birth control, but I needed to have that barrier between us. I never gave him all of me. Ever."

With her admission, my throat clogs with emotion for the second time tonight. But this one I know. Relief floods me and I thrust my fingers into her hair, weaving them deeply as I pull her to me and crash her mouth against mine. Our mouths seal, our breaths become one, and our tongues knit together in desperation, trying to make up for every second lost between us.

I tighten my grip and Spencer breaks the kiss, arching her neck and moaning deeply while she rocks forward, riding me harder.

"Fuck . . ." is the last thing I'm able to mutter before all control is lost.

Releasing my hold, I grab her hips, my fingers biting into the flesh of her ass. They dig deeply as I guide her in stroking me. With her heat emanating through my jeans, I continue to unabashedly push and pull her body, syncing our rhythm with each of my upward thrusts. Her head lolls forward and her hands find my chest. Fisting my shirt in both hands, she begins to drive her hips with such force, with such need, that the only thing I can concentrate on is filling her hunger.

Pressing my body off the couch, I clear the birthday contents with one firm swipe of my arm, then push her back onto the blanket. The nightie falls free from her breasts, lining the sides of her body.

The sight is fucking magnificent.

Rising to my knees, I lean forward to peel the straps over her shoulders. She lifts her arms to assist in their removal, but I leave the gown under her body as I sit back on my heels, hook my fingers into the sides of her panties, and tear them down her legs. Yanking my jeans open with one hand, I use the other to fist the back of my shirt and pull it over my head.

As my gaze falls to hers, she grins, rolls toward the basket, and pulls out . . . a Wonder Woman sleeping bag.

I shake my head. "You're killing me. I think I just lost my erection."

Her laughter fills my ears and the sound resurrects my soul. I can't fight the smile that breaks across my face as I grab the stupid sleeping bag, still shaking my head, and cover my bare back with it before lowering my body on top of her.

As soon as I slide my naked chest against hers, my eyes are forced shut.

"Your erection feels just fine to me." She giggles.

"Yeah, well, it's killing me," I reply, finally opening my eyes.

Her smile steals my breath as she places her hands on the sides of my waist. "I can totally help you with that."

Sliding her thumbs into my waistband, she presses down on my boxers, taking the jeans along with them as they drag over my hips. My cock springs free and I groan with relief before my eyes fall to the lip held between her teeth. Greedy for a taste, I lower my head and suck that lip into my mouth, flicking it with my tongue and nipping it lightly.

Her moan fills the air and vibrates against my chest before she hooks my jeans with her foot and continues with their removal. Once they're lodged at my ankles, I kick them off then realign my body with hers.

Placing my elbows on either side of her head, I cup her face with my hands and gently stroke her cheeks with my thumbs. My eyes lock with hers as I find her entrance. The heat from her core coats the tip of my cock, the sensation launching waves of fiery pulses straight to my balls. I watch intently as she closes her eyes with the shudder of her body against mine. Once she reopens them, her hooded gaze sets me on fire, the same way it did years ago. It's as though no time has passed between us.

She lifts her hand and grazes my cheek. "I love you, Dalton. It's always been you. *Only* you."

I swipe her hair away from her face and narrow my eyes on her stare. "I love you too, Spence. You have always been, and will always be *everything* to me."

I focus my gaze at her mouth, which curves into a beautiful smile, before meeting her eyes once again. In complete awe, I shake my head. "So. Fucking. Beautiful."

As soon as the last word leaves my lips, I slide into her body, taking my time as I fill her. Instead of pain, her face exhibits only pleasure. She draws her tongue across her lips. Her eyes are heavy, laden with desire as I continue to stroke inside her. She groans, her muscles clenching tightly around me, and when I bury myself in her, they begin to quiver with my movements. I hook my arm underneath her lower back and her legs circle my waist, pulling our bodies flush as we grind against each other. I know I won't last long, not after my lengthy celibacy, but this isn't about me. This is about making a new memory for her, and God willing, it's going to be one of the best of her life, so I take my time and pay attention to her reactions.

The way her muscles respond to the strokes I deliver.

The way she moans with each circle of my hips, and the way her fingers tear at the blanket, searching for something to grasp.

I trace her skin, caress her thighs, nip her breasts, thumb her clit . . . all deliberate touches made to drive her to the brink. I pump in and out of her body, and when I find that one spot, the spot that has her clawing my skin and screaming my name, I drive harder. Pump faster. Until finally, her walls pulse, each tense wave caressing my cock with her release.

My own release is imminent, drawn out by her body's greedy demand. And she welcomes it with her muscles still grasping me, drinking me, completely consuming me until I have nothing left to give. Strength is drawn from my muscles and I collapse on top of her, our sweat-lined bodies sliding against each other with our heavy breaths. I will myself to lift my head, and I'm met with the beautiful sight of a satiated grin framed by swollen lips. I cover them with my mouth, my tongue connecting with hers, and I sweep in deeply to devour as much of her taste as I can.

After one more greedy pass into her mouth, I give her a tender peck on the lips, then fall off her body and roll onto my back. We lay side by side, panting as we stare at the ceiling with Wonder Woman clinging to our bodies. I twist my neck and watch her chest rising rapidly, satisfied with her heavy breaths. She turns to me with a wide smile on her face and her eyes bright.

"All that was missing were the stars."

"And Spiderman," I remind her.

She giggles then rolls her naked body to face me. "I have something I want to show you."

My mind begins to conjure up all sorts of things I want her to *show* me, but I keep them to myself.

As though reading my thoughts, she laughs, then covers herself with the sleeping bag before sitting upright and leaning over to snag the basket. I grab my boxers from my jeans and slip them on while she sets a rectangular object covered with a small sheet of fabric in front of me. I watch as she pinches the cloth between her fingers.

"Ready?" she asks, excitement radiating from her body.

I nod with a half-grin on my face.

Slowly, Spencer lifts the sheet, and once it's removed, I angle my neck for a better look. Held within a clear display box are two items. One of the objects I recognize, the other I don't. She clears her throat and places her hand on the top.

"I had another box where I stored stuff from my eighteenth birthday. Actually, not everything. Cassie gave me the picture hanging on the wall in my room. But everything else I put inside a box, because I couldn't look at them. The memories were just too much for me then. But sometimes, randomly through the years, I would pull it out of my closet and look inside as a form of punishment, I think."

My mouth opens, but she shakes her head to silence me. "I was angry. So angry. At you, at myself, at life, everything. And it was that anger that kept me from seeing what was right in front of my face." Her finger points toward the compass. "My mom gave me this that day. It's one of Jim's heirlooms."

I narrow my eyes to get a better look at the compass. I feel like I know Jim from what Spencer has told me throughout the years. He was an incredible man and she loved him very much.

"She gave it to me so that if I ever lost my way, it would serve as a reminder of the important things in life. A way of guiding me back onto my path. And I think this was Jim's way of trying to help me since you left." Her blue eyes glisten as they find mine. "I lost my way when you left, Dalton. But this compass, it's telling me right where I needed to be. Where my path lies, and it lies with you. Look."

I lean toward the front of the case, where the magnetic heart I gave her resides on a stand. Right next to it, the open compass sits in a black velvet box with the needle pointing directly at it. Spencer wipes the moisture from her eyes and I take her hand into mine.

"The magnets," I breathe.

She smiles, then scans my face. "It *might* be the magnets. But it's *always* been you, Dalton. Neither time nor distance could break the connection we share. We're two souls joined. I lost faith in that, lost faith in you. But you"—she shakes her head—"you never did."

I touch my mouth tenderly to hers. "I never did and I never will."

Her lips smile against mine as I wrap my arm around her shoulder, then pull her into my body. With candlelight flickering around us, she nestles her head into my neck and we continue to stare in silence at the box.

After a few minutes, she whispers, "I love you."

My cheek presses into her hair with my smile. "I love you too, *Pencil*."

Her giggle hits my ears and I grin wider. I hold her close, our bond fully solidified as we are rejoined. We are one—in heart and soul, in body and mind.

Yet, as though waiting for the perfect time to ruin this moment for me, for *us*, the dealings at the warehouse earlier tonight invade my mind. The constant heavy feeling draws tight in my stomach. Something is coming, and soon. Unbeknownst to Spencer, as her contented breaths fill my ears and the happiness in her heart warms mine, it's then and there I make my vow.

Nothing will *ever* come between us again.

Not even Silas Kincaid.

I will make fucking sure of it.

Chapter 37

Silas

"Yes, thank you for the information." My voice is clipped as I end the call.

Leaning forward, I hit the "Speak" button. "Bates."

His thick voice reverberates through the speaker. "Yes, boss?"

"Have you transferred the last of my money to the accounts specified?"

"It was done earlier this morning."

Hitting "Speak" again, I inquire, "And my passport?"

"All set."

I nod to myself, then press the button one last time. "I need you in my office."

"On my way."

I ease back into my chair, lost in thought about my long-lost prodigal son.

About his chosen alliances when *he became a fucking traitor*.

All I asked for, in return for my provisions, was loyalty. Loyalty to my organization and me.

From the age of twelve, I made sure he was provided for, that he was protected and had some semblance of family. And this is how he fucking repaid me?

Five years ago I lost him, but he's not the only thing I lost.

The prominence of my organization ceased to exist that very night. Even though I had Juan *silenced* immediately upon his arrival in prison, it didn't matter. My word was void, and fear spread like wildfire that he had leaked information to the authorities. My suppliers and distributors vanished. All respect for me was gone.

The people around me scattered like a struck ant pile. No loyalty whatsoever—spineless motherfuckers.

Sure I continued to sell, but nothing like before.

Then Bates brings forth a promising prospect. One whose reach would provide me the money and respect I deserve with distribution in new, uncharted areas. So imagine my surprise when this prospect arrived in Fuller and I discovered his true identity.

It's amazing what money can buy, and as always, Fuller PD did not disappoint. I know every move he and his "mentor" have made since he's been back. Well informed in advance, I knew exactly how to throw them off my trail. They think they have me, but they don't.

They're not even fucking close.

I've outmaneuvered them plain and simple. The drugs they keep for investigation have absolutely no tie to me. All their precious recordings have been deleted, all marks linking me to any part of this business have been erased, and any leads to my suppliers are false.

I've merely been toying with them until everything was in line. Time was necessary to establish accounts, transfer funds, make new connections—everything needed to make sure I'm able to disappear without a trace.

Not that I wasn't planning on leaving eventually. His presence merely expedited the process. And it also accelerated my plan to execute the girl. Her death for the destruction of my now-crumbled empire was the last thing I planned before leaving Fuller. Whether he was dead or alive, it was going to be done, but knowing he will be there to watch her lifeless body as it hits the ground is pure joy. *Vindication.* The scales of justice must be balanced.

My sweet revenge.

My final *gift* to him before I depart.

I glance at the calendar on my desk and grin. Five years to the day. Almost poetic in nature.

I'm fully immersed in these thoughts as Bates finally enters my office. As soon as he turns to shut the door behind him, I clear my head and focus on the task at hand.

Bates and his eagerness to trust. To be part of something. To have the foundation of family. I preyed on that need at one time, but now it's become a liability. This isn't a business for the weak or lighthearted. This isn't the business for someone like him. And it sure as hell isn't the business for someone who brings a fucking traitor into *my* organization.

So with his back facing me, I relieve him of his duty as my bullet is lodged in the back of his skull.

Grabbing the stocked satchel under my desk, I head toward the door, nudging his limp body to the side as I open it.

Today is the day.

Then I'm gone.

Chapter 38

Spencer

THROB.
  THROB.
  THROB.
  CRINGE.

Waves of pain radiate from the back of my skull and strike the backs of my eyelids as I try to gather my bearings. I attempt to pry my eyes open, but they slam back shut. My mouth remains closed, no matter how much effort I put into trying to cry out. My hands and legs don't seem to want to work either.

"Well, hello there, Ms. Locke. How nice of you to join me."

A deep, malicious tone alerts me to someone's presence on my right. My chin remains attached to my chest when I try to twist my neck to see, so I give up trying to maneuver my failing body and just settle for having to listen to what's around me.

As footsteps begin to echo, I know my captor is on the move. I also know who it is, even without having the benefit of sight.

The infamous Silas Kincaid.

Dalton knew this was coming. He's become increasingly agitated and gradually more paranoid over the past couple weeks. And I have a feeling he's going to be super pissed that I decided to make a run to my car in the middle of the night. While he was sleeping.

Sure, Krav Maga is great when you have the chance to use it. But when you don't even see your assailant before he clocks you in the back of the head and knocks you out, it's kind of useless. It also helps when you have active use of your limbs.

Probably something we should have considered during my training.

The increasing volume of his steps tells me Silas is approaching. I hear slight shuffling, then his voice right next to my ear. "I gave you a little something to sleep until the festivities begin. Don't fight it. Soon enough, we'll be at our destination and I'll make sure you're wide awake so you don't miss anything."

As soon as the words fill my ears, I feel myself begin to slip out of consciousness. I try to fight it, to hang on, but it's pointless. Helpless against the drugs in my system, I slowly begin to drift back to sleep, but not before I feel it.

The burst of heat as it detonates within my chest.

The explosion of unadulterated fury.

Anyone else in this situation would be terrified, but for some reason I'm not in the least. In fact, if I could smile, I would. Because that explosion, that insatiable burn for revenge, that's not me.

That's Dalton Greer.

And he's on his way.

Chapter 39

Dalton

"FUUUUUUUUUCK!!!!!"

I pinch the bill of my cap as hard as I can between my hands and grind down on my molars, trying to calm the rage that I've kept contained for so long. But this—this overrides anything I learned during anger management and therapy sessions.

The fucking patrol unit isn't here.

Spencer. Is. Not. Here.

I should have been standing guard at her goddamn door instead of sleeping in her bed. I should have fucking *known* it would be tonight.

April 23.

Her birthday.

Five years to the day.

That motherfucker has her, and I know exactly where he is.

Whirling around, I sprint to my Rubicon while grabbing my phone out of my pocket. Clenching it with all my strength, my hand quakes as I try to control my anger. I stop right outside my door and close my eyes while attempting to swallow the knot forming in my throat.

She's mine.

The words re-etch themselves in my heart, deepening my fury.

Clearing my throat, I hit send, then immediately hear, "Greer."

"Where's your fucking unit?"

Losing control, my voice is frantic as I fling open my door and fall into my Jeep. With the phone cradled against my shoulder, I lean to the side and grab my Glock G43 and a full clip. Slamming it into place, I cock it and slide it into the back of my waistband. I curl my fingers tightly around the steering wheel, squeezing until I have no more feeling in my hands. The rage is boiling, but I know I need to maintain control.

"My unit? What the fuck are you talking about, Greer?" I can hear the anxiety rising in Lawson's tone. He knows exactly what I'm talking about without me even having to say it. The fact that I can hear him getting dressed attests to that.

"No one is outside Spencer's apartment and she's fucking gone. Your people are nowhere to be found."

Lawson mumbles something unintelligible over the line before clearly stating, "Murphy and Johnson were on rotation tonight."

Fucking *Murphy*. I *knew* something was off about him.

"Yeah, well, they're not here now." Flipping the key, I rev the engine and throw the Jeep into reverse. "The woods. Silas has her in the woods. I know it. Grab whoever you can for backup. I'm heading over there now."

Pressing the gas pedal to the floor, my tires protest before finally finding traction.

"Greer. You have the shot; take it. Take him fucking *out*. And Spencer—"

"On my life, Lawson, nothing will happen to her."

A heavy breath hits the airwaves. "I know. Just make sure nothing happens to *you* either. This is what you've been waiting for; you only get one chance. Keep a leash on that anger of yours, kid. It makes you irrational, and you need to have a clear head or you'll miss your opportunity to do this the right way."

So don't go on a killing spree without just cause. Got it. But I sure as fuck can't guarantee anything, so my only response is, "See ya there."

Pulling onto the main highway, my knuckles are completely white as I continue to clench the wheel with every bit of strength I have.

"Be safe, kid."

I disconnect the call.

Due to my speed, mere minutes pass before I turn onto the road that led me to the place where this crusade began five years ago. This will be the last drive I will ever take on it.

Because tonight I *will* finish this.

I follow the path until I see the brake lights of a very familiar Mercedes AMG CLA45, their red hue giving the appearance of demonic eyes watching my approach. *With Satan himself standing outside.*

It doesn't escape me that this car hasn't been in use for a very long time, and I'd be a fool to think anything other than its presence on this particular night is intended to make a statement.

Well, I hear him. Loud and clear.

My Jeep skids to a halt next to his car before I launch myself onto the ground. With the clearing now illuminated with both sets of headlights, it's impossible not to see Silas Kincaid standing behind an extremely drugged Spencer, his green eyes narrowed on my face. She's wearing the same tank top and shorts as she was earlier tonight, and I'm relieved to see both are intact with no signs of tearing from the use of force.

Spencer's head lolls to the front, just like Rat's sister's did that night, and I breathe deeply to restrain my anger. The edges of my vision blacken, and a familiar fury begins to ravage my entire body. My knuckles pop in succession as I clench my fists, and my fingernails dig into the skin of my palm, but there is no pain. I feel nothing other than the need for vengeance as it ignites, launching its flames clear down to the marrow of my bones.

Instinctively, I crack my neck as I approach. "Subtlety has never really been your forte, 'Caid."

"Nor yours, boy." His lips break into a satisfied smile.

"I'm not your boy."

His brows hit the night sky as his mouth dips in the opposite direction. "You were, though. At one time, you were mine, and in return I gave you everything you needed. Yet this betrayal is how you repay me?"

My jaw tightens at his words, but I force composure into my voice. "I took what was given to survive. And yes, you provided that, but at what price?" I shake my head. "Not a price I was willing to pay. Not for Rat's life, and sure as hell not for hers."

At that, Silas tugs the hair at the back of Spencer's head, and her neck bends as though she has absolutely no control. My teeth grind down so hard I'm sure one, or all, of my molars just cracked in two. My nostrils flare. I'm barely containing the red-hot rage that burns below my skin.

I don't know what the fuck he gave her, but she's not well. Her head falls back way too easily, and her speech is slurred as she tries to form words.

Silas grins down at her before looking back at me. "So you would give your life for her?"

"I would," I respond.

His eyes dart down to her blonde hair within his grasp before he states, "I never would have believed you so weak. You used to be strong. Resilient. Resourceful. Now you're just a love-struck joke. It makes me *sick*."

The muzzle of his gun is pressed to the side of Spencer's head as he speaks, and I fight the initial reaction to run to her. Deep down, I know he's taunting me. If he wants to play, I'll play. But not at her expense.

Spencer leans forward as though she's going to puke all over the ground in front of his pretentious Gucci loafers.

"Speaking of sick, I need to stand," she slurs. "Please, or I'm going to vomit all over these woods. *Exorcist* style." She waves her hand drunkenly toward the branches surrounding us. "Pea soup on the pretty trees."

Yet when her blue eyes rise from underneath her hair to meet mine, they're focused. Maybe a little hazy, but she's not nearly as drugged as she's pretending to be.

It's then I know.

She's trying to get him to let her stand so she will have an offensive advantage, and fuck me, I might kiss Grady for his brilliant Krav Maga instruction.

Silas fists the back of her tank top and hauls her body upward, keeping hold while she struggles to get her footing. Obviously the drugs aren't completely out of her system, but hoping that Silas gave her something that metabolizes quickly, I try to bide her more time.

"So, this is your brilliant plan? Killing her as a form of revenge? Why not just shoot me and be done with it?"

He moves to stand behind Spencer, most likely to protect his shoes if she does in fact get sick, then scowls at me over her shoulder. "Shooting you would be too easy. Too quick. There is no pain worse than watching someone you love die. It's pure torture. It eats at you from the inside, the agony of the loss clawing until there's nothing left. You will feel it for years, and I find great satisfaction in that."

I know that pain. I've been living with it for the past five fucking years.

A menacing chuckle fills the air as he presses the gun against Spencer's head. "I lost everything when you deserted my organization. Power. Respect. Money. All because you decided to grow a fucking conscience."

Spencer leans forward and he forcefully pulls her back into his chest, the anger in his voice when he begins to speak unmistakable. "To think you and your substitute *daddy* wasted all your time trying to take down my organization when it doesn't even exist. Not here anyway. There is nothing given to you that can be connected to me. I made sure of it. I *paid* to be sure of it. In fact, all evidence you have against me is being wiped clean as we speak."

"Murphy . . ." I mumble under my breath.

"You're still smart, kid, if nothing else. But not smart enough to know that I saw you coming. Your little infiltration scheme was a farce."

At that, I laugh without absolutely any humor in my tone. "I could give two fucks about your organization. About its livelihood or its downfall. Because *my* plan, the one that's actually going to come to fruition tonight, the one that *you* didn't see coming, doesn't have anything to do with your regime. It was never about taking you down; it was about taking you *out*. For me. For Rat. For every other helpless victim who's fallen prey to your sick forms of manipulation."

I break my stare to glance at Spencer, who seems more lucid as she listens to our exchange. Her face is intense and her stance is strong. She nods discreetly and my eyes remain on her as I continue to speak. "And by bringing me out in the middle of nowhere, holding my girl hostage, well . . . you've pretty much just given me a get-out-of-jail-free card."

From under the bill of my cap, I shield my eyes from Silas then dip my head, giving her the signal she's been waiting for.

And then she executes our perfected move.

Before Silas has time to register her movement, her arm flies across her body and she grabs the barrel of the gun. In one swift motion, she twists the muzzle in Silas's direction as she launches her body forward. Taken by surprise, he falls off center and she uses it to her advantage, throwing her arm backward until it lodges under Silas's. She then whirls around, hooking his arm with hers and twisting the gun out of his grasp with the other hand. I reach back and draw my Glock from my waistband, ready to take the shot I've been waiting to take for years.

I aim it at Silas as Spencer begins to shuffle backward as she's been trained to do, and that's when it happens. Still unsteady, her legs tangle with her steps and she falls backward. And as she does, her hold on the gun falters. Everything begins to slow as it makes its descent, and it's not until the dust stirs with its landing that my instincts take over. I raise my Glock and point it directly at Silas, only to lose sight of him as he dives toward the ground. Spencer launches her body forward at the same time, and I watch in horror as they begin to grapple for possession of the gun.

Panic thrums through my entire body. "Spencer, get back! Let it go!"

My voice seems to register because she stills, then begins to crab walk back in my direction. Silas takes hold of the gun and my heart lurches into my throat.

Pressing off the ground, she climbs to her feet then spins in my direction, her panic-stricken face slicing my heart wide open. I haul my entire body forward, and with my arm jutting straight in front of me and my gun trained on Silas, I fire a shot just as Spencer lands safely against my chest. Wrapping her tightly with my free arm, I curl both arms around her and turn our bodies, using mine for a shield right as another shot pierces the air.

All control is lost as my legs give out beneath me and I crumble to the ground, taking Spencer with me. Pain splices through my entire body as though it's being ripped in two. I grit my teeth and try to focus on my breathing.

Spencer's screams fill the air. "Oh my God! Oh my God! Dalton! NO!"

I try to console her. To tell her not to cry. To assure her I'll be okay. But nothing fucking works. Shock takes over and I'm helpless against it. *Can't talk. Can't hold her.*

The last thing I feel are the warm tears that strike my face as she leans over my body, holding me against her chest.

The last thing I hear is her soft, soothing whimpers as she cradles me tightly.

And the last thing I smell is the scent of Love and Happiness.

I'm finally home.

Eventually, I'm forced to succumb to my body's demands. As I disappear into the darkness, I breathe in one last time and pray to God that it isn't the last breath I'm granted. Yet as I take that breath, I find comfort in the fact that if my time here on Earth has come to an end, there's no place I'd rather be than in the arms of my angel when I go.

Chapter 40

Spencer

Rage.

I've never known how powerful it can be when unleashed to its fullest extent. But as it takes control of my body, as every single muscle burns and trembles with its presence, it blankets the agony shredding my heart as I hold Dalton in my arms.

I know now why Dalton found comfort in the sensation. Why he took solace in its existence.

And just as he once did, I welcome it.

A wheezing sound slowly filters into my mind as it echoes behind me. I glance over my shoulder to find Silas Kincaid lying on the ground, not even five feet away. Blood trickles from the hole left by Dalton's shot, and his eyes call to me for help, but I have nothing to give.

Not to him.

My brain completely shuts off, then I turn back to Dalton. Fury dictates my movements as I reach over his body and take the gun from his grasp. I glance once more at Dalton to solidify my decision, then release him and turn in the opposite direction.

Slowly, I drag my heavy legs behind me, crawling until I'm inches away from Silas's body. He grasps blindly at his throat and rolls onto his back, his inhales for air becoming more prominent with the movement.

Raising the gun, I place it right in the center of his forehead. My entire arm is shaking, barely able to keep the weapon steady, so I press it firmly against his skull to reinforce my hold.

"Spencer."

A familiar voice flitters in then out of my hearing.

"Spencer."

The voice is stronger now, firm and demanding, and a familiar hand curls over mine, covering my hold on the gun. Warm tears cascade down my face as I stubbornly tighten my grip.

"I need to finish this for him. I need to do this. I *have* to do this. For Dalton." My voice is unrecognizable as sobs wrack their way through my throat.

"No. It's done, sweetheart. Look, he's finished it already."

I peel my eyes away from the gun and direct them at Silas's face. There is no strain. No pained effort to breathe. There is only death as it relaxes his features.

I turn to face the gentle, kind eyes of Kirk Lawson, and the intense look on his face brings me back to reality. I release the gun.

"I'm sorry. I don't know . . ."

"I do. I know exactly what you're going through right now, Spencer. And it's more than okay to feel that way, but Dalton needs you. I need you to focus that intensity on helping him. You need to remind him of what he's been fighting for all along. You need to keep him alive until the paramedics arrive."

I bite my bottom lip so hard I taste blood. Tears continue to fall and I sniff them back while nodding my head absently. "Okay." Looking back at Dalton, I breathe, "Yeah, okay."

My body seems so heavy, but I force it to move back to Dalton. *Back to Dalton.* Taking him in my arms, I cradle his head in my lap, rocking him as I cry. Anger finds its release and I speak through gritted teeth. "You *promised* me. You promised you would never leave me again."

I continue swaying back and forth, willing him to open his eyes. "I just got you back. You can't leave me. Not again. Not today. You fucking promised!"

Reaching forward, I take his hand into mine and press my lips against his skin, relieved when I feel the faint beating of his pulse. Slowly, I uncurl his fingers, then place his palm flat on my chest, hunching myself over his body once again. I lower my voice and begin to whisper. "Come back to me. Come back to me. Come back to me."

I lessen my grip so he can breathe. "Please, Dalton. This life you wanted to live is so close. It's *so* close. I just need you to fight for it."

Refusal sets in and I move so I can whisper directly in his ear. "You said there is nothing you wouldn't do for me. Well, I need you to fight. I need you to find your way back to me. Please do that for me because I need *you*. I cannot exist without you, remember? I. Do. Not. Exist. Without. You. In fact, I *refuse* to exist without you. If you go, I go. That's the deal."

A few seconds pass before a loud gasp sounds from below me. Dalton's beautiful blue eyes fly open and I immediately shout, "Kirk! Kirk!"

Rushing footsteps sound from behind me. "The paramedics are here."

Before I know it, I'm ripped from Dalton's body and placed into Kirk's arms. I bury my head in his chest, refusing to hear anything other than his affirmations that Dalton will be okay. I refuse to accept anything else other than that. He will be okay. He *has* to be okay.

Because he made me a promise.

Because he loves me.

Because I know there's nothing he wouldn't do for me.

And as my heart beats frantically in my chest, I know he's doing just that.

He's going to war.

And he *will* make his way back to me.

Chapter 41　✺

Dalton

Six months later . . .

My eyes land on the wheelchair on the porch, resurfacing memories of the night I fought the toughest fight of my life. Fragments from Silas's bullet were splayed all over the left, lower part of my back, nearly severing my spine. I was told the closest one came within two centimeters of causing permanent damage. They did manage, however, to create a shit-ton of swelling, which left me temporarily paralyzed from the waist down. After a couple months, and with some intense physical therapy, I was eventually able to walk again. So now the only thing the wheelchair holds is a pumpkin-headed scarecrow with a vat crammed with candy waiting patiently for the kids to arrive.

Spencer and I bought this house a little over a week ago, and she went right into party-planning mode. Tonight we're hosting the First Annual Ghostly Get-Together, a party for kids from the abuse center, a place where Spencer and I spend a lot of our time. The eyeballs floating in a clear tub of red punch were messing with my mind, so I decided to come outside and wait for Spencer. I swear they were watching me.

An involuntary shiver creeps across my skin, but my thoughts are pulled away from their disturbing presence as I hear the familiar growl of Spencer's Mustang just down the street. Closing the book in my lap, I wait, then smile when she pulls into the drive.

She's so giddy; she's practically bouncing in her seat as she eyes the scarecrow in front of her. I grin wider and shrug. I always said there's nothing I wouldn't do for her, and that includes spending hours stuffing straw into my clothing and carving a face into a pumpkin.

"Oh my God. I love it," she exclaims as soon as her flip-flops hit the pavement. Her hair is in a messy bun on top of her head and her shirt is a retro Joplin throwback that matches the style of her hip-hugging bell-bottom jeans. And, as usual, they drag the ground as she makes her approach.

Her eyes are lit with excitement. *So beautiful.* After all these years, the sight of her happiness still robs me of my breath.

"What are you doing out here?"

I pat the porch. "I need a sunset."

She nods and takes a seat next to me, inhaling deeply. "Me too."

We sit in silence until she turns and tugs my hair with her fingers. "You need a haircut."

I reach up and drag my hand through my messy hair. "Yeah, but at least the beard is gone. Fucking itchy, that thing."

She grins. "I kind of liked it. The contacts though"—she shakes her head—"I was glad to see them go. I missed *your* eyes."

I pull her into me and press my lips against her temple.

"Cassie and Grady will be here around eight." Her giggles fill the air. "I can't believe they moved in together."

I chuckle. "I can. They're a perfect fit. My gut feelings never steer me wrong."

She sighs. "Yeah. Speaking of lovebirds, Mom called earlier. She and Kirk will be over around that time with the kids too. I can't believe they're getting married next month."

Lawson. I grin at the mention of his name. Kirk Lawson did, in fact, find some very useful information on Silas's suppliers when he raided the abandoned warehouse. After stripping it clean, he obtained names from a stash of papers hidden in Silas's office, then handed the info over to the DEA. After that, his investigation into Silas's activities was officially closed. Obviously.

We still work together though. Not undercover, but I'm working my way up to detective under his guidance and mentorship. He's become a very important man in my life, and I owe him so much more than I'll ever be able to repay. I made *several* attempts by trying to explain to Spencer's mom that Lawson had the best of intentions in mind when he withheld information from her regarding Spencer's safety. I'm pretty sure he slept on the couch for a month straight, but eventually, she forgave him. She's a smart woman, and she'd be a fool not to see how much Kirk Lawson loves her daughter. But that doesn't mean she didn't give him hell just to prove a point.

And as I glance at the blonde-haired beauty sitting next to me, I know exactly where she gets her stubborn streak.

Spencer gasps from beside me, breaking me from my thoughts. "I totally forgot to tell you. Mom received a letter today from Penny. They're doing really well. They only live a couple of hours from here, so we should go visit them sometime. I know she would love to see you. She told Mom that Lawson checks in with them every now and then and that she heard about the accident."

My heart aches as I watch the sides of her mouth curve downward. I know she continues to blame herself for dropping the gun that night, no matter how hard I try to convince her otherwise.

She stares off into the distance briefly, then her grin reappears and she meets my eyes. "She told Mom to tell you that she always knew you were a hero."

I chuckle and shake my head, draping my arm over her shoulder and pulling her into my body. Her scent fills my nose and I breathe it in deeply before whispering in her ear, "She also said that *you* would save *me*. So that kind of makes you a hero too."

I pull away to look into her sky-blue eyes. "Because you *did* save me, in so many ways. From a life I wanted no part of, from becoming a person I loathed, from living a life completely void of emotion. You saved me from all of that. And now here I am, sitting on the porch of a house I love, with the girl I love, in a life that I absolutely love. *You* saved *me*, Spence. Never forget that."

Her smile widens and the bridge of her nose begins to crease. I laugh and brush my mouth against hers, unable to do anything else when she makes that expression. She sighs, then nestles her head in the crook of my neck. Her hand touches the book in my lap as she asks, "What is this?"

I smile. "A book."

She huffs. "I know *that*, doofus."

I glance down and trace the worn cover with the tips of my fingers. "Dante. I read it from time to time."

She giggles and my heart ignites with the sound. "I can tell."

I pull her closer and we fall into silence with the setting sun. And at this moment, as she sits next to me on the porch and we watch it set in silence, I'm drawn deeply into my memories.

The crackling sounds of gravel catch my attention, but I don't look up. I just want whoever it is to go away. As I'm transported to yet another home, I find comfort in the fact that at least this time around I'll be able to protect myself, even if it is emergency foster care.

My entire body still aches with the effects of my fight with Bill. The one I provoked in order to make a statement, to let him know he no longer had the upper hand. The same one that got me kicked out of his miserable house.

But I still hurt. Inside and out. I'm so tired. I just want to be left alone.

"Hi."

As soon as the word hits my ears, a feeling that I've never felt before begins to warm my chest, and the ache that's always there begins to disappear. I breathe in deeply but keep my focus on the ground below me.

"My name's Spencer. What's yours?"

My body freezes with her voice. It's the voice of the person I've dreamed about so many times over the years. I keep my eyes on the dirt because I don't want to look up. I've seen this angel so often in my dreams, I'm scared it won't be her. But eventually, I look up and finally catch sight of her glowing presence.

I narrow my stare, surprised at how much she resembles the girl in my dreams. My angel as the sun shines behind her, her light-blonde hair blowing almost in slow motion as her sky-blue eyes lock onto mine. I look her over, and as my heart begins to pound with hope, I squash it and state in a cruel voice, "Spencer? That's a boy's name."

I refuse to believe it's her. And the only way to keep that stupid hope, that ridiculous need to hold onto something that will only lead to disappointment yet again, is to make her go away.

But she doesn't go anywhere. She just nods and says, "Yeah, not the first time I've heard that one."

Frustrated, I focus my irritated gaze on her. But as I continue to watch her lack of reaction to my anger, I find myself wanting to reach out and hug her. To hold her in order to know she's real. Which is stupid and weak.

I look back down at the ground, hoping she'll just go away and leave me alone. But she doesn't. She just sits next to me, and I find myself fascinated by her stubbornness.

It reminds me of me.

I don't say anything though, and neither does she. I'm strangely comforted as we sit side by side in silence. Together we watch the sun make its descent, and as we do, I gear myself up for another set of foster parents, silently hoping she'll at least be close by.

The thought of being able to see her whenever I want makes me smile. My first real smile in as long as I can remember.

"So . . . Spencer, was it?" The sound of her name coming out of my mouth feels so natural. Surprised with the ease, I say it again, along with the only way I know how to tell someone I like them.

"Well, Spencer. Wanna get high?"

Back in the present, the sun lowers, finally disappearing for another day. And despite Dante residing in my lap with his tales of hell, purgatory, and heaven, I can't think of anything else other than the angel sitting next to me.

I draw her in closer and breathe her straight into my lungs.

Every last bit of her.

Her strength. Her love. Her ferocity.

She was the only person capable of rescuing me from the depths of my own personal hell. *Only her. Always.*

She thinks I saved her, but she truly has no idea how much she saved me. I grin as I hold her tight against my chest, because when I asked her if she wanted to get high, I had absolutely no idea how high she would actually carry me.

In her arms alone, I found the true meaning of heaven: heaven on Earth—sitting on this porch watching the shifting colors of the horizon with her by my side.

I live and breathe because of her, and I will continue to do so making sure that each day, she understands the depths of my love for her.

Nothing else matters. In fact, nothing else *ever* mattered until the day I met her.

I was captivated by her eagerness.

Influenced by her willingness to love.

And under *that* influence, I fell helplessly for the gift she so willingly offered—uncompromising love—the gift of giving and receiving.

A love that buries itself in your soul as it solidifies completely and wholly with another person.

A love that forever binds, whether it be in life or death.

And in that love I find comfort.

I find strength.

I find existence.

I find *her*.

And she's all I need.

Forever and always.

My air.

My angel.

My Spencer.

THE END

Chosen Paths continues with ...

Out of Focus

Turn the page for a sneak peek of *Out of Focus*!

Prologue

Only twenty-three years old, and I'm so goddamn tired.

I used to be so much stronger. I somehow kept the voices at bay, the memories locked away safely, contained within the confines of my mind. But with each passing day, I feel the glow of my once-luminous strength fading. Darkness encases me now, bowing the walls of protection I put into place years ago. My past is an ever-present nightmare, repeatedly tapping, slowly fracturing the window of my sanity.

I have no doubt that it's only a matter of time before the glass finally breaks. Blackness will eventually seep through its cracks and deliver me from the safety of my façade into a reality that will destroy me.

My reality.

I've done my part. I've kept the secrets thrust upon me with dedicated believability. My portrayal of who I am has become a blurred, hazy version of the once very distinct Cassie Cooper.

I read an ungodly amount of trashy romance novels.

I'm the overtly sexual and foul-mouthed friend who will say anything to get a laugh.

And I have exactly zero fucks to give to what anyone else thinks about my actions.

But the reality, the actuality, is this:

I read obsessively to escape my own world. To live the dreams of others when, for so long, the reoccurrence of my nightmares has been *my* reality. I read to fall in love and find a happily-ever-after, even if it is purely imagined. With each story I read, I'm able to *live* and *love* vicariously through the characters in my books. It's the only plausible way for me to survive.

I threw away my virginity at the age of thirteen just to prove something. And when I found that proof, that vindication I was looking for, I sought it every chance I could. Sex is about control for me. Nothing more. The act will never be about making love, like it is for the heroines in my books. I will never be granted the beauty of that gift.

I use humor as a form of avoidance. I draw upon laughter to block the pain. And I smile to mask the agony of the eight-year-old soul who weeps within me.

And the fucks . . . well, that's not entirely accurate either.

I have given two to be exact: One to my best friend of seventeen years. She knows nothing of my past, and although she so willingly disclosed the horrors of hers, mine remains hidden for no other reason than to avoid the pity she would undoubtedly cast my way if I were to ever tell her. I don't want her pity. I would sooner die than have her look at me in any other way than with pride.

The other died with the person to whom it was given. Anthony "Rat" Marchione. He was one allowance of naïveté. The one person I actually *wanted* to touch me, to hold me, to love me. He was going to rescue me from my brokenness as though I were a character in one of my books. Young and senseless, I thought he was to be my eventual happily-ever-after, but tragically, he was murdered five years ago.

Black coldness waits in vain to leech the void where his once beautiful existence filled the pieces of my irrevocably shattered heart. Where he temporarily healed the hurt of the innocent child and quieted the voices that tormented her.

He's gone now. I've accepted that. And in turn, I have relinquished all dreams associated with finding the light at the end of this miserable tunnel.

I will keep trudging through this life . . . this *sentence* handed to me for someone else's crime, my payment shackled by secrets and weighted with lies. I will continue to do so with the same fraudulent smile on my lips and play the part of the strong heroine so convincingly, that even I believe it.

It's only a matter of time before my fictional strength wears out—when I'm no longer hidden safely inside my protective blur—and I have to face the very real and lucid image of my past.

But until that time comes, I'll do all I can do.

All I have ever done.

I will pretend.

Chapter 1 ✦
Bonded

Past—Six Years Old

The sun hits the tops of my new black dress shoes, making them shine with each step I take as I cross the street. I'm skipping with excitement, and my smile is as big as the poufy skirt of my dress. It's my most favoritest Sunday dress. It's yellow and happy and I love the sound it makes each time one of my feet leaves the ground.

Swish.

Swish.

Swish.

Five *swishes* later, I finally step onto the sidewalk.

I grin so wide, my cheeks ache. I knew I would finally wear Mommy down. As soon as I saw the yellow-haired, skinny little girl pull a huge My Little Pony stuffed animal out of the moving truck, I knew we were gonna be best friends. So I bugged Mommy all day long, asking her when I could go across the street to meet my new friend—at breakfast while munching on peanut butter toast, at lunch while eating a big bowl of ravioli, at dinner while chomping down on a burger my daddy made on the grill outside, and a couple hundred times in between.

Finally, she threw up her hands—*really*, she did—and told me I could run over after and introduce myself, but only if I finished my dinner first.

I've never eaten so fast in my life.

As soon as the burger was gone, I jumped out of my chair, put my plate in the sink, then ran upstairs to my room and threw on my prettiest dress. On my way out, Daddy yelled that I only had half an hour until bath time before the door slammed shut behind me.

My long dark hair, in a ponytail that I did *all* by myself, swings as I walk down her driveway and skip around the back of the moving truck. As soon as I pass the bumper, I see her. She's sitting on the top step of her porch, wearing the same pink glittery T-shirt and blue jean shorts I saw her in earlier today.

I start to say something, but my mouth slams shut when I notice shiny tears as they roll down her cheeks. My smile falls straight to the ground, and my eyebrows pinch tightly together. I slow my steps, not sure if *now* would be the best time to introduce myself to my new best friend. My feet stop moving and I still, watching her for a second or two before deciding against it. I lift my shiny shoe and slowly begin to take a step backward, but a dumb twig cracks as soon as my foot hits the ground. I freeze, just like I do when Mommy catches me stealing cookies out of the pantry right before dinner.

I'm pretty sure I'm even making the same *Crap!* face.

Her teary blue eyes meet my dark-brown ones, and I just stand there, still like a statue with my arms stuck midswing. I don't know what else to do, so I begin to move like a robot, making the same *er-er-er* sounds my daddy does to make me laugh.

She watches my moves, and after a couple of seconds, she finally giggles.

My body relaxes, a relieved grin tugging at my lips to match hers. I can't help it.

I straighten my body, then take a step in her direction, and another, and another. When I finally come to the porch, I reach forward to shake her hand, finally making the introduction I've been waiting to make *all day long*. "Hi, I'm Cassie Cooper. I live across the street." My thumb points over my shoulder as I speak.

She wipes the tears onto her jean shorts, then stands and links our hands, giving them a good shake before answering, "Hello, Cassie. I'm Spencer Locke."

Spencer looks down as the breeze blows, and another *swish* fills the air. "I like your dress." Her voice is soft, and she tucks her hair behind her ear.

I smile my thanks and curtsey, while her pretty blue eyes—thankfully now dry—grin back at me. "And you can do the robot *almost* as good as I can."

My smile becomes a laugh, and she turns to take her spot on the porch, then pats the area beside her. I sit, happy to have a funny friend.

After a few seconds, she looks at me and says, "I'm sorry I was crying. I, uh, well . . ."

The screen door behind us creaks open and I turn my head. Behind me stands a beautiful lady around Mommy's age with glasses on the edge of her nose and light-brown hair in a pile on the top of her head. Her eyes are the color of her hair, and they crinkle at the sides when she smiles at us.

They don't look anything alike, so I'm not sure if this is Spencer's mommy or not. I don't know what to say to her, but she takes care of that for me.

"Hello, I'm Deborah, Spencer's . . ."

She pauses to glance at Spencer, who says in a strong voice, "*Mommy.*"

Her mommy's mouth dips down at the sides and her chin trembles. Now tears are in *her* eyes.

Why is everyone crying?

"Yes," Mrs. Locke continues, "I'm Spencer's mommy." She says it almost to herself, then looks to me.

"I'm Cassie." I point across the street. "I live over there."

Her mommy smiles back at me. She has a really pretty smile.

She glances back to Spencer. "Well, it's good that you'll have a friend so close, isn't that right?"

Spencer nods her head and Mrs. Locke adds, "Spencer, can I talk to you for a second?"

"Yes, ma'am." Her voice is soft when she answers. Mrs. Locke steps onto the porch when Spencer stands, and the screen door bounces a couple times before it finally shuts behind her. She's wearing a fluffy, pink robe and ties it around her waist as Spencer walks toward her. That makes me smile. As soon as Spencer stands in front of her, she places her arm gently around Spencer's shoulder and leans to whisper in her ear. Spencer nods and whispers back. This continues until they finally stop and smile at each other, as though they've decided on something.

Mrs. Locke hugs Spencer then lets her go, looks at me, and winks. "Nice to meet you, Cassie. I think you and Spencer will be very good friends."

A man's voice calls her name from within the house, and she smiles again at both of us before she leaves. I glance shyly at Spencer, who's taken her seat next to me. She lets out a long breath, then she looks back at me. She tucks her hair behind her ears again, brings her knees to her chest, and lays her cheek on them before finally speaking.

"She just wanted to tell me it was okay for me to talk about why I was crying. I wasn't really sure if I was allowed to tell people, but she told me if I wanted to tell you, that it was okay with her. And I want to tell you, because if we're going to be friends, we shouldn't keep secrets from each other. If you still even want to be my friend when I'm through."

I place my cheek on my knees just like she's doing and give her a happy smile to let her know I will still be her friend. "Well, I live across the street, so *I'm* not going anywhere."

At that, her face splits into a wide grin, before she clears her throat. I watch her smile as it falls and slowly disappears. "It's not easy to talk about, so it might be hard for me to say."

My happy face turns into a sad one, but I stay still and wait for her to start.

And then she does.

I always thought when grown-ups whispered about someone's heart being broken, it was just something they said. Like, when Mr. Keyes *kicked the bucket* or when Grandpa tells me he's *fit as a fiddle*. I had no idea that a heart could actually break. I didn't know that by just listening to Spencer share her secret, I would feel real pain in my chest.

But I do.

My heart hurts for her as she tells me how her mommy isn't really her mommy, that Mr. and Mrs. Locke adopted her because her real parents didn't want her. It crumbles into tiny pieces when she shares how her new mother found her. Her own parents had locked her in a pantry for weeks with very little food and water. And when I realize that's *why* she's so skinny, my heart breaks a little more. She tells me how scared she was in the darkness, and how she cried for days, but they never let her out. She doesn't understand what she did to deserve her *punishment*, but she says that Mr. and Mrs. Locke always hug her and tell her she didn't do *anything* wrong.

By the time I know everything there is to know about Spencer's secret, Daddy is calling me to come home and *both* of us are crying. I reach over and pull her into the tightest hug I've ever given, promising in my mind that I will be strong and protect her. I will never let anyone hurt her again.

We both let go and smile as we wipe away our tears. The wood beneath me creaks as I stand, signaling to Daddy with my finger that I'll be home in *just a minute*, then look at my new friend and smile. "Wanna come over and play tomorrow?"

I think she's surprised by my offer to still be her friend because she answers me by widening her eyes. The pain I felt earlier is gone, replaced by a warm feeling as I watch happiness fill those wide eyes.

And I'm *proud* I did that. *I* did something to make her happy.

"I would like that very much. Thank you, Cassie."

I nod excitedly and turn away from her, looking both ways before I cross the street and walk toward Daddy, who's *still* on the porch. I fight to not roll my eyes—that'll get you into heaps of trouble at my house—and as my steps carry me farther away, a new feeling begins to spread throughout my chest. One I've never felt before.

Pulling is the best way to describe it, I guess.

Like two invisible ropes, hers and mine, tying a knot to keep us together.

I let out a heavy breath and keep walking.

I'm relieved when the feeling is still there once I make it to my house. Daddy holds the door open for me and I turn to give her one last wave good-bye before entering in front of him.

The last thoughts I have before climbing into bed are wondering how far this rope-thing actually stretches, and being thankful I live across the street.

Because as I still feel the strong pull in my heart when I shut my eyes, I know it's in no danger of breaking anytime soon.

And that makes me very happy.

LOOK FOR *OUT OF FOCUS* AT YOUR LOCAL BOOKSTORE OR BUY ONLINE!

Other Books by
L.B. SIMMONS

Chosen Paths Series

Into the Light
Under the Influence
Out of Focus

Mending Hearts Series

Running on Empty
Recovery
Running in Place

Author's Note

The subjects covered in this book were not easy ones to tackle. Domestic violence is far more prevalent than we know, most likely because so many victims feel trapped and don't speak out. If you or someone you know is a victim of domestic abuse, please call the National Domestic Violence Hotline at 1-800-799-7233 and speak to an advocate. You are not alone.

And for those of you interested in helping a child in foster care, you can do so by becoming a Court Appointed Special Advocate (CASA). As taken directly from the CASA For Children's website, "CASA volunteers are appointed by judges to watch over and advocate for abused and neglected children, to make sure they don't get lost in the overburdened legal and social service system or languish in inappropriate group or foster homes. Volunteers stay with each case until it is closed and the child is placed in a safe, permanent home. For many abused children, their CASA volunteer will be the one constant adult presence in their lives." You can make a difference. If you would like to learn more, visit the CASA For Children's webpage: http://www.casaforchildren.org.

Acknowledgments

Acknowledgments for me are always bittersweet. They mark the end of my writing journey, but they are also a powerful reminder of the support given along the way. Without the tremendous positivity and encouragement provided along the way, this book would not have come to completion. I am so truly blessed to have these people along with me for the crazy ride. People that have been with me from the very beginning and people I love with all my heart. My supporters. My readers. My teachers. My friends. Each one of you has impacted my life in ways you will never be able to understand. I love you all.

My hubby. You are an amazing man with the patience of a saint. Not only because you give me the time I need to continue living my dream, but because you do so without me having to ask. You sacrifice so much so I can sit at a computer for hours on end, taking care of our girls while I'm merely feet away lost in another world. I love you so much for supporting me wholeheartedly, and your belief in my writing never fails to astound me.

My babies. I love you girls so much. I do this for you, to show you that you can do anything when you put your mind to it. I wanted to write a book, so I did. Now I've written five. Find what you love, your passion, what drives you . . . and do it. Because I know you can.

Jena Eilers. Good Lord. I would not have finished this book without you by my side. It was hard but you stood by me, encouraged me, and supplied me with endless amounts of Diet Mountain Dew, all because you believe so strongly in my stories. Your friendship continues to amaze me on a daily basis.

Luna Sol. I love you so much. It's funny how I can say that when you're on the other side of the world, when we've never even met, but it's true. Your unwavering support, your passion for reading, and your love for the characters within those books is what I admire so much about you. You have this uncanny ability to see inside my head when we discuss my books. You just get it, and then you translate it beautifully. And you make me giggle. A lot. I will never be able to truly express how much your friendship means to me.

Hang Le. Woman. This cover stole my breath, and when I saw it for the first time, I knew you understood what I was trying to say. I could not have asked for a better representation of Dalton and Spencer's story than the beautiful image preceding their pages. It's breathtaking. It's emotional. It's perfect. You amaze me.

Lisa Paul. It's been a rough year, but your constant sticker messages and voice messages kept me laughing . . . out loud. You never gave up on me. And that's the definition of true friendship right there. Thank you for being my friend. You are truly a gift in my life.

Nicole Jacquelyn. Another dear friend who I will be forever grateful entered my life because of this crazy world of self-publishing. You are real. You are genuine. And I love you for it. You never hesitate to help me mold the idea of my stories, to steer me in the right direction, and to offer advice when needed. But moreover, you are an amazing friend. Peas and carrots.

For all the beautiful ladies of L.B. Simmons Books. I LOVE YOU ALLLLLLL! I know I tell you this often, but you really have no idea how your support and excitement gave me the drive to finish this book. Thank you so much for believing in me as much as you do. Thank you for the constant laughter in the group. And thank you for being absolutely incredible individuals. I am blessed to know each and every one of you.

To the many bloggers, who spend hours on end reading and reviewing the plethora of books out there, thank you for taking the time to read mine. Without your help and support, no one would read my stories. Plain and simple. And I feel you don't get thanked enough for that. So thank you from the bottom of my heart.

And to my readers. YOU ARE AMAZING! Thank you so much for taking your time to read my stories. I know life gets busy, and the fact that you choose to take time out of your day to read my words will always humble me. As always, thank you for your support, your letters, your messages—all that you do reminds me why I continue to write. Thank you.

About the Author

Two Sons Photography

After graduating from Texas A&M University, L.B. Simmons did what any biomedical science major would do: she entered the workforce as a full-time chemist. Never in her wildest dreams would she have imagined herself becoming a *USA Today* best-selling contemporary romance author years later.

What began as a memoir for her children ended up being her first self-published book, *Running on Empty*. Soon after, her girls were given reoccurring roles in the remainder of what became the Mending Hearts series.

L.B. Simmons doesn't just write books. With each new work, she attempts to compose journeys of love and self-discovery so she may impart life lessons to readers. She's tackled suicide, depression, bullying, eating disorders, as well as physical and sexual abuse, all while weaving elements of humor into the storylines in an effort to balance the difficult topics. Often described as roller coaster rides, her novels are known for eliciting a wide range of emotions.

Connect with the Author

L.B.'s Website:
    http://www.lbsimmons.com/

L.B.'s Facebook Page:
    https://www.facebook.com/lbsimmonsauthor

L.B.'s Twitter Page:
    https://twitter.com/lbsimmons33

L.B.'s Instagram:
    https://www.instagram.com/Lbsimmons33/

Contact L.B.:
    http://www.lbsimmons.com/contact-me